"*Chrissie's Run* will take you on an amazing ride. The author has an incredible ability to make the characters and the story come alive. This is the first novel I've read that captured me so completely, it felt as if I were watching a movie. It is a suspenseful, compelling read that weaves the message that life is precious throughout the story. You won't be able to put it down!"

—Tina Underwood
Author of *Captive No More*
Captive No More Ministries

CHRISSIE'S RUN

CHRISSIE'S RUN

S.A. MAHAN

TATE PUBLISHING
AND ENTERPRISES, LLC

Published by Tate Publishing & Enterprises, LLC
127 E. Trade Center Terrace | Mustang, Oklahoma 73064 USA
1.888.361.9473 | www.tatepublishing.com

Tate Publishing is committed to excellence in the publishing industry. The company reflects the philosophy established by the founders, based on Psalm 68:11,
"The Lord gave the word and great was the company of those who published it."

Published in the United States of America
ISBN: 978-1-62902-501-8
13.11.06

DEDICATION

For Ella Shalom

ACKNOWLEDGEMENTS

I want to thank my friends and family for their encouragement and support. A special thanks to Tina Underwood for believing in this book. Thanks to Dr. Richard Tate and all of the people at Tate Publishing for their support and encouragement. A thank you to my husband, without whose support this book would not have been possible. And a very special thank you to Mark and Bette Hollingsworth, the parents of a very special little girl, Ella Shalom. Ella was born with tremendous physical challenges, and, now as a beautiful little girl, she faces those challenges with an indomitable spirit. She truly is a living testament that every single life is precious. Ella served as my inspiration for this book.

PART ONE:

MOSES

CHAPTER ONE

In the rare moments when the drugs seem to be wearing off, I question everything. What I thought were dreams become memories for me. Faces with names materialize, and I know that they are the faces of people who died. People who fought for me. People I loved.

In these moments, I rise from my cold prison bunk and seek out the dim sunlight that filters in through the heavy steel bars of my window. It is difficult to stand; my body is weak from the constant onslaught of drugs that the ugly giant injects me with on a daily basis. I let the faint warmth of light wash across my face; then I look down at my outstretched arms and gasp at the ugly blue-black needle tracks that march across my skin.

In my dreams, my arms are healthy, solid, and strong. My legs ripple with muscles, and I know that I have the ability to run all day long if I want to. But in my dreams, I don't run. I stand and fight my pursuers. I fight with an incredible skill that comes from…where?

In prison, one day fades into a week, which fades into a month. I have long since lost track of time. I am not even sure how old I might be. I only know that twice a day, the hideous giant will open the door, pin me to my bunk, inject me with drugs, and then wheel me down on a hospital gurney to the bright white room. There, the lady doctor with the big green eyes will shine the blinding strobe light in my eyes, and the loudspeaker in the ceiling will scream over and over again.

"*What is your name?*"

And then, when I don't utter a word, it will answer for me:

"*My name is Christina Wright.*"

"*What do you want, Christina?*"

"*I want to be a productive, law-abiding citizen of the New Republic.*"

Hour after hour, it will blare. There is no escaping from it. And all the while the lady doctor with the green eyes sits next to me and stares at me and takes notes on her electronic clipboard.

"*What is your name!*" the speaker screams.

"*My name is Christina Wright,*" it answers when I don't.

"*What do you want, Christina?*"

"*I want to be a productive, law-abiding citizen of the New Republic.*"

The loudspeaker, the strobe light, the drugs absorb me. And all the while, the lady doctor stares at me with those huge green eyes, like she is studying a giant bug. Even in my sleep, in my nightmare dreams, she stares at me.

Back in my prison cell, I hear noises. A phantom toddler seems to have free run of the hallways outside of my heavy steel door. Sometimes, I peek through the slot where the giant shoves trays of food to me and catch a quick glimpse of him as he rolls by on a four-wheeled scooter. I feel like I should know him, but I just don't know. Is he real or is he just part of my dreams?

How long have I been here? Weeks? Months? Years?

Sometimes the warden pays me a visit. He is a strong young man with sandy blond hair. He seems to be strikingly handsome, but I can't tell for sure because of the big mirrored sunglasses he always wears, even when he sits in the darkness of my prison cell.

He asks me a lot of questions, which I never remember because of the drugs, and sometimes I get really mad at him. But he seems to be trying to help me. I should trust him, but I don't because he also shows up in my dreams.

In my dreams, he is a monster and I hate him.

Today, I must have done something right because when the giant opened my cell door, he did not drug me. He handed me a bundle and told me to get dressed. I wait until he leaves and then I open the bundle to find that I am holding a beautiful red evening gown, polished red high heels, a hair clasp, and a necklace.

I shrug out of my one-piece orange prison jumpsuit and try the dress on. It fits perfectly. Then I shakily sit down. The residual effects of the drugs have weakened me and a strong spell of dizziness washes through my head. My body shakes uncontrollably for a few minutes. Outside my cell door, I hear the toddler scooting by and laughing. I stand up in spite of my dizziness and peek through the door slot, but he is gone. Was he real?

Then much later, I am sitting in that dress at a big banquet table. The table in front of me is filled with an enormous amount of food, and directly across the table, the warden sits and watches me.

"Christina," he says and I snap fully alert. "I have forgotten my manners! We have started eating, and I haven't even introduced everyone to you."

He sweeps his hand around the table, and I glance at the faces staring back at me.

"This is my assistant warden, Mr. Sasaki." He gestures to the man to his left. The Asian man smiles and bows politely.

"And farther down my side of the table, you have the lovely Doctor Mendenhall."

The doctor lady with the huge green eyes smiles and nods at me.

"I credit her with curing you," the warden continues. He continues down the table, naming different prison guards.

Then the warden stands and raises his wineglass.

"Ladies and gentlemen," he says, "a toast to Jason and Christina, our guests of honor. I received the confirmation just this afternoon. The president plans to grant them both a full pardon. He is personally flying down tomorrow to escort them home."

The dinner guests rise and raise their glasses.

"Hear, hear." They toast us. "To Jason and Christina!"

Jason is a handsome teenage boy who sits next to me. He seems vaguely familiar, and I know that I should know him.

The food and wine is beyond belief, and I have no qualms enjoying it. Then over a dessert of cake that melts in my mouth, the Asian man makes conversation for the first time. First, he looks at me, and maybe I imagine it. An image of a jackrabbit flashes across my mind, but it is only there for an instant before it fades. Then he turns to Jason.

"What is your name?" he asks Jason in Spanish, and I detect a hint of an additional exotic accent.

Jason looks up from his plate and smiles at the Asian man.

"My name is Jason Morson."

"What do you want, Jason?"

"I want to be a productive, law-abiding citizen of the New Republic."

"Very good, very good!" the warden cuts in, beaming at Jason. He ignores Mr. Sasaki and turns to me.

"What is your name, dear?" he asks me, and I can see my own gaunt face reflected in his mirrored sunglasses.

Take off those damn sunglasses and I'll tell you, Stingray! my mind shouts out.

Where did this thought come from? This reaction surprises and alarms me, but I muster up a smile and answer aloud.

"My name is Christina Wright."

"What do you want, Christina?" he asks.

I want my baby! my mind screams out. I try to control my thoughts, but my mind continues to scream in my head. *And I want to kill you, you murderer! I really want to kill you! For Moses, for Samson, for Angel, for the villages you bombed, for all of the villagers of San Hidalgo you killed!*

I try to calm myself, and answer aloud, sweetly, "I want to be a productive, law-abiding citizen of the New Republic."

The warden cocks his head to the side and grins at me with a strange, crooked grin.

He leans over to Mr. Sasaki.

"Tomorrow is going to be quite a day," he says to him.

"Yes, indeed," the Asian man quietly agrees. "Quite a day!"

As I finish my last bite of dessert, I become aware that Mr. Sasaki is watching me, studying me intently.

CHAPTER TWO

Two years earlier.
His name is Daniel. Daniel in the lion's den. That is what the voice calls him, the voice that whispers to me in my mind late at night, when I am drifting away into sleep. I try to picture what a lion's den might look like. If it is as bad as what I picture, Daniel is definitely in it.

I know for sure he is a boy. That is the first thing they tell you at the Parlor. Right before they give you the other news.

They even tell that news to somebody like me, sixteen and unwed. My young age does not bother them; other things bother them. The fact that Daniel is not normal bothers them, even if it does not bother me.

"It is deformed, dear," the redheaded woman with green eyes tells me, as if she is giving me the time of day. "It is missing its right foot, part of its right hand, and it probably has a mental deficiency."

I hold in my emotions. I stare back at her with a blank face. I know all about the people at the Parlor. Later I cry, a week later, as I pack my things in a backpack. Tomorrow is abortion day for me. The law is the law. After the abortion, the nice people at the Parlor will sterilize me. They will also sterilize Jason, my boyfriend. You cannot be too careful, after all.

Jason is relieved. He told me so last night. I throw an extra shirt into my backpack, right on top of the dried fruit and wheat bars I took from the pantry. Maximus purrs, stretches on my pillow, and curls up again. He watches me through his half-closed, blue-gray Siamese eyes. He loves me more than Jason does.

Jason is going places. For him, sterilization is a small price to pay. He told me so last night before I screamed at him and stormed into my house. He is a genius at math and science, and the university headhunters are already out after him. I am not so lucky. I stink at math and science. I love to read though.

I toss a small book into my backpack. It is not a novel, or a fairy tale that would transport me to another, happier world. It is a mini atlas full of ancient names and ancient places, something more practical. I like the feel of its strange, antique paper pages when I thumb through it. It has a vastly different feel from the plastic viewers everybody uses. Real books like the atlas are hard to come by, terribly expensive and, for the most part, usually illegal; but I did not feel bad when I swiped it from the illegal stash of ancient books hidden in my father's desk. My father collects and studies them; but he is so high up in the government nobody cares.

I throw two one-liter bottles of water on top of everything else. Put the heaviest things on top, I know. I backpacked with Jason outside of the city once or twice. Back when I was still in love.

Maximus meows softly and looks up at me with inquiring eyes. He glances at the backpack.

"No, kitty," I tell him. "I have to do this alone."

It is long after midnight, way past city curfew, and I will have to sit and wait for a couple of hours until curfew is lifted for early morning commuters. The night police are too good. They would catch me for sure at this hour.

I sit still in the heavy quietness of early, early morning and think about my parents. I was hoping that my stepmother would at least betray some emotion when she found out I was pregnant, but she only gave me a puzzled look. No talk, no advice, not even a hint of disappointment. Father, coming in late from his government job, sat in his easy chair and looked at nothing. It was that way for the next three months, until my stepmother insisted on taking me to the Parlor. She said I was beginning to show and we had to avoid legal action. This, at least, she was emotional about. She threw such a tantrum, I finally gave in.

So she was relieved last week when they told us the news. An uncomfortable problem solved for everybody involved. Except Daniel.

I look around my bedroom, still the bedroom of a little girl. I still have my stuffed animals, my *One Star* photos that automatically change when each new winner is announced. It all reminds me of a book I read on my viewer when I was really little, about a little worm in its cocoon. My bedroom is a cocoon.

There is not one thing in my bedroom, not even in the house, for that matter, that I can use to protect myself. My stepmother uses an autocooker, no need for knives. You have to try to get a government permit to purchase a real knife anyway. No sense in risking hurting yourself if you don't have to.

The hours slowly slide by, and at 3:30 a.m., I catch myself dozing off. I resort to slapping myself to stay awake. Maximus has snuggled close to me and is snoring lightly.

At 4:00 a.m., I pick him up, hug him and give him a kiss.

"Good luck, kitty," I whisper to him. With me gone, there is no telling what my stepmother will do with him. But it is impossible to take him along.

I wipe the tears from my face as I work my arm through a strap of my backpack. *No crying, Chrissie*, I tell myself. *This is for Daniel.* I open my bedroom window as quietly as I can and slip out into the damp, early morning Frisco air.

CHAPTER THREE

It is going to rain today. With fall approaching, it is going to be an uncomfortable, chilly rain. A light mist is already growing, dampening my hair and face. There is a small park at the far end of my street where the road dead ends into a larger road that leads through the guard gate out of the government neighborhood. I stick to the shadows of bushes as I make my way, house to house, toward the park. I scoot past Madison's house, my best friend growing up. She has known about my pregnancy, and I know I should at least leave her a note. But I can no longer trust her or anybody else. Two police cruisers float by as I cross the street and enter the park. They are so quiet and dark when they are roving, you cannot see them until they are next to you. It does not help that they cloak up, camouflage to their surroundings like chameleons. It is only their motion that catches your eye.

"You need some company, sweetheart?" a metallic voice asks from the nearest one. They are the special government police who guard my neighborhood, and I figure they are probably approaching the end of their shift. I shake my head no and keep walking. Curfew is over and I know I am safe for now; they will not arrest me even if it is still early.

"Maybe later," the other policeman chimes in.

"It's a little early, school's not for another four hours." The voice in the first cruiser grows serious. "What are you doing out this time of morning, kid?"

Trouble. I have to think quickly.

"I had a fight with my boyfriend!" I cry out, truthfully. There is obvious anger in my voice.

"Lucky guy," the other policeman chuckles. "Okay, be careful, sweetheart. Checking. Just a moment, please. Christina Wright. Okay, you're clear."

I get a pass. Later on, I know I will not be so lucky. I walk away from the cruisers, into the park, and sit at a table that I have sat at playing since I was a little kid. The gravity of my situation starts to seep into my mind like the cold, damp mist that hangs in the air, and I know that I have to think clearly about what to do next. As hard as I try to avoid it, I can't help but think about Jason. Okay, he is a royal jerk. But I did love him, and my feelings are all mixed up. *Get over him, Chrissie*, I tell myself. You're never going to see him again. Still, I feel the loss.

I wiggle my toes in my hiking boots. The dampness has not penetrated, and my feet are warm and dry. This is good, I decide, the boots work. I open my backpack and dig for my light jacket. I pull it out and put it on over my sweatshirt. It is waterproof and, more importantly, it has a hood. Later, I know, I will need that hood for more than just the rain.

I have to get to a store as soon as one opens while my credits are still good. I've made out a list of things I'll need on the inside back page of the atlas. I could have used my viewer for this, but I left it behind. It can be tracked. I'm hungry, and I am feeling slightly nauseous from the onset of morning sickness. I decide to save my food and wait until I can buy more at the store. I hold my upset stomach and think about Daniel.

At 5:30 a.m., dawn is breaking through the mist as a dull, gray glow on the horizon. It is time to move, late enough to walk anywhere without raising too much suspicion. I take one last sweeping look at my childhood park and a flurry of memories rushes through my mind. I'm sad again, and I sigh as I walk out to the street and leave the last sanctuary from my childhood behind.

An hour later, I'm on the sidewalk entering old downtown Frisco and the shopping district. Boards are everywhere, of course, bright with colorful moving images, advertising the latest of everything. They have other, darker purposes too. I ignore them and their relentless commercial onslaught as I head for the only store that I know opens at seven. It is mainly a convenience store with really very little to offer, but it will have to do.

I am amazed and dismayed at how long it actually takes to get anywhere on foot. What takes me an hour to walk can be covered in a few minutes in our car. I am in what I consider fair shape for my condition, but I realize that in the days ahead, I am going to have to toughen up. My feet are already sore.

The store scans me as its front glass door slides open.

"Good morning, Chrissie!" It greets in a friendly young male voice. It always uses a young female voice for my father. "Out early this morning?"

"I have the day off," I answer truthfully. "Display medicals, please."

The blank white walls of the store come to life and display all types of medical products in categories. I am obviously the first customer of the day; otherwise, the store would already be displaying in general customer default.

"Getting a little exercise?" the store asks conversationally as I browse. It has already noticed that I have no car outside.

"I like to walk," I lie. I find the analgesics.

"This, this, and this." I touch the balms, aspirin, and a tube of Blister-Rid. "Hardware, please."

"Eighty-five credits, dear."

The walls change. Not much hardware to be had here, but it will have to do. *Keep it small,* I tell myself. I seriously wish that I had saved more money.

"How many do I still have?" I ask.

"Two hundred and twenty one."

I select three small spools of nylon twine. It was useful on camping trips, and you can burn through this variety, unlike the stronger stuff. I have no way of cutting it yet. Then I pick a small roll of duct tape, a small poly screwdriver and a pair of poly pliers.

"Snacks, please."

"Fifty-eight credits, Chrissie. You have one hundred sixty-three left. What a shopping spree!"

I try to act like I'm ignoring it.

"Snacks, please!" The walls change again.

I pick out a packet of beef jerky. Synthetic, of course, but it is tasty and guarantees its food value. Hard candy. More food bars, high protein. Now, to the hard stuff.

"Vitamins." The wall switches to display hundreds of brands. I select a general-use multivitamin, three hundred tabs in a small bottle.

"Eighty credits left, dear. Looks like you'll be walking home?"

I have to play this one just right.

"Any camping gear?" I ask nonchalantly.

A small section of one wall lights up. *Get it right, Chrissie*, I say to myself. I wish more than ever I had saved more money. I casually glance over the items, all but ignoring the two things I want more than anything else in the store.

"I'll take that little flashlight," I finally point out. The smallest one, but bright and guaranteed to stay lit for the rest of your life.

"Forty-five credits left, Chrissie."

Good, no probing questions on that one. Here goes nothing.

"And how about, uh, okay…how about that Perma Lighter?"

"One minute," the store answers. "One minute."

I know it is going into its full background check mode, sweeping through my history, checking my family, my clearances, and possible violations.

"Chrissie, are you planning to go camping this late in the year?"

It is a human voice, an older man. I've been patched through to the central police station. Be cool, I tell myself and try to answer calmly.

"Yes, and it's a present for my boyfriend."

"Celebrating?"

I bite my lip. He means about the Parlor.

"Of course!" I blurt out. Wonderful!

"Let's see here," the voice is searching. "That's Jason Morson, right?"

"Yes."

"One minute, please…" They are checking Jason out. I try to look as if I'm slightly perturbed. After all, they know who my father is. If they only knew how I really feel. I try to suppress my emotions; they might be scanning my bios. An eternity passes.

"Okay, honey, you're clear," he finally answers, now in a slightly bored voice. The store voice pipes right back up.

"Two credits left, Chrissie," it says cheerfully. "Anything else?"

"No, thank you." I answer quietly. A hatch in the front wall slides open, and my bag slides out across the store countertop, sealed neatly, with plastic grips at the top. I grab it and head for the door.

"Thank you for your patronage, have a wonderful day and come back soon," the young male voice drones as I head outside. "Have a great time at the Parlor, Chrissie. Reminder, your appointment is at ten o'clock, sharp!"

"Get lost!" I mutter under my breath as I head down the sidewalk, turning back in the direction I came from. At 10:01 a.m., I will be officially declared a runner, an enemy of the state. I will be a fugitive hiding in the middle of the capital of the New Republic. I will have to get out of sight from this store before I can double back and go where I need to go.

CHAPTER FOUR

The rain is coming down harder now. The falling drops give me a small sense of security; rain helps reduce the effectiveness of the invisible cameras that are hidden everywhere. I know that I don't have much time before I am reported missing and they start to look for me. When I don't show up for my appointment at the Parlor, all hell is going to break loose.

I find a green metal bench that has been placed in a nook between two old red brick buildings partially sheltered from the rain. It is a good place to stop for a minute and rearrange my backpack. I am on the outskirts of central downtown, far uphill from the bay where a heavy fog is starting to roll in. It has taken me a full hour to circle back away from the store and reach this point. I know that I am running into the heart of danger instead of away from the city, but right now, I don't have much choice. There are things that I have to find out, and find out quickly.

I open my backpack and hunch over it to keep the raindrops out. There is plenty of room for my new items, so I pull my water bottles out and start packing the food and medicines in. I take the poly screwdriver and a handful of the hard candy and stuff them into my left jacket pocket. My pockets are deep. The Perma Lighter will fit nicely into my right pocket. I hold it up in front of me and dial it to its "full torch" setting with my thumb. I can't risk even testing it out here; that would bring a police cruiser for sure. I sigh and stuff it into my right pocket. I tear open a snack bar and quickly wolf it down. My stomach still feels queasy.

Then I close my backpack, stand up, and swing it back up on to my shoulders.

The old inner city is always dark. Even on the sunniest days, it is always blanketed in deep shadows cast from the tall ancient buildings, like the narrow canyons up in the mountains far to the east. I pass a few early pedestrians as I follow the sidewalk that leads toward the center of the city. That is where I will start my search.

Every schoolchild has heard the myths by the time they are ten years old. For me, it was even earlier. I remember hiding on the stairs when I was seven, listening to my parents talk in hushed whispers about my aunt. She was a runner. She ran with her unborn baby ten years before I was even born.

"Rachel is dead by now," my father whispers. "There is no way she could have even made it halfway to Haven. Stupid, stupid girl!"

My mother is crying.

I have never been able to picture Rachel, my mother's older sister. We have no pictures of her in the house. Runners are never mentioned, never remembered as having even lived. But my mother sometimes talked to me about her when we were alone, with father off at his government job. This was when I was still very young. This is when my mother still told me secrets about places like Haven. Where you could go to be safe and have your baby if you wanted to. Where there were no Parlors.

She told me these things, a lot of which I don't even remember now, and she would always finish by doing something strange. She would look deep into my eyes, touch my forehead lightly, and make a sign by tracing her finger up and down then side to side. Then she would sigh and kiss me goodnight. This was all before…

There is another rumor fresh in every schoolkid's mind about a fabled underground. According to this rumor, an even older city exists underneath the streets of Frisco.

The boys love this rumor. Every boy wants to find the underground and wants to go there to be an "outlaw." The teachers insist that nothing exists beneath the streets of the city but rotten sewage tunnels and electrical lines, but for some reason I have a strong sense that the rumor might be true. And I have to find out if I am right. It's my only hope for finding the information I need.

I pull up the left sleeve of my jacket as I walk and take one last, long look at the silver bracelet dangling on my wrist. It is the bracelet that Jason gave me on my sixteenth birthday. Even in the rain, it shines like new. *Don't get sentimental*, I tell myself. *Don't even go there, it's just a bracelet.*

I enter an alleyway deep in the heart of the city where the sidewalks are filling up fast with people now. It is nine thirty in the morning, and I know that the types of people who hang out in the dark, back alleys are the types who can't get regular jobs. Three scruffy-looking types are loitering in this particular alley, leaning against the rain-soaked brick walls of the tall, old buildings that disappear into the mist far above my head. Two of the men are leaning against one wall, well apart from each other, while the other one idles on the other side of the alley farther down. They don't appear to be friends with each other.

I approach the closest one who is wearing tattered gray slacks and a dark hooded jacket. They all wear hoods that hide their faces in shadow, and this one is reading from an ancient plastic viewer that he holds just beneath his long, graying beard. He probably pulled it out of a waste bin. He doesn't even look up at me.

I turn and scan the area behind me, and then I whisper to him. "Underground?"

"Beat it, kid" he mutters and keeps reading.

Fine. I approach the second guy, and he flinches and quickly turns away from me. I walk down the alleyway to my third and last chance here. This guy is a real prize. He appears to be older than the other two and awfully thin, hands shoved deep into his pockets. He turns slightly away from me as I approach, and while I am still at least ten feet away from him, I nearly faint from his bad smell.

"Underground?" I whisper when I am close enough to him.

"What've you got, missy?" he rasps in a half growl. He turns and leers at me with dark, shiny, beady eyes.

I slip my bracelet off my wrist and hold it up for him to see.

"I have this," I say.

He yanks his right hand out of his pocket and opens it to reveal a jeweler's lens. Unbelievable.

"Real McCoy," he whispers as he examines my bracelet. "Rich little girl, eh?"

"No."

He grabs my bracelet and quickly shoves it in his pocket. I realize that I am too trusting, that he could just walk away with my jewelry and then where would I be? But he doesn't.

"Follow me," he whispers in his raspy voice.

The rain is easing up as he leads me out of the alleyway, downhill on a city sidewalk for five blocks and makes a right turn into an even darker alleyway. As we walk, he constantly shifts his eyes back and forth, scanning the streets. He has scored big time, I realize, the bracelet probably represents a months' worth of food to him and he doesn't want to have to give it up.

Halfway down the alley, I spot where he is headed. Ahead of us stand a pair of heavy, rusted metal doors that lead into the side of a huge, crumbling old brick building. He quickly swings one door open and leads me down a dark set of stairs. I instantly regret packing my flashlight away. The stairs descend forever, and after a little while, my eyes start adjusting to what was utter darkness. We have to be a hundred feet below the surface of the alley when we reach a giant metal door on a landing at the bottom of the steps. My guide stops and bangs loudly with his fist on it. A giant hulk of a man opens the door from the inside. I slow a little and try to make out what he looks like, but it is too dark.

"Hounddog," my guy grunts. Fitting.

"Pass!" the figure growls back. He swings open the heavy door. I studied mythology in school, and I know that we have descended into Hades. The underground is a stark contrast of darkness and brightness to my adjusting eyes. Dark, because deep shadows stretch everywhere into pockets of sheer blackness. Bright, because dozens of little campfires burn along the tiny streets with dirty, skinny figures huddled around them. The whole place stinks of human waste and stale smoke. The streets are lined with ancient, black-stained, moldy buildings; some, I can see with candles burning from interior rooms, lighting windows from the inside. Overhead, I can hear the faint, dull roar of city traffic on the streets above us.

"Keep moving, missy!" my guide orders as he starts down a street. After hesitating, I follow him. But I am wary and terribly claustrophobic from the inescapable feeling that I am trapped in a giant, foul cave. The rumors were true, the underground exists. I doubt that the police would even bother coming down here. I sigh heavily. In my civics courses in school, I was taught that you either contribute to the common good of society or you die. Down here, stretching away from me into the darkness, I see a third option.

We head down an impossibly narrow street. What kind of vehicles could have used these passages to travel by, I wonder, as we turn two corners until we are entering the remnants of a neighborhood filled with collapsed houses and dirty old storefronts. Broken old bricks and any trash that cannot be burned litter the street. Filthy, wretched men and women look up at me from their fires like I am a newly arrived fresh piece of meat. I ease my hands into my pockets as I stare back at them.

"This way!" my charming tour guide growls and leads me into an uncomfortably dark back alley. I hesitate, staying close to the better-lit street we have just left. Two figures emerge from the darkness and join my guide, who has turned back toward me.

I take in a deep breath as they slowly creep up together. They are hideous.

"My, my, Smithy," one of them hisses, "what have you brought me?"

"A present," my guide answers and gestures grandly in my direction.

"Don't try to run, honey," his friend says. I can see him in the firelight now. He is a little younger than my guide but incredibly ugly with crusty dark eyes and the hollow look of a starving man.

His partner laughs. At least I think he is laughing. It is more like a cackling, like the black crows that have just found a fresh, smelly feast in the garbage bin at my neighborhood park.

"There ain't nowhere to run to!" the first man assures me. They continue toward me, and I really start backing up.

"How much?" the first one asks.

"Oh, she's not cheap," Smithy chuckles. They pick up their pace, and Smithy reaches out to grab me with his grimy hand. I pull my right hand out of my jacket pocket, and an intense, white-blue flame lights up the alley.

The Perma Lighter's flame extends out almost a foot from its tip, and I easily burn Smithy's hand with it. He howls in pain and yanks his blistered hand back. I wave the lighter at the other two, who are quickly backing up.

"That's right," I growl. "I'm not cheap! Anybody else?"

The Perma Lighter is doing its job. They don't want any part of me now. I glare at Smithy who is groaning and sucking on his hand.

"I gave you the bracelet," I tell him, letting my anger radiate. "We had a deal!"

I turn and run out of the black alley, letting the Perma Lighter's flame die down as I go. I can hear the voice of Smithy's pal as I run, but it isn't directed at me.

"Bracelet?" he asks Smithy. "What bracelet?"

I wipe the tears from my face as I run.

CHAPTER FIVE

Who am I trying to fool? Sure, I backed them off; but still, I am really just a scared little girl with a Perma Lighter. I want to be anywhere but in this horrid, stinking garbage dump, and I know that my time is running out. Somebody down here is going to get me.

But for now, there is nowhere else to go; and if Haven exists, somebody down here is probably enough of a criminal to know about it. I have to find that person. I have to know if Daniel and I even have a chance. I have to keep moving.

I check my watch and see that it is 10:30 a.m. By now, all the machines are in motion, and there is probably a citywide alert out about me. I can just imagine my picture flashing across the public boards with PUBLIC ENEMY NUMBER ONE plastered beneath it. I wonder how my parents are handling the situation. Most likely, they are freaking out. Runners are always big newsmakers, and I imagine that it will be up to my father to handle the spotlight. My stepmother will be too mortified. There have not been very many reports of runners this year, only three or four that I can recall. The government is really cracking down on them and captured runners face abortion, sterilization, mandatory prison, and even death sometimes when they are caught and dragged back— if they are brought back alive. If they are brought back dead, you get to see their bodies displayed on the public boards for weeks. If a live one is executed, you get to see that too.

But some of them are not brought back at all. Do they make it to Haven? Is Haven real?

I walk along the main street, and it is a relief to be back in a relatively brighter place. There is no sign that Smithy and the boys are pursuing me; they probably don't carry any weapon that can trump a Perma Lighter. I have to stay on guard though. They might go and get something better, and then lay a trap for me. They don't strike me as the types who will just give up.

I really start to observe the people who huddle around the street fires, trying to ward off the cold and damp, smoky air. It smells like a pigsty down here, and I wonder how so many of them came to be here. Were they enemies of the government? They look like starving skeletons when they glare up at me or cringe away like feral, beaten animals. I know that I must look like an alien from another world to them. At least half of them look insane.

As if to confirm my suspicions, a little old lady wearing a dirty little girl's dress, her face smeared with old, crusty makeup, dances in front of me and sings to me in a high-pitched little girl voice, a song that is completely unintelligible. I quicken my pace to get around her, but she is persistent and stays right in front of me, invading my space. I begin to sense danger again; there is something sickly sinister about, her, and I feel her herding me toward something. Where ever it is, I definitely don't want to go there. The Perma Lighter comes out again, but I don't ignite it. I just wave it in front of her grotesque face, and her shiny eyes finally light up with fear. As she turns and runs off screaming, the people huddled around the nearest fire howl with laughter.

What if this place is Haven? I wonder to myself. The very thought makes me sick to my stomach.

I keep walking. I feel like I am broadcasting information to these people like a walking public board. "Look, a rich little girl with a backpack full of food, carrying a very valuable Perma

Lighter." It would probably fetch a pretty price down here, and I know for sure that I would.

I continue down the street until a well-lit, slightly run-down storefront catches my eye. Through yellowed white lace curtains in the windows, I can see shelves of books. Old, ancient books with hardcovers and real paper. This is what I have been searching for, hoping to find. Old books are illegal for a reason; they contain illegal information. Tentatively, I walk up the steps and knock on the door.

"A minute, please!" a high-pitched male voice calls out from somewhere inside the house. The front porch starts to shake, and I hear him rustling the front door open. He is a huge, fat man, completely different from anyone out on the street, wearing a slightly yellowed, daintily laced shirt and black trousers, probably leftovers from an old tuxedo. His graying brown hair is long and curly complete with greasy bangs that nearly hide his small, dark eyes. There is a glint in his eyes, even tucked away as they are in his flabby face.

"An angel!" He appraises me. "Come into my wonderful store, dear angel."

He motions inside with a sweep of his hand, and I tentatively enter, keeping my eye on him as I do. I hold the straps of my backpack tightly with my hands. The place reeks of stale perfume, and I almost sneeze.

"Oh, don't mind that!" he exclaims as he ushers me in, sensing my distress. "My perfume vanquishes the musty smell of old paper!"

He leads me between overstuffed bookshelves packed with volumes of wonderful old books. It is an amazing sight, to see such obvious wealth. But it is wealth with a price. On the city streets above, this man would spend the rest of his life in prison. If they let him live.

"The angel looks like she has enough money to buy one of my books!" The fat man happily announces to no one that I can see. "Does the angel have a name?"

"Chrissie," I answer. I run my right hand along the spines of the books, feeling the textures of old leather and cloth. "My name is Chrissie."

"What a wonderful name!" he exclaims as we enter an office-like area nestled behind the bookshelves, cluttered to high heaven with stacks of books and old papers. "I have always loved the name Chrissie! Please, call me Perryman. Merriwether Perryman at your service!"

He bows slightly and then motions to a crumbling leather chair that sits in front of a broad, wooden desk. At least I think it's a desk. It is buried in old books. I recognize the lamp nestled in the middle of the desktop as a Tiffany-style lamp from pictures that I've seen on my reader. If it is authentic, it has to be priceless.

I carefully take my seat, leaving my backpack on, and Perryman throws himself into a giant leather chair behind his desk. With practiced frenzy, he shoves books and papers aside so that he can see me. I see that he has a midsized viewer sitting to one side on his desk.

"Now then, beautiful little Chrissie," he says and smiles broadly at me, "relax, relax! Now tell Perryman what brings you to his fine bookstore?"

As he talks, his fingers dance across the screen of his viewer like a musician's hand, with his eyes riveted on its display instead of on me. I take a deep breath.

"Maybe you have the answer here," I say, unwilling to commit further.

As he continues to study his screen, a slight frown crosses his face.

"The answer, the answer, the answer," he says. "Oh, little dear, you'll have to tell Perryman more than that!"

I sigh and squirm out of my backpack. Perryman turns and watches me as I unzip the top, reach in, and pull out my father's atlas. Perryman gasps out loud as he sees it.

"Oh, that's a find, dear! A genuine atlas from the twenty-first century, it looks like. May I see it?"

"It's just an old atlas," I say, sensing how much he wants it. "It belongs to my father."

"A lucky man," Perryman gulps. "A very, very lucky man."

"He's a policeman," I lie. "He is just down the street, working undercover. He brought me down here to do my research."

"Research, yes, yes," Perryman says quickly. "For school, I bet, little girl, can I see it, please?"

He reaches out with his fat hand. I hesitate for a moment and then hand the atlas to him. He nearly yanks it away and then rapidly thumbs through it before returning to his viewer.

"Very nice," Perryman says, "very nice, indeed. How much, Chrissie? How much do you want for it?"

"I'll ask my dad," I promise him. "He does want to sell it, and it looks like you're the expert. But I need for you to show me something first."

"Oh yes, yes," Perryman answers. "Fine. I have plenty of customers up above who would pay through the nose for this. Tell your dad we could split the profits. Why, the president himself might want this!"

"Okay, Perryman," I answer. "I'll go out and ask him in a minute. But first, can you show me where Haven is located on it? That's what my report is about. I want to solve the mystery about Haven."

"You'd get an A, that's for certain," Perryman exclaims as he studies his viewer. I watch his eyes. They pause on the screen and he freezes, transfixed on what he sees. Whatever it is, his eyes betray him. I see the flash of fear cross his puffy face.

"Dear, dear," he says, and looks directly at me. "Haven is not a real place, Chrissie. But we can pretend that it is, if you want to. You can certainly embellish your report. Who would know?"

My heart drops at his words, but I freeze into my best poker face. Something else is going on here, I sense.

Perryman jumps up.

"Where are my manners, dear girl?" he exclaims. "I haven't even offered you tea! A moment, please!"

He rumbles off like an elephant into the dark recesses at the back of his house, and I hear dishes clanking. Quietly, I move around his desk to see his viewer. The screen is black; he has blanked it out. If it is like my viewer, I can pull up a recall. I work the screen.

"The water is boiling, dear!" Perryman calls out. "Patience, patience!"

There it is! The screen wakes up to show me a full-blown picture of myself with an alert printed below it. Assigned "possible runner status" at 10:30 a.m., it says. Fifty thousand credits for her safe return, it also says. I grab my atlas.

"Coming, Chrissie," Perryman calls out, and I can feel the wooden floor shake beneath my feet. Frantically, I yank my backpack out my chair and sprint through the rows of bookshelves.

"Where did you go?" I hear Perryman call out behind me. *No way can he catch me*, I reassure myself. He's too fat. The whole house starts to shake.

"Chrissie, come back!" Perryman pleads. His voice is definitely fading behind as I reach the front door. *Please*, I pray, *don't let him have autolocks on his door*. Sure enough, I hear the tell-tale snapping noise in the doorframe. I ball up my shoulders and slam into the door with all my might, hoping that the locks haven't fully engaged yet. It hurts and I grit my teeth, but the door gives way, and I run across the front porch and back out on to the street. I look back to see Perryman leaning out of the broken doorway.

"Come back here, you girl!" he screams, his voice deep and ugly now. Then he turns to the people out on the street.

"She's a runner, get her!" he screams.

A dozen of the skeletal figures spring into action, and I feel hands grabbing at me. They pull at my arms, and someone yanks away my watch. I scream and run faster. They outnumber me, but they are weak. As I run, I pull out the Perma Lighter and light it up. The skeletons start to fall back.

"A thousand credits!" Perryman screams. "Get her!"

There are so many of them. The hands are hanging on tightly now, and I know that they can overpower me. I wheel around and burn them with the Perma Lighter, hearing them howl in pain. The Perma Lighter scares them, and they start to give up.

Three blocks later, I'm sure that I have left them behind. I have to get out of here. The street looks familiar to me, and I think that I might be able to find my way back to the big entry door. I stop to catch my breath. The people on this street stare at me and cringe away from my Perma Lighter. I extinguish it and shove it back into my jacket pocket.

Another street up and around the corner, I am sure, is where Smithy brought me in. I start walking slowly toward it, glaring at anybody who dares to look at me.

"Password!" the guard at the entry growls at me as I approach him. He is a huge dark man and looms at the door like an immovable mountain. Why can't I get a break? I rack my brain. The password to get in was "Hounddog," I remember that. I take a chance.

"Kittycat," I whisper to him.

"Go back!" he growls, frowning at me.

I have to go back. For hours, I creep along the dark streets, keeping to the black shadows and hunting for any face that looks even half sane. *Good luck*, I finally tell myself. I can feel hundreds of eyes leering at me from the huddled groups around the street fires. In my mind, I picture myself in a deep cave, surrounded by hundreds of hungry, feral wolves.

CHAPTER SIX

There is no way that I can blend in, and my mind is racing desperately for a way out of here. Someone is laughing at me, and I realize as I turn the corner to another street that I am crying again. I wipe my eyes and wet, black soot covers my hands.

"Don't cry," I hiss at myself. "Don't show them any weakness."

I am lost now. I doubt that I can even find my way back to the big guard at the entrance. I am starting to wander aimlessly through the underground.

Then I can hear Perryman's shrill voice somewhere out there in the darkness.

"Five thousand credits!" he is yelling. "She is down here somewhere!"

He is shouting out an exact description of me. I run down the street and turn another corner into a wide area that almost looks like an old playground or courtyard. There must be more than a hundred hideous people gathered here. They all hear Perryman's shrill voice. They are all looking up at me from their fires.

Almost on cue, they jump up and charge me. I scream and turn around to run back to the street I just left, but another crowd of skeletons is coming up behind me. I pull out my Perma Lighter and light it. I have to stand my ground, and I hold the sharp blue-white flame up high for everyone to see. This time, they don't seem to be deterred by it. Five thousand credits would make any one of them rich for life. I am trapped.

As they creep closer to me, I recognize Smithy and his pals standing at the front of the crowd. I guess the bracelet wasn't enough for them. Their beady eyes shift back and forth between me and the Perma Lighter I am waving at them. Now a hundred hungry faces circle me, drawing closer and closer like moths toward my little ball of blue-white light.

Somewhere out in the darkness, I hear a blood-curdling shriek. The skeletons surrounding me gasp in unison and twist their necks around to see what is coming. Another shriek, even louder, reminds me of the big cats at the zoo.

The crowd parts and fades away into the darkness as she approaches me. I have never seen anything like her. She appears to be in her twenties, lithe and strong as she walks up to me. Her hair is jet-black, short, and spiked where it falls around her face. Her eyes glow unnaturally red in the light of my Perma Lighter, and she glares at me with undisguised malice. But she is also grinning.

She wears a tight bodysuit that accentuates her trim, muscular body. It is black and yellow and reminds me of a tiger's stripes. Everything about her radiates power and a ferociousness that is totally out of place with the pathetic skeletons I have been running from.

I freeze with fear, like a rabbit caught in headlights, with a death grip on my only weapon and doubting seriously if it will make any difference at all. When she reaches me, she answers my question by slapping me so fast and so hard across the face that the force of her blow lifts me off of my feet. I go tumbling through the thick, black soot blanketing the crumbling pavement of the street.

The force of her strike is unimaginable. I see nothing but stars as I hear her shriek again. When my sight returns, I see her crouching above me, glaring down at me with her wicked grin, her fist clenched and ready to strike again. I curl up in a ball in the soot and wait for her to pounce.

Out of the corner of my eye, I sense movement. A large black man comes out of nowhere, crosses over me, and like lightning, attacks the woman. She hisses, raises her arms to block him, and I can see that her forearms are shielded by some sort of protective covering. Like lightning, the man strikes at her again and again. She blocks his attacks, spins away, and leaps back at him like a wild animal. They move so fast, I have a hard time following them as they battle.

He blocks and finally connects with a hard blow to her head, sending her reeling. She shrieks and jumps at him again. I huddle as I watch. I could run, but I am still too dizzy to get to my feet.

The man is silent as he parries and blocks the woman's terrible attack. Then he moves in, and in a flash, he has her, his arm braced around her neck. She screams, struggles, and thrashes around, kicking the street soot up into a black cloud. He eases her to the ground as he keeps her locked up in his strong arms.

Now he is on his knees. The woman has stopped breathing, and so have I as I watch the red light fade from her eyes.

The man gently lays her down on the ground. He looks sad. With his hand, he closes her eyes, whispers something that I can't hear, and then makes a sign with his other hand across her body. Then he turns and looks directly at me. His large eyes are brown, and have a kind of gentleness about them.

"She was called Medea," he quietly says to me. "She was a closer. She was going to kill you, Chrissie."

He takes a step toward me. His clothing is dark, coarse, and worn. He blends in down here.

"Let's have a look at you, child," he says as he kneels next to me.

"Nothing broken," he appraises and then lightly touches my stomach with the calloused palm of his hand. I feel Daniel jump in my belly. The man closes his eyes and sighs.

"Daniel is okay too," he says. "Can you stand up?"

Gingerly, with the big man's helping hand, I struggle to my feet. I am still dizzy, and I can't feel the left side of my face where the woman hit me. My left eye has already swollen shut. Once on my feet, I sway back and forth, my body determined to tumble over into the soot again.

With a firm grip, the man holds me steady.

"We can't stay here, Chrissie," he says. I look around at the dark town square and see that he is right, the skeletons are moving toward us again.

He wraps his big arm around me and leads me toward a side alley. As we enter it, confusion crosses the skeleton's faces.

"They vanished!" I hear Smithy yelling from somewhere behind us. "Find them!"

"Somebody up above wants you dead right now," the big black man whispers as he hurries me down the deserted alley. "And that is not the way this game is played. They always give runners a chance to come back on their own for at least a day or two. Then the police mobilize their search. Closers are always a last resort. They never ever send in a closer this soon."

We work our way back and forth down back alleys until the man is satisfied that we have lost the crowd. He sits me down against a soot-covered wall. My face and jaw are hurting so bad that pain shoots up the side of my head with each step that I take, and I am glad that we stop. But I still want more than anything to get out of this place.

As soon as I sit down, I am overcome with fatigue. I haven't slept in several days, and it is catching up with me. The big man watches me.

"It's just as well you sleep now," he says quietly, seeing my state of exhaustion. "It is late evening up above."

Has it been that long? Have I been down in this snake pit that long?

"Too many cruisers up above," he continues as he rubs his big hands together, "hunting for you, girl. Maybe even another closer or two. Our best chance is to go up into the city and blend into the sidewalk crowd in the morning. You'd better sleep now."

I want to sleep, but I have questions.

"Who are you?" That's the obvious one.

The big black man sighs and looks down at me. I can tell that he is older than I first thought now that I have a chance to study him up close. His short black hair is peppered with gray and white, and his face is heavily wrinkled. But I can tell from the wrinkles around his eyes that he must smile a lot in better times. Tonight, he just looks worn out and sad.

"I'm your guide, Chrissie," he answers. "I'm here to help you get to Haven."

So there is a Haven after all?

"How did you know about me? How did that Medea, whatever she was, know?" I ask.

"I've known about you for a long time," he answers. "A long, long time. But I don't know how Medea knew so soon, unless..."

"Unless what?"

He doesn't answer.

"What is a closer?" I ask. I shift my back against the wall and my head throbs. My one good eye is growing heavy with sleep, and everything around me is taking on a dreamlike quality. None of what has happened seems real to me now; maybe I am already dreaming.

"Closers work for the government," the man tells me. "They are specialists, independent contractors. They are hunters, the best of the best, trained to catch runners."

"Assassins?" I ask. Medea had death in her eyes.

"Yes, sometimes, and sometimes, even worse than that. They work alone most of the time. The police are mostly afraid of them and usually stay out of their way. They play by their own rules."

I don't get it. I know that I have officially been designated the status of a runner by now, but my dad is important. Really important. He would make sure no one would be out to kill me. He would only send the police, wouldn't he?

"Like I said, Chrissie," the big man answers, like he is reading my mind, "they want you bad, and they want you dead. They want you and Daniel. No matter what you might believe. And they have their reasons."

He said it again. Daniel. I am really suspicious now.

"How do you know my baby's name?" I ask him. "I haven't told anybody his name, not even my best friend!"

He chuckles, and his deep voice jolts me awake a little.

"You know who told me," he answers.

The voice, I think to myself, *he must be talking about the voice.*

"You're right, Chrissie." The man nods his head, as if I had actually spoken out loud to him. I know for certain that I didn't.

"The voice told me Daniel's name. That's why I am here today, Chrissie. That's why you are still alive."

Now I know that this is a dream, probably a nightmare. I'll wake up in my bed at home, any minute now with Maximus curled up in the blankets next to me. I want to wake up in my bed, in my safe house, in my safe neighborhood. All of it is not that far away from here, from this impossible place. How could this even exist?

But the nightmare continues.

"Somebody is going to find us," I say.

The big man shakes his head.

"Nobody is going to find us. Nobody is even going to see us. Sleep, child."

"Who are you?" I ask again, yawning, "What is your name?"

I can't help it; even though I don't fully trust him, I slump heavily against the big man's warm shoulder. Darkness is settling over me. I am really drifting off now.

"Moses," I hear his deep voice answer in my dream. "My name is Moses, child."

He sighs a deep, heavy sigh. A sad sigh.

"Moses…leading his children to the promised land…"

CHAPTER SEVEN

I know that I am lost in a deep sleep, dreaming. I open my eyes, and I am lying in a bed, with a thick, white silk blanket spread across me and my head resting on a fluffy pillow. My mother sits next to me in a white rocking chair and smiles at me as she gently rocks back and forth. She is wearing a snow-white dress, and her face radiates with something greater than just her natural beauty. She leans toward me, reaches out, and makes the sign of the cross on my forehead. My forehead is little, I realize. I am a little girl again.

"His name is Moses, Chrissie," my mother tells me as she rocks back and forth in her white rocking chair. "And he is a good man. You can trust him."

I nod my head and smile back at my mother. It has been so long. I miss her so much.

Light erupts. It flows from a single point above my mother's head and grows until it engulfs everything around us. It literally flows like water and behaves like it is alive. I can feel the warmth of its life, of its overwhelming presence. And it contains deep, deep emotion. And then I hear the voice that spoke to me about Daniel.

"You have chosen the hard path, Chrissie," the voice says to me. "You have chosen well!"

My mother nods in agreement with the voice and smiles her gentle smile at me again. Then as she and the living light begin to fade away from me, a tear runs down her cheek…

I am startled awake to the sound of snipping scissors. I must have really slept; my mind feels cloudy and a little bit disoriented. My left eye is still swollen shut and my head aches horribly. It is so dark here.

The scissors are clipping away at my hair! I wince and turn around to look right into the big, brown eyes of the man who calls himself Moses. So he wasn't a dream after all.

"What are you doing?" I ask, still waking up. Moses is perched against the wall behind me, scissors in hand.

"Getting you ready, Chrissie," he calmly says and smiles a warm smile that could melt your heart. "If we go outside with you looking like you did, the police will be on us in five minutes."

I settle back and let him cut. All around me, long strands of my light brown hair lay scattered on the damp concrete. He is cutting my hair short, almost like a boy's.

"How long did I sleep?" I ask, yawning.

"You slept a long time, girl," Moses says with a chuckle and continues to cut away.

"What time is it?"

"Morning," Moses voice lowers a little. "Is Jason your boyfriend?"

"He was," I admit in a lower voice.

"You talked about him in your sleep," Moses tells me and, gently grasping my shoulders, turns me around to face him. He is looking at my hair.

"Just a few more cuts," he says and studiously snips away at my bangs.

"Chrissie," he says, "you are going to have to forget all about him, child."

I sigh. My mind is reeling. Before I fell asleep, this man actually read my thoughts. I am certain of it. How is that possible? I accept the idea that he might be a clairvoyant. I have read about those people, old enemies of the New Republic and supposedly long dead, but I never quite accepted the idea of someone really having the ability as something I might have to deal with.

Moses makes one last cut and carefully appraises his work.

"There," he says, "not too bad."

"Do you have a mirror?" I ask, and it makes him laugh. I like his laugh; it is warm and makes me feel secure.

"You'll have to trust me," he says. "And now, for the finishing touch."

He has a bottle of something in his hand and tells me to lean forward and look at the ground. As I comply, I realize that I am no longer wearing my backpack. I glance from side to side, and there it is, leaning against the wall.

"Now, close your eyes," Moses instructs, and I feel a cool liquid flowing through my short hair. It smells acrid and fizzles; I wrinkle up my nose and sneeze. Then Moses is carefully rinsing my hair with what must be water and then drying it with a small towel.

"Okay, Chrissie," he says, "you can look up now."

I look back up into his eyes, and he is smiling at me again. He gives me the thumbs up.

"It will do," he says. "And your swelled-up face will help for sure. Now, let's take a look at that backpack."

Quickly, we empty the contents of my backpack out on the concrete. Moses makes two piles. In the smaller pile, he places the medicine, a handful of food bars, the hard candy, one water bottle, and that's about it. I look from one pile to the other. I am hungry, with the first mild waves of morning sickness, so I grab a food bar and open it.

"Where we are going you won't need any of that," he tells me as I eat, gesturing at the big pile. I look at it longingly. My dad's atlas is lying on top.

"What about that?" I ask, pointing at the old book.

"You definitely don't want to take that, Chrissie." Moses shakes his head. "You can't carry anything that can help identify you. Don't worry, I'll teach you how to find your way."

"I'm going to need water," I challenge, eyeing my other bottles.

"Yes, you will," Moses agrees and hands me a foot-long sipping straw. It is light and pliable in my hand.

"We developed these in Haven," Moses tells me. "All of the guides carry them. Water is where you find it. Sip it through this straw, it will be pure. Trust me, child, it's much better than that bottled stuff."

Moses reaches behind his back and pulls out a dingy gray little knapsack, fully stuffed. I haven't seen it before.

"You can keep your socks and boots," he tells me, handing me the knapsack. "But everything else has to go. I'll turn my back. You change into these clothes."

I take the old knapsack. It contains scruffy old clothes, workers clothes. Moses turns around, and I shrug out of my jacket, my shirt, and untie my boots. The clothes feel scratchy against my skin, and look like they feel, but Moses is right. In these, I could be anybody.

"Okay," I say. Moses turns, looks me up and down, and grins.

"You are ready," he announces. He stuffs the little pile of my belongings into his old knapsack, hands it to me, and proceeds to fill my backpack with the discarded big pile.

He gives me a sideways glance as he works.

"Okay, it's time to get down to business," he says, and I feel myself tighten up.

"Why did you decide to run, Chrissie?"

I slump against the wall.

It's a family tradition, I want to tell him. I want to tell him the story about my Aunt Rachel, how she ran, and the hell it created for all of us. I want to tell him how I grew up, always dreaming about her, wondering if she was still alive, and if so, where she had gone.

I want to tell him about my real mother. About the sign she used to trace every night on my forehead when I was a little girl. "This is the sign of the cross," she told me. How she promised to tell me when I was old enough what the sign of the cross meant. It was something that I could tell to no one but my own children when the time came. It was something that could get you killed. It was something that she never got a chance to tell me about.

"Daniel is deformed," Moses continues. "Abortion is the rule of law around here, especially for deformed babies. The government makes that clear. You could have solved all of your problems in one easy stroke, girl."

I still don't know if I can fully trust him. But I have to try.

I tell him about *the voice*. I tell him about how it told me that Daniel is in the lion's den and how I am the only one who can save him. I can feel Daniel inside of me, and I love him more than anything else in the world.

"I will not kill my baby!" I exclaim. "In the Parlor, I saw his heart beating. How can anyone kill their baby after that? And what gives them the right? Why do they get to decide if Daniel lives or dies? I hate them for that! I hate all of them!"

Moses hushes me and looks deeply into my eyes. Is he reading my mind? He looks into my eyes for an uncomfortably long time.

"Okay," he finally says. "That's good enough for me, Chrissie. And you are right, Daniel is definitely in the lion's den! And you and I are going to do everything we can do to get him out of there."

He picks up the rest of my gear and then bundles it up.

"Wait!" I exclaim and take my jacket from him. I take the Perma Lighter and the poly screwdriver out of the pockets and shove them into the pockets of the dirty old jacket that came with the knapsack. Concern flashes across his face, but Moses nods his head.

"Take those if you must," he says.

I must. I hand my jacket back to him.

We make our way out into the dark, cluttered street square. Nothing has changed except for the fact that there seem to be even more crazies huddled around the campfires. I know that we are going to have to pass by places that I don't want to see again anytime soon. The wicked little girl/lady comes dancing up to us, still singing, and Moses hands my discarded backpack to her.

"Go away, Barbie!" he tells her firmly. She looks at the backpack and squeals with delight, dancing away. We keep moving. On one street, I see Smithy and the boys crouched against a wall. They take one look at Moses and slink into the shadows. I slip my arm into Moses's and glare at them. I am in good hands.

The lights are turned off in Perryman's bookstore, and I briefly wonder about it but not enough to investigate. We are headed for the entryway. The big hulk stills guards it. Moses walks up to him and whispers, "Hounddog."

"Right on, Moses," the big man says quietly. "You be careful out there."

The giant looks down at me as I pass by.

"You be careful, too, Jackrabbit," he says to me, and bows slightly. Daniel jumps again, deep in my belly. I am thunderstruck.

We climb the stairs, out into the big city alleyway. Moses carefully checks out the area and then takes my hand. His big, dark hand is warm.

"Let's go, child," he says.

The rain and mist have ended, and bright shafts of sunlight flood the back alleys, creating a stark patchwork of light and dark. We step out on to the bright, busy city sidewalks, and I have to put on my sunglasses. Downtown Frisco is bustling with crowds of people rushing to work, street vendors setting up their wares beneath the old towering skyscrapers that shoot high up into the crisp blue sky, and street people who look only a little better off than the lost souls I saw down in the underground. I look at Moses in the sunlight. He is a tall, strong, lanky man who walks with an uncommon ease, but he blends in with the street people like I do—two grubby vagabonds wearing tattered clothes, carrying old knapsacks on our backs.

Halfway down the block, I spot a large public board suspended in the air above the sidewalk and watch to see if it flashes up the time. It does. It is nine fifteen in the morning. Then I gasp in horror as a flurry of colorful news images shoot across it. A picture of Jason and me at the homecoming dance. A portrait of me with my father and stepmother. A still shot of me in the convenience store buying the Perma Lighter. The words "KIDNAPPED!" plastered below everything. The words *Last seen in the company of a large black man!* pop up as we pass by the board. My last glimpse is of my father giving a tearful interview.

I reach out and firmly grasp Moses's hand.

"I'm so sorry," I whisper to him, "I'm putting you in terrible danger."

"Uh-huh," Moses says. "That's how they are going to spin it, girl. That way, if you get killed, they can blame it on me. That's the game they are playing."

We head up one street, buried in the work crowd, past breakfast vendors and morning coffee shops, before Moses doubles back abruptly and leads me back down the same street. Still holding my hand, he darts into an alleyway, past several grubby loiterers, and we emerge farther uphill on to another street, moving away from the bay. As we pass by a big picture window on a store, I glance at the sharp reflection of myself. I see a dirty, bleached-blond girl, black and blue, swollen face partially hidden by her big, dark sunglasses. She looks like a street urchin. I don't recognize her.

"Water, shelter, food, Chrissie," Moses says quietly as we progress at an even, almost casual pace. "There is a lot for you to learn."

"Are you going to teach me?" I ask.

"As much as I can," he says.

We cross another street and then turn down another alleyway. Deep shadows cut across this one, and I can't see much through my sunglasses. I take them off.

"No, child, leave them on," Moses says. "You can't see them, but trust me, even the alleyways have cameras."

We emerge even farther uphill. We are leaving the business district behind, heading west.

"Water, shelter, food, in that order," Moses continues. "That is your order of priority, do you understand?"

I nod my head. The sidewalk is thinning of people, and Moses jerks his head up and looks behind us. I start to turn, but his strong hand is pulling me down.

"Freeze!" he says, and we huddle together.

"Be still, child," he whispers. I slowly turn my eyes and see the telltale mild distortion moving along in front of the stores across the street, like a gentle, clear swell of bay water washing ashore. A cloaked police cruiser. It passes by and floats up the street.

"Why didn't it detect us?" I ask Moses. I know that they couldn't possibly have missed us. They don't even need to see you. They can sense your bios, your infrared body heat, respiration, even your heartbeat. Then they scan your DNA. Then it's over.

"This is my gift," Moses whispers back, "the ability to hide in plain sight." We stay motionless for another few minutes, and I start to worry about somebody bumping into us. Moses must be worried too because he has us inch toward a wall. Then the coast is clear.

"Let's go," he whispers.

CHAPTER EIGHT

I am four years old. I have learned the fine art of sneaking around the house when I am supposed to be watching my viewer or taking a nap.

I creep like a cat out of my bedroom, tiptoe down the stairs and across the hall toward the kitchen where Mommy hides the cookies. Along the way, I creep past my parents' bedroom. The bedroom door is slightly ajar, and I hear voices.

My mommy and daddy sound like they are arguing. Unusual. My daddy is supposed to be at work at the government.

"Why didn't you tell me?" My daddy sounds very angry.

Mommy is sobbing.

"Because I didn't know for sure, but the latest home test confirmed it," she says. "It is a girl, after all."

"They don't let you have two girls! You know that! You should have visited the Parlor months ago for gender confirmation!"

My daddy stomps around on the floor of the bedroom.

"It's been five months now, you are really showing! It's an actionable offense now, Mary!"

My mommy is really crying now. I peek in through the crack in the door and see her sitting on the bed, holding her face in her hands.

"I can't kill her," she sobs.

My daddy rips off his gray jacket and throws it on the floor.

"I don't get it," he says angrily. "First your sister, and now you?"

He opens the closet and pulls out a suitcase.

"Get packed, Mary, while I call the Parlor. They will take care of it."

He throws the suitcase on the bed and opens it.

"They are going to crucify you, Mary," he says. "And you are going to take it. I'm not having any part of this! You should have checked in with them as soon as you knew you were pregnant!"

"I can't kill her," my mommy sobs, but my daddy grabs her by the arm and pushes her toward the dresser.

"Get on with it!" he tells her.

On the way to the Parlor, they drop me off at the little kids' place. I get to play with the other kids, but I keep crying.

Later, as I grow up, I watch my mother turn from a lively, happy woman to a quiet, sullen shadow of what she once was. When she is with me, she smiles and tries to make the best of things. But when she is around Father and the others, her face is blank.

For the next five years, she has to go to the Parlor five days a week for "reeducation." At first, she drops me off at child care, kisses me, and runs her hand through my hair.

"I'll see you in four hours, Chrissie," she tells me.

"Why do you have to keep going, Mommy?" I ask her when I am seven. She smiles less now. She wears her dull, blank face, even for me.

She has no answer for me. But I find out when I am older. I find my mother's name on the offender registry on my viewer. Even my father's position in the government can't keep her off the registry.

She is a felon. It was mandatory sterilization for her, and even for father. You don't cross the Parlor, not even once.

She disappears off the registry when I am twelve; but she still goes to the Parlor twice a week. She rarely talks, and I am so lonely.

I am sick of my viewer, so I talk a lot to my little sister.

I know that she is really dead; they aborted her at the Parlor, but because mother and I are ostracized by everybody else in the government neighborhood, she is the only playmate I have had for years. I probably made her up, I don't even remember for sure. All I know is that she has been with me for a long time.

Her name is Ruthie, and she is so pretty. She always shows up whenever I need somebody to play with, and she can sit for hours, with her little face in her hands, and listen to me. She looks like one of those beautiful fairies that I like to look at on my viewer, tiny with long, blond hair and sparkly blue eyes. Those eyes light up whenever I smile at her.

She shines, even in my dark room, and she always wears a bright white dress. She always wears pretty flowers in her hair. Sometimes she hugs me, and she always cries when it is time for her to go. I cry too.

When I am ten, Madison moves in next door. She is exactly my age and, unlike all the other kids, she actually plays with me. Her father works for my father, and he has been promoted, so they no longer have to live in an apartment.

"We are so lucky, Chrissie," she tells me. "This is the best place to live in the world! Our fathers are so important."

Ruthie doesn't come around as much because I spend more and more time with Madison. When she does appear, she is shy and keeps to the shadows of my bedroom. She only shows up when I am really sad, when Mommy is sitting in the kitchen, staring at the blank wall.

Then one day, I am old enough to realize that Ruthie has to be make-believe. She exists only in my imagination. Still, I cry. She never visits my bedroom again. For weeks, I grieve over the final loss of the beautiful little sister I never had.

I never tell anybody about Ruthie, not even Madison.

One day, when I am eleven, I hear my father lecturing my mother.

"It should have been a boy," he is saying. "A boy would have been okay. They would have let you keep a boy, Mary."

My mother is quiet. She is always quiet. And she is wearing her blank face.

"It's time to snap out of it, Mary!" My father is saying. "People are talking about your behavior. Important people! And you know I can't afford that."

My mother is just sitting there, wearing her blank face.

"Chrissie."

I am running to my bedroom, crying. And I feel like somebody bad is chasing me.

"Chrissie."

Somebody dark and terribly evil. Somebody who wants to hurt me.

"Chrissie."

I can't get away.

"Chrissie!"

I snap awake, breathing hard. I am sweating. I open my eyes and look up into the warm, kind eyes of Moses. The sun is setting as night approaches.

"Chrissie," he says gently, "you were having a nightmare again."

I rub the tears out of my eyes. We are huddled together under a makeshift lean-to of brush and old tree branches. We are four days outside of Frisco, heading south on foot, toward the coast. That is the plan, to get down to the beach where we will be picked up by Moses's friends.

Moses sits next to me with his legs crossed, his face totally relaxed from doing what he calls "praying and meditating." I know what "praying" is. It is a superstitious ritual that was practiced by the ancients. It has been outlawed for centuries, but Moses doesn't seem to care at all. He looks up slowly, reaches into his pocket, and hands me a food bar.

"You're okay, honey," he tells me as I tear it open. I sigh heavily and take a bite.

"You had the same dream again," Moses says as I eat. I am so hungry.

"Yes," I agree. "Mostly the same one. Something chases me, but I can't see what it is."

Moses shakes his head. He shifts his weight to his side and leans closer to me, looking me straight in the eye.

"Maybe it isn't a dream," he says, "maybe it's a vision, Chrissie."

He shrugs his shoulders, and his expression melts to one of concern.

"I have to get you ready, just in case," he says to me.

"If you mean ready for that thing chasing me in my dreams," I say as I chew my food bar, "good luck!"

"Not only for that," Moses answers. "I have to prepare you for the problems that might lie ahead. I have to teach you where to find food and water."

He closes his eyes for a long moment and then sighs.

"I have to teach you how to find your own way when something happens to me."

I stop chewing.

"When?" I ask incredulously, "Did you say 'when something happens to you,' Moses?"

Moses sighs again.

"I'm sorry, Chrissie. 'If' something happens. It was a slip of the tongue, that's all."

I already feel like I have known him all of my life. I feel like we are old, old friends. In the past four nights, we have slowly, carefully crisscrossed our way out of the suburbs and headed south. We always travel when it is dark and hide during the daylight hours. Moses does have a gift for hiding. Sometimes, people look straight at us, and it is obvious to me that they don't see us.

"How do you do it?" I ask him.

"It has to do with thought," Moses explains as we travel. "Not my thoughts so much, but their thoughts. You would be surprised,

Chrissie. People usually only see what they want to see. All I do is help them out a little bit."

"Can you teach me?"

"I can try," he promises as we go. A few moments later, we flush a sparrow as we wade through some dry brush. I watch it as it rapidly flaps its wings and flees. Then when I look back at Moses, he simply isn't there. I try to find him, but he has vanished.

"Chrissie," he finally says, and I suddenly see him standing next to a small stand of scrub oak. I could swear he wasn't there a moment before.

"All thoughts have substance," he explains as we continue to walk. "And you can project your thoughts in a way that directly influences the thoughts and perceptions of other people, even from great distances. I am pretty good at it, other people are even better."

He chuckles as he watches the sparrow disappear into the shadows in the distance.

"The bird distracted you," he continues. "And I used that distraction to confuse your thoughts. Your world has been full of distractions all of your life, Chrissie. People here in the New Republic are literally drowning in distractions, from media, from marketing, from the noise of technology. And they don't even notice, and they have lost the ability to think clearly. They live like blind, deaf mutes, ignorant of the true world. They have lived this way for a long, long time."

I am confused. The high technology of the New Republic is mankind's greatest achievement. In school, that was pounded into my head.

"Yes," Moses agrees. He is reading my mind again!

"The 'greatness of technology' was pounded into your head by that technology itself, wasn't it?"

I have to agree. From the time I was old enough to hold one, a viewer was crammed into my hands. Not a day went by that I didn't use one to learn, to talk to Madison, to watch *One Star*, to shop, to be talked into shopping, and on and on. I think about it. What have I enjoyed most about the past few days with Moses? The serenity.

"Where I come from, it is very peaceful and quiet, Chrissie," Moses says. "And people are better able to think for themselves. You will see. Where I come from, it is not so easy to confuse the thoughts of others."

"Haven?" I ask as we cross a field of tall grass.

"Yes," Moses answers. "And don't be too hard on yourself, Chrissie. Your mother started you on the proper path years ago."

That said, he reaches out and traces the sign of the cross on my forehead.

"This has been your first lesson."

Last night, I spotted a board floating above a farm road. I have definitely been kidnapped, according to the media spin, and the reward for my safe return is now set at one hundred thousand credits. Moses also has a price on his head. Fifty thousand credits. "What an insult," he tells me.

Police cruisers can float and don't need roads, of course, and several have passed too close to us. Moses always seems to sense their presence before they have a chance to detect us, and we hide. So far, so good.

"How can you tell when they are near?" I ask him.

"It is another part of my gift, Chrissie," Moses tells me, his brown eyes sad. "I can see things that other people can't see. Things that are going to happen. Your world calls it clairvoyance, but it is actually something much more than that. Even so, my gift has its limits. I can't see everything that will come our way, not by a long shot. But I can see enough."

Clairvoyants were all killed in the wars, well over two centuries ago. I learned about them in school and how an army of them rebelled and nearly destroyed the New Republic. The skin on the back of my neck starts to crawl.

"The clairvoyants are all dead," I say sheepishly. "Everyone knows that."

"Not by a long shot, child," Moses says with a sigh. "And you should know by now not to believe everything you read on your viewer."

"What do you see now?" I ask quietly.

Moses is quiet, pensive for a long moment.

"While I meditated, I felt someone blocking me, trying to disrupt my thoughts," he finally answers. "And not many people are capable of doing that to me. I can't see what happens when we get to the beach, Chrissie. But we will stick to our plan and continue for the beach. If the beach does not work out, there is another way."

A silver half-moon is just cresting the far horizon, to the east of us, I think. It is going to be a clear night, mildly illuminated by the moon. We pick up our pace.

"Another way?" I ask.

"The long way," Moses answers. "We go south, across the New Republic."

I think about home. My stepmother is probably still freaking out, and my father is most assuredly working with the police. That is his job anyway. I was not too far off the mark when I told Merriwether Perryman that he was one.

As we enter an area of grassy, rolling hills, Moses asks me about my father. He nods his head when I tell him how high up in the government my father has climbed. Next in line to be the minister of information for the Northern Province, he is quickly becoming an elite member of the president's inner circle.

"Even so, you were right to run, Chrissie." Moses says to me. "Where I come from, everybody knows about you and how special you and Daniel are. Everybody is happy that you made the right decision, child. Where I come from, of course, everybody rejoices when any runner decides to run. That is why we help."

"How did they even know about me?" I ask.

"You know how we knew," Moses says, giving me a serious look. "The voice told us. That's how I knew that you had decided to run to save Daniel. And by deciding to save Daniel, you created a ripple. Kind of like throwing a little pebble into a pond, you see. That ripple spreads out wider and wider and crosses the ripples created by other peoples' lives. And people notice a strong ripple like yours…if they are not too distracted by other things. Every single life has infinite value, Chrissie. And every life creates a ripple, spreading and touching every other ripple in the water. Do you understand?"

"But you killed that closer, that girl named Medea," I point out. "What about her ripple?"

Moses looks down, shakes his head, and my heart drops. I can actually feel his acute pain in my own heart.

"It is never my wish to kill," he tells me. "But sometimes, I have no choice. A terrible evil is growing, Chrissie, and I have chosen to fight it. To save people like you and Daniel from those who would kill you without a second thought."

He stares at the ground pensively and then whispers.

"So many innocents have been slaughtered…how many more?"

Then he stays quiet for a few moments. When he finally looks back up at me, he changes the subject.

"For now, let's talk about you, Chrissie," he responds. "We can talk about other things later."

I wonder if there will be a "later." Briefly, my cat Maximus crosses my mind. He is such a wonderful cat, and I wish that I had him snuggled in my lap right now. *What has happened to him?* I wonder.

The night sky is as dark as it is going to get, and Moses stops and picks up a long, straight, hardwood branch.

We start to move out again, but first, Moses grasps my shoulder and points the stick up at the stars.

"Do you recognize that constellation, Chrissie?" he asks, pointing to a group of stars that every schoolchild has learned at the planetarium.

"The Big Dipper," I answer, nodding my head.

"And why is the Big Dipper so important?" he asks. "What can you always find by using the Big Dipper as a guide?"

I'm stumped, and Moses smiles and shakes his head.

"Look, child," he instructs, and points with his walking stick. "Look at the star I'm pointing at. Follow the two front edge stars of the Big Dipper to that star. That is called the North Star!"

"I see it."

"Can you find it again and again?" Moses asks.

"Of course I can," I tell him. It's easy to find.

"Good," Moses says. "If you have to head south, always walk with your back to the North Star, whenever you can see it at night. And also, when the sun rises in the morning, turn your left shoulder to the sun, and you will be pointed in the right direction."

We walk a few feet through the grass. A light breeze blows in from the west, and I can smell fresh salt. Crickets are starting to chirp.

"And if you are not with me?" I ask quietly, remembering our earlier conversation. Moses looks down at me and I can see starlight sparkling in his eyes. He looks like a big fairy king from a fairy tale I once watched on my viewer.

"Other guides will find you, honey," he assures me. "I promise."

"Now, come along," he says. "We have to keep moving. That monster you keep dreaming about is real, and he probably isn't far behind us."

The next day, I sleep fitfully under a primitive shelter of tall grass. Moses can't be getting much sleep with me tossing and turning the way I do, but he never complains. Whenever I open my eyes to look at him, he is sitting quietly with his head bowed. And then he just pats me on the shoulder and whispers to me that it's all right, it's all right. When we rise in the early evening under another spectacularly clear, moonlit night, Moses refuses to allow me to eat one of my remaining food bars.

"Save it, Chrissie," he instructs me firmly. "Tonight, we forage for our food and water."

In the moonlight, Moses moves quickly through the tall, dry grass like a big, lanky panther. He looks at the ground as he walks, he looks ahead and behind us; he studies every minute feature of our surroundings. I try to copy his movements, but I feel like a baby elephant stomping through the brush. We are definitely approaching the coast. The smell of sea salt permeates the damp, musty night air.

As we progress, the nightmares of my restless sleep take shape in my mind like the bad memories of the Frisco underground. One image in my mind's eye appears over and over again, and I realize that it is the image that has so deeply disturbed me. Almost on cue, Moses stops just ahead of me and turns to stare at me. He is staring at me but with a faraway look in his eyes.

"Nightmares again, Chrissie?" he asks me quietly.

"Bad ones," I admit. He slowly shakes his head.

"You are seeing something real, child," he tells me, and I can almost feel his mind probing my thoughts. How does he do that? He hands me his walking stick.

"Draw it in the dirt for me, Chrissie," he says. "Draw what you are seeing in your nightmares."

It is a creature, something that I have never seen before. I draw its sleek wings, its terrible eyes, and its sharp, pointed tail. Moses squats down and studies it carefully in the moonlight.

"Do you have any idea what that is, Chrissie?" he finally asks me.

"Not a clue. It must be some kind of strange bird."

"No," Moses corrects me. "It's a sea creature. Those are its fins, and that tail, that is its stinger."

He shakes his head.

"The stinger of legend that a son once used to kill a great king…this creature is called a stingray, Chrissie."

Moses shakes his head again and wipes his forehead. His thick brows glisten with sweat, and I can see the worried look in his eyes.

"Okay, Chrissie," he says, standing up and kicking my drawing smooth. "It's time to give you a few things that you are going to need."

I start to ask questions and protest, but Moses just hushes me and reaches into his trousers pocket. When he pulls out his hand, he is holding several beautiful gems that sparkle in the moonlight.

"Diamonds, Chrissie," he explains. "They won't work on closers, but you might be able to buy off a few policemen with these, and they are easy to hide. Now come here."

I do as Moses says, and after he hands me the diamonds, he grasps me by my shoulders and pulls me close.

"Hold still, child," he instructs me. He leans forward and touches his forehead to mine. I feel a mild shock and jump back in surprise.

"What was that?" I demand.

"Don't be afraid, child," Moses says. "I've only reminded you of a gift that you already possess. It is a gift that runs strong in your family. You won't be able to use it very well first off, but by and by, it's going to come in handy."

I feel a little dizzy and slightly nauseated. Is it the morning sickness? Daniel hasn't jumped or anything, he must be asleep. Moses squats down again and pulls up a handful of something green out of the ground. He studies what he is holding and smiles.

"Wild onions, Chrissie," he says. "Not as tasty as a food bar, but they are easy to find, even in the dark."

I root around in the grass under his direction and come up with another handful. We clean the small onion bulbs off with our hands and continue to walk. I bite into one, and the taste is stronger than the onions I am used to, but not too bad.

I pull my scratchy jacket tight around my shoulders, and we continue on—southwest, I think, from the position of the North Star in the night sky. There is a cool ocean breeze caressing my face, blowing gently through my bleached hair. The ocean has to be near.

Every couple of hours, Moses stops and roots around in the ground. He pulls up an array of edible roots, and I am amazed at what he can find. He has done this many times before, obviously. Some of the roots are bitter to the taste.

"This one will keep you alive," he instructs me as I try to chew it. "It is better if you grind it into a paste, flatten it, and cook it in the sun on a flat rock, but we don't have that luxury."

He's right. I have the Perma Lighter strictly for protection. Use it to light a fire out here, and the police cruisers will swarm us in an instant.

Carefully, we cross a big, six-lane highway brightly lit by hundreds of giant media boards that stretch out over the lanes as far as the eye can see. Information and advertisements stream from board to board in a sequence that plays like a never-ending movie. Something to keep you from getting bored as your self-guided car shoots beneath the boards at well over a hundred miles an hour. On the far side of the highway, beyond the bright lights, I can see big, dark bluffs looming in the distance, and Moses heads for them.

"Now," he says, "it's time to find some water."

We approach the base of a coastal bluff and start to circle to the north of it, walking due west now.

"Always check out the north-facing side of a hill or a bluff," Moses points out. "And if you're lucky, you might just find a little brook of water. If you're real lucky, you might find some edible lilies or roots in the water or the mud."

This area, so close to the coast, is actually pretty dry, and we aren't lucky enough to find much more than grass growing in a mix of sand and dirt. Moses studies the lay of the grass.

"Chrissie, see where the grass grows thick and green there at the bottom of that slope?"

I do see what he is pointing at and watch as he starts to dig with the sharp point of his stick. It takes a while, and I find a sharp rock and help.

"There," he finally says, and we sit back and watch as a little water seeps into the hole we have dug out.

"You have to work hard out here," Moses says. "But you can always find what you need. Now take your straw like this."

Moses lies on his belly and sips a little of the muddy water through his straw. I kneel low, holding my stomach, and try it. The water is cool and sweet. We dig a little more and drink enough to quench our thirst.

"Sun will be up soon," Moses says. "Come along, child, we have to find a place to sleep."

CHAPTER NINE

It happens when I am thirteen. My mother has become more and more sullen. She sits alone every evening and stares at nothing. She just stares. She is still a pretty, petite woman with her large, brown eyes and long, golden brown hair that falls around her shoulders, but she is worn out.

One morning, she hugs me for a long, long time. She drops me off at school and blows me a kiss. Today is her last mandatory visit to the Parlor.

Then just after noon, they pull me out of the lunchroom.

At the hospital, I stand next to the cold, steel table in the middle of the bright white room. Everything smells like strong disinfectant, and I can hardly breathe. My mother's hand falls out from under the white sheet that covers her body. I take her cold hand and hold it tightly to my chest, trying to warm it up.

"It was a terrible car accident," my father tells me through his tears. "She was on her way back from the Parlor. She didn't suffer, Chrissie, she died instantly. There was nothing anybody could do."

I reach up and slowly pull the sheet back from her face.

"Chrissie, you shouldn't," my father says, but I ignore him. Through my own tears, I look at my mother. Even in death, she is wearing her blank face. And out of the corner of my eye, I think I catch a quick glimpse of my imaginary little sister, Ruthie, standing in her white dress in the far corner of the room with her little arms crossed and tears streaming down her cheeks. But when I look closer, the corner is empty.

Just three months later, my father remarries. She is a much younger woman, very pretty, the daughter of an important government official…

◈ ◈ ◈

Dawn is breaking, now, in the early morning, casting a deep red hue over the tall grass that surrounds us on all sides. We hunker down near some tall cattails growing along the edge of a small pond that is miraculously standing in the middle of nowhere. Before we rest, Moses teaches me the fine art of selecting edible water lilies.

"I know," he says as I crunch down on the wet greens, "you've eaten better. But these will keep you alive. Actually, they are better than most vegetables you will find in your stores nowadays."

Moses is a veritable walking survival encyclopedia. A moment does not pass that he is not teaching me something.

"Listen to the morning song of the cicadas!" he exclaims. He reaches down into the shallow, muddy pond water to snatch up another lily. The muscles in his arm ripple. I have noticed how scarred-up his arms are, but they are as hard as steel.

"When the cicadas stop singing, Chrissie, you know that there is something…"

The cicadas stop singing.

"Get down!" Moses whispers. I crouch down as low as I can in the water.

I hear nothing but dead quiet. Moses stands up straight and sniffs the predawn air. Then he nods.

He leaves me where I am, wades to the edge of the pond, and walks out into a large clearing.

"Hello, Ashur," he says. "I could smell you a mile off."

A massive young man emerges from the dark bushes nearby. He is giant and bald, with lunatic green eyes. He wears filthy black leathers and has massive silver shields on his arms, like the shields that Medea wore.

"Hi, Moses," he says, "long time no see."

His voice isn't friendly. As big as he is, he trots through the deep grass with the grace and agility of a hunting wolf. He approaches Moses rapidly and swings his fist at him. It is like swinging a giant club, and Moses easily ducks under it.

"Where is your blaster?" Moses asks him.

Ashur laughs.

"I decided that blasters are for babies," he growls. "And I sure don't need a blaster for an old man like you. Where's the girl?"

He lunges for Moses, trying to grasp him in a bear hug. Moses clips him in the throat with the edge of his right hand and ducks again.

"Nice move!" Ashur says, choking a little.

"Who sent you, son?" Moses asks him as the giant man rubs his throat.

"I only have two hundred thousand reasons," he rasps as he rubs.

The bounty on my head is increasing.

"No," Moses says, "somebody sent you. Who?"

Ashur lunges again and this time, he moves so fast that he gets lucky. He picks Moses up off the ground, and I can hear ribs cracking. Moses strains for a moment then relaxes and kicks Ashur hard in the crotch. Ashur cries out as he drops Moses. Moses rolls and springs back, hitting Ashur with a flurry of strikes that would kill any ordinary man.

Ashur gasps as he drops to his knees.

"Now tell me," Moses says again, "who sent you?"

Ashur jumps back up. His eyes are crazy, more feral than those of any of the skeletons that I saw in the underground.

"You'll have to kill me to find out!" he screams.

"Come on, son," Moses sighs. "You're not that good, and I don't want to kill you. Not today, anyway."

Ashur reaches into his pocket and pulls out his blaster. He fires and Moses jumps to the side with his arm raised to block the shot, but not quickly enough. The blaster catches him in the shoulder.

Moses screams in pain and lunges directly at Ashur before he can fire again. My eyes have trouble following him. He hits Ashur in the throat at least twenty times. At first, Ashur tries to strike back because his blaster now lies uselessly on the ground. Moses keeps hitting him until he falls on his back, moaning and trying to breathe.

Moses kneels down, leans in close, and Ashur whispers something to him. Then the giant stops breathing. Moses sighs and, like he did with Medea, makes a sign with his hand over Ashur's body.

"Come on, Chrissie," he says as he stands back up. "No time to sleep now, we'd best be moving on."

I rise up and wade out of the pond. The cicadas start to sing again.

"Who was he, Moses?' I ask as I walk out into the clearing. Moses rubs the blaster burn in his shoulder and winces.

"He was called Ashur," Moses answers. "A closer just like Medea. They all like to name themselves after the old gods and demons. Sometimes, I think they might fancy themselves to be gods and demons. But they chose wrong, Chrissie, they chose wrong."

"Is he the monster I've dreamed about?"

"No," Moses painfully shakes his head. "Not by a long shot."

"You're hurt!" I exclaim. I reach into my old knapsack and hunt for the burn balm. Moses stops me.

"Time for that later," he says. "We have to make some distance now."

"Can we hide him?" I ask. Moses shakes his head.

"He's too big to move, Chrissie," he says. "And my shoulder is gone. We'll throw some brush over him. Might buy us a little time, but not much. Others will be on the way."

I help Moses gather old brush that is lying around, and we cover the body as well as we can. It is really no use. Ashur is so big, the pile really shows.

I can tell that Moses is in real pain by the way he moves, but he keeps walking, and soon we are heading southwest again.

"That thing you did with your hand over his body. I saw you do that to Medea, too."

"I said a prayer, child," he tells me. "I prayed that he might be forgiven and shown mercy."

A prayer to whom? I wonder. In school, I learned the old myths about the Greek gods and the Roman gods. Which of them does Moses pray to? Moses turns and looks at me.

"Those aren't the gods I pray to, Chrissie."

"My mother used to make a sign like that, but smaller, on my forehead. You did it to me too. She called it the sign of the cross."

"I know, Chrissie."

"Did Ashur tell you anything?" I ask as we walk.

"Not enough, Chrissie," Moses says. "Not near enough."

CHAPTER TEN

Throughout the day, Moses keeps heading us toward the coast. Night falls, and I am feeling sick and exhausted, but we continue to travel west. My pregnancy is holding me back, making me slow, and I can see the concern in Moses's eyes. Still we push on as if he is trying hard to outrun something. Finally, early the next morning, when I am just on the verge of collapsing, I can hear the distant roar of the ocean.

We reach the beach, and Moses sits us down under a cluster of dry mangrove bushes that grow just below a sandy ledge. The beach is deserted, and from our vantage point, I can see three- or four-foot waves rolling in and thundering into the shallows with a steady rhythm that immediately makes me drowsy. A few seagulls crisscross back and forth in the air along the beach. They are probably hunting for the little crabs that I see scurrying across the sand. "This is where help will arrive," Moses tells me. "This is where we leave the New Republic behind."

Ignoring Moses's protests, I rub burn balm into the wound in his shoulder. It takes care of the pain, and soon he is moving his right arm more easily.

"I learned all about the gods in school," I say as I work the balm in. "The Greek gods and the Roman gods. But they were all just made up by ancient people. They taught us that gods were nothing more than somebody's imagination."

I am probing, and Moses knows it.

"I am sure they did," he answers. "But you want to know the truth, don't you?"

I nod my head even though Moses is facing away from me.

"That's right, child," he says. "And you need to know the truth."

He stays quiet for a moment, and then he turns and looks intently into my eyes.

"Someone is coming into your life who will tell you the truth. But for now, just thinking about this truth will get you caught and killed," Moses warns me with a solemn voice. "And until you are taught how to guard your thoughts, you are safer not knowing yet.

"Okay, child," he whispers. "Get some sleep."

Soon, leaning against Moses's strong shoulder, I start to drift off to sleep. I start to dream.

I am in a place that can't possibly exist. I am holding Daniel tightly against my chest, hiding in the shadows somewhere incredibly high up in impossibly sheer, jagged mountains. The night air is thin and crisp, and I am trying like crazy not to breathe. Daniel stirs and whimpers in my arms, and I desperately try to shush him. Something is stalking us. It moves silently through the rocks, not making even the slightest sound, but somehow I know that it is near.

I seem to possess some kind of sixth sense. I follow my pursuer's movements with my mind's eye. The thing that is after us does not search from side to side; it comes straight on toward Daniel and me. Is it a wolf or a big cat? It is too dark to tell.

In complete desperation, I back into the shadows of a terrible, towering cliff wall and crouch down behind a pile of giant, tumbled rocks. The thing presses nearer, and I know that I have backed my way into a trap with no way out. I can hear it breathing, and I hold Daniel tighter to my chest. Don't move a muscle, I tell myself.

I am so afraid. I shut my eyes tightly as the thing turns the corner, growls at me, and pounces.

Something nudges me, and I hear a voice in my mind. "Chrissie!"

Another nudge and the voice again. It is not "the voice." It is a voice. It is the deep voice of Moses, whispering to me in my dream.

"Jackrabbit," he whispers in my dream. "Never give up, child. Now you will feel alone, but you never, ever walk alone!"

◈ ◈ ◈

Moses nudges me awake. How long have I slept? I don't know, but it feels like long, and I can feel the hot sun beating down on us from high overhead. It has to be close to noon. It is so hot, even the shade of the mangrove bushes provides little, if any, relief.

Moses is holding the palm of his hand gently across my mouth, signaling me to keep quiet. Keeping my head perfectly still, the way Moses taught me, I scan the beach in front of me with my eyes. What I see causes my heart to leap in my chest.

There is a man on the beach, less than fifty feet away from us, stretched out on a fold-out beach chair like ones I've seen at the public swimming pools. He is a young man, somewhere in his twenties, wearing just a pair of red swimming trunks and blue rubber flip-flops on his crossed feet. He is not a large man, but powerfully built, with golden bronze skin and wickedly blond hair that he slicks back away from his forehead. He looks extremely handsome to me, from what I can tell. Some of his facial features are hidden by a set of mirrored sunglasses. He casually flips the pages of a book that he reads. Music plays from a quaint little radio placed in the sand next to his chair, and over the crashing noise of the ocean waves, I can tell that it is classical music. Probably Mozart or Chopin.

He could be anybody spending a day outside, taking in the sun's rays, enjoying the salty air, and watching the hypnotic ocean waves; but something is wrong. This guy is facing directly toward us with his back to the ocean.

As a wave crashes ashore, Moses removes his hand and whispers to me.

"His name is Stingray, Chrissie. He is a very special closer, the baddest of the bad, and he's here for you."

I inhale sharply and feel panic tightening my chest. Stingray! That was the sea creature I drew in the dirt with Moses's walking stick.

"That's right," Moses whispers when the next wave thunders. "He's the monster you've been dreaming about."

"What do we do?" I whisper back, shivering even though I am roasting under the white hot sun.

Another wave crashes. If the man hears us or knows exactly where we are hiding, he doesn't show it. He just casually reads his book.

"There's not much we can do," Moses whispers with the next wave. "He holds all the cards."

"Do you know him?"

"We've crossed paths."

For the next hour or so, we stay huddled together under the bushes, not moving a muscle. The man just reads his book and listens to his music. Occasionally, he pulls a water bottle out of his red-and-white striped beach bag and takes a sip. Each time he does that, I lick my parched lips, remembering how deadly thirsty I am.

It is obviously a waiting game, and he seems to have all the time in the world. Moses leans to me and whispers again.

"Chrissie," he whispers, "the help I told you about isn't coming now. If something happens to me today and you can get away, hike back up to the highway. Walk south along it until you find mile marker 543. That is the other plan. Somebody will pick you up there. But whatever you do, stay hidden."

"How will they see me?" I whisper back.

"Don't worry," he whispers, "they will know how to find you."

Then slowly, he reaches out to me with his hand and traces the sign of the cross on my forehead.

Another agonizing hour passes, and the man turns the last page of his book and snaps it shut. For the first time, it occurs to me that he has been reading a real paper and cloth-bound book, an illegal, valuable antique. He drops the book into his beach bag, pulls out his water, and takes a long swig.

"Damn, that's good," he says, seemingly to no one.

Moses grasps my shoulder tightly.

"Shh!" he warns with the next crashing wave.

Stingray seems to be looking directly at us now.

"Come out, come out, wherever you are, Moses," he calls out casually, almost playfully. "Unless you want me to come over there and get you."

Moses sighs and gives me a long, sad look. *Don't move a muscle*, his eyes say to me. Slowly but deliberately, he slides out from under the mangroves, stands up, and walks across the sand. Stingray smiles and stands up.

"You look good for an old man," he says as he stretches. The muscles in his bronze chest ripple in the sunlight.

Moses stops in front of Stingray, at arm's length. He looks directly at the man's mirrored sunglasses, which flash blindingly in the sharp, white hot sunlight. And suddenly, the whole beach has a surreal, hard-edged look about it. The flying seagulls, the crashing ocean waves, and the blue sky all disappear; and all I see and sense are the two men standing, facing each other. Two men engulfed in white heat.

"How are you, Stingray?" Moses asks quietly.

"I came out to invite you to the funeral," Stingray answers and laughs. His laugh is chilling.

"I'm in mourning, you know," he says.

"Oh, yeah?" Moses asks. "In mourning for whom?"

Stingray grins. His mouth is slightly crooked to one side. An old injury?

"You killed my girlfriend!" he answers, and his grin turns into a scowl.

"Medea?" Moses asks innocently.

Stingray glares at him.

"She had it coming," Moses says.

"Give me the girl," Stingray says. Moses looks up and down the beach.

"Girl? What girl?" he asks.

Stingray frowns, looks down at the ground, and slowly shakes his head.

"Do you really want to do this, old man?" he asks. Moses smiles at him.

"More than anything else," he answers.

I watch in horror as the two men fight. Moses is unbelievably quick, moving and striking Stingray with a fighting style I can barely follow with my eyes. But he is favoring his injured shoulder, and with every strike, the younger man counters effectively and hits Moses even harder. Stingray laughs, and his laugh sounds like the hiss of a rattlesnake to me.

"You're too slow, old man," he chides. "I'm going to have to kill you."

He strikes Moses hard, and Moses falls to the ground. Before he can climb back to his feet, Stingray strikes a crushing blow to his head, and that is it. Moses falls and doesn't move, doesn't even breathe. Stingray hunches over his crumpled body and studies him.

"You should have stayed in Haven," he says. "I might have let you live."

My body starts to shake uncontrollably. I feel like Daniel is turning over and over in my stomach. Stingray has retrieved something small from his beach bag. He kneels next to Moses's body and goes to work. He is using a laser knife! He is carving something into Moses' forehead. I recoil in horror.

Out of nowhere, a police cruiser materializes next to Stingray, and he stands up and walks to it. A passenger door opens, and a cop steps out, dressed in black police body armor with a black helmet and visor.

"Get our new buddy out and have him help you throw this body in the trunk," Stingray orders the cop. The cop is holding what looks like a dog's leash in his hand, and he gives it a strong yank. A boy tumbles out of the backseat of the cruiser and rolls in the sand, the leash attached to a thick steel collar around his neck. Jason!

Jason has been beaten. His cheek is badly bruised, and he has two black eyes. His left eye is nearly swollen shut. The cop slaps him hard across the face and orders him to his feet.

"You heard the man!" the cop yells at him. "Get your butt out of the sand and give me a hand!"

I can hear Jason crying, but he does as he is ordered and helps the cop heft Moses's body up and throw it in the open rear trunk of the cruiser. Then the cop shoves him back into the backseat. I can hear Stingray laughing as he slams the trunk shut.

Stingray starts to climb into the front passenger seat and stops.

"Wait!" he says to somebody inside.

He climbs back out, opens the trunk back up, and pulls something out of it. Slowly, he turns and walks toward me, casually, holding in his hands two severed heads by their hair.

"Chrissie!" he calls out as he looks directly at me through his mirrored sunglasses. "I could kill you right now! I could kill you and that little mutant growing in your belly anytime I want to! But that wouldn't be any fun at all, would it?"

He stops less than ten feet in front of me. He has to be able to see me! He has a wicked grin on his face.

"Smithy and Perryman wanted to say hello."

He tosses the two heads at me so that they land just in front of me. They slap the ground with a sickening thud and the one with a thin, gaunt face is lying on its left ear with a cruel, sad expression. The other head is bigger, its fat, flabby face and beady eyes staring up at me. It looks as if it must have died in sheer terror.

Each head carries a mark burnt neatly into its forehead with a laser knife. An immaculately carved image of a stingray, like the one in my dreams. I look back up at Stingray, and I can feel his cold eyes boring through his sunglasses into my eyes. I can feel his cold, intense menace. I know that I am dead.

"Run as hard as you can, little girl," he says to me conversationally, as if we are having tea together. "And let's play a little longer before you have to die."

He grins, turns around, and walks with a light step back to the cruiser.

"Let's go," he orders as he climbs in.

CHAPTER ELEVEN

"Chrissie, I foresee a time when everything you are carrying will be taken away from you. That is why I'm going to teach you how to get by on nothing but what you can harvest from the land."

I can remember Moses saying those exact words in the wee hours of the morning, when we were bushwhacking our way toward the coast. Now, cruelly, everything has been taken from him. His life.

For the next hour, I huddle alone on the beach, frozen beneath the mangroves, miserable and baking in the heat. I can't stop crying.

Moses is dead, and it's all because of me. I've never felt more alone in my life. Poor Moses, dead because I decided to buck the system, to say no to the rules. For his death, I'll never forgive myself. How many people are going to die because of Daniel and me? I feel trapped, and I hate myself for the feeling.

Watching Moses die has shaken me to the core. A sick, scared thought flashes through my mind for just an instant that maybe I should go back, go home, and go to the Parlor where that sick, smiling, redheaded lady is prepping the abortion table for me. Then I can maybe endure "reeducation" and maybe even marry Jason and make my parents happy. They could forgive all this, and the government would promote my dad. "Chrissie just lost her mind for a little while," they would all say. Just like her mother did. Just like her aunt did. Carrying a deformed baby can freak anybody out, they would all agree.

Immediately, I hate myself for thinking.

And Daniel kicks my belly hard, as if he is saying, "Don't listen to them!"

That's my problem; I have listened to them all my life. Listen to them long enough and you start to think like them. Everything will be fine as long as you follow our rules, even if all that we want you to do is murder your baby. That's the system: follow the rules and commit murder; keep up all the fine appearances, and you can become one of us. Cross us, and we will send Stingray after you. We will kill you.

Just a few feet in front of me, flies and tiny crabs are swarming Smithy's and Perryman's faces—a vivid reminder of what the government is capable of doing to you. In death, their faces are even more grotesque than they were when they were leering at me alive. The smell is almost bad enough to make me faint. Still, I stay frozen in the mangroves. I don't move a muscle.

Smithy and Perryman didn't follow the rules and look what happened to them. Stingray happened to them. I know in my heart that unless there is a miracle in my future, Stingray will happen to me too.

How do you even deal with someone like him? He can't be human. I have never seen a human move as fast he did. I have never experienced anyone as cold and ruthless as he is. Okay, maybe the lady at the Parlor takes a close second place, but Stingray definitely wins out. With Stingray, Moses never had a chance, bad shoulder or not.

What rips my heart out is the realization that Moses knew. He knew he couldn't win, but he fought Stingray anyway. To protect me.

And what will become of Jason? They have him, and they are beating the living daylights out of him! How can they do that? He isn't even involved with this! I cry again when I think of how pitiful he looked, cowering on the ground at Stingray's feet. Are they going to kill him? Jason can act like a jerk sometimes, but he doesn't deserve this! I chose to run, not him!

The terrible thought returns and reasserts itself. I can hike back to the super highway, flag down a truck, and just go home. I can turn myself in.

It's all over, Chrissie, I say to myself. You have to go back; you have to save Jason. You don't really count in all of this and neither does Daniel.

Daniel stirs, kicks me harder, and snaps me out of my despair.

You're right, Daniel! I think of him as if he is already a fully grown boy. I have to figure out how to do the kicking. Moses gave his life for Daniel and me. I have to figure out how to make it out of here. If they want to murder my baby, they have to kill me too. Of course, that is what they plan to do. But I'm not staying on this beach another single minute.

I stand up and take Moses's walking stick in one hand. I look away from Smithy and Perryman and start to climb up the sandy ridge away from the beach. I don't even bother to use the cover of the bushes now; what's the use? Stingray knows exactly where I am, and evidently, he has decided to play with me the way that a cat plays with a mouse. Running up the bounty on my head to the highest price possible before he finally pounces.

A small, two-lane road runs along the top of the sandy ridge; and as I reach the crest, I am startled to find two government news media cars sitting there. A full camera crew is waiting, leaning against the cars, reading their plastic readers and drinking bottled water. I don't have time to get back out of sight. As I turn to walk down the road away from them, they spring into action.

A man sprints up alongside of me, and I recognize him from the news network. He wears heavy makeup and has the most perfect jet-black hair I have ever seen on a real human. And bright turquoise eyes—fake, of course. His face has been frozen by cosmetic surgery and makeup so that he smiles perpetually.

"Chrissie, wait!" he calls. I pick up my pace, and his camera crew catches up to us. I am surrounded by six people now, walking down the road with me.

"We aren't with the police, we just want your interview, please!" he pleads with me. A flurry of cameras are catching me from all angles, zooming in on my tiniest expressions.

"Go away!" I yell at him, "Get lost!"

"Just a little interview," he repeats, "so your Mom and Dad will know you're ok."

"Then make it quick!"

I want to get a message to my parents. I want to get a message to the government.

The reporter runs a comb through his perfect hair and trains his turquoise eyes at the closest camera.

"Breaking news! This is Bob Roberts, reporting live, and I have, surprise of surprises, Chrissie Wright! She has just escaped from her kidnapper, and she is live, right here with me, along the Pacific Coast Highway!"

I know that I look like a mess. The camera crew doesn't seem to care.

"Tell us, Chrissie," Bob Roberts asks me. "Now that your kidnapper has been apprehended, why haven't you cooperated with the police? They are standing by to take you home now. Every single person in Frisco wants you back home.

"I wasn't kidnapped," I tell him. "The man who was helping me was murdered by the police."

Bob Roberts stops in his tracks.

"What are you saying, Chrissie?" he asks, sounding positively stunned for added effect. This is going to play great on the news. I can picture the millions of people glued to their viewers right now. My face has to be plastered on every board in the country.

"I said, I wasn't kidnapped!" I repeat. I walk up to the nearest camera and look directly into its lens.

"Tell my stepmother and father that I am running, just like my aunt did. Tell them that I love them, but I also love my baby!"

The entire camera crew has stopped dead in their tracks. They are stunned.

"And you tell the government to stop sending their monsters after me!"

"Stop the cameras!" Bob Roberts orders his crew. His eyes frown at me through that stupid, frozen smile on his face. He places his hands on his hips, and he studies me.

"This isn't smart, Chrissie," he tells me quietly. "I have this report on a time delay. Okay, let's do another take, and you had better do it smart if you know what's good for you. Do you get me, dear?"

I scan the area behind the camera crew. I see nothing but pavement, sand, and weeds. Where is Stingray? Is he anywhere near, ready to take me? I don't see any sign of him, but that means nothing. I start to walk. I have to get away from these people before they all decide to grab me and take me in for the reward.

"All right, Chrissie," Bob Roberts hisses through his frozen smile. "Here is how it works. I tell you exactly what to say, and you say it into the camera there. And you smile while you say it. I can turn this all around for you. Do you get it? I can make you the hero."

I turn and glare at Mr. Perfect Smiling Bob Roberts. I will never be a hero. Moses was a hero. Heroes die for people like me. I am trying to look brave, but my stomach is turning over and over again.

"And what about my baby?" I scream. Bob Roberts's eyes frown deeper. He looks at the ground.

"You have your interview! Now get out of my face!" I growl. I raise Moses's walking stick, ready to hit him with it. He shrieks and backs away. I turn and run off the side of the road, away from the beach. Then when I am less than a hundred feet away, I stop and freeze. Looking back, I see that they aren't chasing me. The entire camera crew is searching around, shielding their eyes from the sunlight, and looking for me. But they can't see me. *They can't see me!*

"Where did she go?" Bob Roberts yells out. They keep looking and shrugging their shoulders in disbelief.

"Do you want to know, Chrissie?" Bob Roberts finally calls out, squinting in the sunlight, trying to find me, "The price on your head? It's a million credits, dear little girl! Everyone in the world is coming to get you! Dead or alive!"

An hour later, the camera crew loses interest. One by one, they pull out their viewers and stare at the little displays. Some of them start to aimlessly punch away at the viewer screens.

Bob Roberts loses his cool.

"Come on, people, we have the biggest story of the year here!" he shouts. His crew responds by reluctantly putting down their viewers and searching for me again. As I stand frozen, one of them walks within two feet of where I am standing.

"Come on, Bob!" One of them finally exclaims. "She got away…if she was ever really here."

Bob Roberts looks crushed. His shoulders slump, and soon he has joined his crew, tapping feverishly away on his own viewer.

"Let's get out of here," he finally says. "And check that recording. Maybe she was here, and maybe she wasn't."

As soon as they drive off, I head away across the hot sand, turning east through the scrub brush toward the super highway. I have to find mile marker 543. Plan B is to go south across the New Republic. "Keep the North Star to your back," I remember Moses saying. The path to Haven heads south. But south beyond the borders is where the dark lands lie, I learned in school. Savage, desolate lands filled with nothing but barbarians and hideous mutants left over from the old wars. Left to fight each other and die.

But if the barbarians and mutants are anything like Moses, I am all in. They can't be any worse than Bob Roberts and his crew, than Stingray, Medea, and Ashur, can they? I hug my stomach, and Daniel, tightly as I run.

CHAPTER TWELVE

I hike due east for at least five miles before settling down in the middle of a grassy field. I can see rows and rows of vineyards in the distance and decide that I should check them out after sunset. The only thought that makes me hesitate is the possibility of dogs that might be guarding the grapes. Still, I am desperately hungry, and I think I should at least take a look.

I have at least a night's journey ahead of me to get back to the super highway, and then who knows how far south I have to go to find that mile marker. I am tired, morning sickness is still a problem, and my feet are killing me. After over a week of nonstop hiking, my boots are breaking in and holding up fine, but the sheer distance I am covering has made my feet rub and blister in a number of hot spots. I have medicine that helps a little, but I don't like having to deal with blisters. Not now when that monster is somewhere close.

There is a low spot in the middle of the field with a small, brackish pool of water lying at its lowest point, and I lie down on my side and sip the water through my straw. Then I pull my one plastic water bottle out of my backpack and refill it to the brim.

Remember, Chrissie, I can hear Moses saying, *a time may come when you will lose everything you are carrying.* I fish around in the water and pull up a handful of roots. They are edible, even sweet, I discover, as I wash them and take small bites. How did I know that they would be? Moses never showed these to me. After I eat my fill, I move a good distance away from the pond, knowing that it is the obvious place for someone to hunt for me, and set up a crude lean-to in the grass. I still have a couple of hours of daylight before the sun sets and night falls. Then I can move out under the cover of darkness. For now, I need to try to get some sleep.

They didn't see me. Why didn't they see me? It haunts me. I am not Moses, but I can hide.

Sleep does not come as I lie beneath the shelter. Another question burns in my mind that I just can't get over. Stingray obviously saw me. Why did he let me go? There was already enough money on my head, and he had me dead to rights. I had absolutely no protection except for my feeble Perma Lighter, and I clearly saw what he was capable of. Moses was completely at his mercy, and Moses died. All he had to do was scoop me up off the ground.

He is the big gun that the government has sent after me, and I can't figure out why. I know that my dad is important, but this? I am just another runner. I just don't get it.

And Jason. Who would beat up an innocent teenager like Jason? Part of me still loves him. I can't help it, and I don't want to see him suffer because of me. Stingray obviously works with the police, and there are laws. How can they allow him to do that to Jason?

Closers have their own rules, I can hear Moses saying, *and he's the baddest of the bad, Chrissie.*

Like Stingray said, a game is being played here, and I don't understand the rules. All I know for sure is that Stingray can grab me at anytime, anywhere. And he will. And I am alone.

I don't really know when I drift off to sleep, but I am dreaming. My stepmother and father are watching my interview with Bob Roberts, gasping with their hands covering their mouths. I love you, I am telling them from the screen, but I also love my baby! As I talk to Bob Roberts, I am cradling Daniel in my arms. He looks to be a few months old. I have him swaddled in a blanket, and all you can see is his little face looking up at me. He has bright, blue eyes.

"Oh dear!" my stepmother gasps, and Bob Roberts is sitting next to her on the couch and patting her on the shoulder, his perfect hair slightly mussed. My father is sitting in his easy chair and shaking his head. Then my stepmother turns her head to look at someone who is standing behind her. She sees someone who is emerging from the shadows behind her couch, and she shrieks.

"He's here," she screams. "He's going to kill us!"

I jerk awake. For a confused minute, I search around for Moses with my hands. Tears stream down my face as I remember that he is not here, that he will never be here again.

It is dark, and the moon is just breaking over the horizon, so I know that I got at least a few hours of sleep. Still, I feel exhausted. I eat a handful of roots that I stashed in my backpack. I am saving my remaining food bars for an emergency, but I take a small sip of water. I am eating for two people, I remind myself, and food is my priority now. I have to take a look at those vineyards.

Water in irrigation ditches reflects the moonlight in perfectly straight running lines as I approach the first vineyard from the north. I creep as quietly as I can, not wanting to alert any guard dogs that might be around. There is a small farmhouse in the distance, about a quarter mile to the south, and a light glows through its windows. I reach the nearest irrigation ditch and realize that it is wider and deeper than it appeared from a distance, and I don't want to swim across it. I walk south along its elevated dirt border until I find a road that crosses over a gray metal water gate valve.

The vines are chock-full of grapes, big, plump grapes. I cram one into my mouth, and the juice runs down my cheek. It is a semisweet grape, I have no clue what kind, that seems edible enough. I pull off my backpack and open it up to pull out a plastic bag I have kept for food. As I fill it up, I eat a handful of the grapes. "Not too many," I warn myself. "They might make you sick."

Satisfied that I am well enough provisioned, I rise up to take the road back across the ditch when I hear them. At least six dogs are running along the border of the vineyard, barking and closing in on me fast. In the moonlight, they look to be a mix of Dobermans and pit bulls. I race for the ditch crossing, but the dogs are too close and too fast, and I know that they will either catch me here or follow me to the other side of the ditch. I do the only thing I can think of and jump into the irrigation water.

The water is shoulder deep and freezing. I inhale sharply at the shock to my body and wade to the middle of the ditch as the dogs pace back and forth above me, snarling and barking their heads off. A porch light flicks on at the small house, and I see a tall man with a flashlight walk out on the front steps.

There is a fairly strong current running through the cold water, and it is pulling me toward the gate valve. I decide to let it carry me with it through the valve and under the ditch crossing. Over the commotion of the dogs, I can hear the footsteps of the man as he approaches, and I grab some old metal piping to stay in place under the crossing.

The dogs are pacing up and down both sides of the crossing now, howling and pawing the dirt in my direction. The bright beam of a flashlight sweeps across me. I don't move a muscle. *You don't see me,* I project the thought out as hard as I can. *You don't see anything!*

"Good, boys," the man says to his dogs with a deep voice. "Must have been a fox or a coyote, but he's gone now. Good, boys."

The man turns to leave, but the dogs keep barking at me.

"Come on, boys," the man says to his dogs. "That coyote is long gone now. You're just smelling him."

He walks back to the house and calls the dogs. They howl and cry, but they finally give up and follow him.

I let the water current carry me out from under the crossing, and I hunt for handholds on the other side. It takes me a few attempts, but I am finally able to scramble up the dirt bank. Quickly, I head north away from the ditch and out of the dogs' territory. It was close call, and I am not feeling good about it. At least, I got some food out of the deal, even if I am cold and soaked to the bone.

As I skirt around the north side of the vineyards and continue toward the east, I wonder if I can travel a path that stays close to these fields of grapes and water. There are hazards, to be sure, but at least I have figured out how to deal with the dogs. What really worries me is that Stingray has probably already thought of this. He would know that I would be hunting for food. It probably doesn't matter; I wouldn't know the first step in how to avoid him and, in the meantime, I need to eat.

I cross little dirt farm roads as I head east, and I watch as the moon slowly crosses the sky and sets below the far horizon. I can see the first hints of sunrise in the east, and I search for a safe place to bed down for the coming day. I feel as though I am looking at the lay of the land through Moses's eyes, and I finally settle on a broad, vacant field of tall grass, several miles away from any farms or vineyards.

As the day breaks, I have an easier time relaxing and falling asleep. The hiking has really worn me down. Two things happen before I drift off. I feel Daniel move in my stomach like he is also settling down to sleep. Then just before I nod off, I have a brief vision of standing in front of a giant board next to the super highway. There, in ultrahigh definition is my face, looking haggard, bleached hair and all. An announcement is displayed next to my face. Reward: Five million credits!

CHAPTER THIRTEEN

You can actually feel the super highway before you see it or hear the traffic on it. Its invisible, magnetic "wave field" makes the hairs on the back of your neck stand straight up. I am looking down at its metallic black pavement from a high, grassy bluff. Occasionally, cars flash by; but I mainly see a continuous procession of big, long, turbine-powered trucks that are carrying food and goods between the New Republic's Northern and Southern provinces. As the trucks streak by at well over a hundred miles an hour, I can hear the high-pitched whine of their electric turbine engines and the rush of air that they push out of their way. I look at the endless procession of gigantic boards that float above the highway, much bigger than the ones in the city, streaming endless advertisements mixed with government announcements mixed with my face and "Chrissie alerts."

I was wrong in my dream about the size of the reward on my head. It is actually up to twenty million credits now, a tremendous fortune. Somebody is pulling out all the stops to bring me in. Every closer, cop, and bounty hunter in the world has to be hunting for me by now. But if any police cruisers are patrolling the super highway looking for me, I have yet to see any sign of them.

It has taken me nearly a week to find mile marker 543. And then for the past three days, I have hidden in a dark crevice on the side of a bluff above the mile marker. I don't really even know what I am looking for. All that I see below me is the endless, monotonous flow of traffic.

And I have discovered a new enemy…heat. I am losing weight at an alarming rate, even though I continue to scrounge for edible roots and plants and raid the vineyards that lie just a few miles off to the west. It just doesn't seem to be enough to sustain me, and it can't be good for Daniel. I know that something has to happen soon, or I will be forced to disregard Moses's advice and continue south, hoping to find real stored food in a cellar or a warehouse that I can raid.

My nightmares are more intense than ever. Stingray stalks me in them, approaches me even when I am completely hidden and cowering. He puts his face next to mine and grins that wicked, crooked grin of his, and I can see my face reflected in his mirrored sunglasses. My face is dark and dirty, my eyes are filled with fear, and I almost don't even recognize myself. The same thought always grabs me as I look into those sunglasses. How can I kill him?

Where do they find these monsters? Where do closers come from? Why hasn't he just shown up, beaten me to death like he beat Moses, and thrown me into the trunk of his cruiser?

It is well past midnight. I have developed my own sense of time from watching the movement of the moon and the stars at night. I lie down on my back and watch the Big Dipper when I hear a sound that doesn't seem quite right. Down on the highway, a giant southbound freight truck has pulled over at the mile marker and is idling on the shoulder of the highway. I freeze and watch.

A huge fat man with a heavy black beard opens up the driver's door and slides down out of the cab. He is carrying what looks like a toolbox in his left hand and proceeds with haste to the right rear tires below the refrigerated trailer, sets the toolbox on the ground, and squirms underneath the axle. He opens his toolbox and starts to work on something, but from my hiding spot, I can't tell what.

Is he here for me, or is this just a coincidence? I can't be sure, and I'm not going to move a muscle to find out. A giant board hovers twenty feet directly above mile marker 543, and its bright display has shifted from an advertisement for soft drinks to a full-blown picture of me standing next to Jason at the prom. Jason is dressed to the hilt in a white jacket and trousers, and I am wearing a white lace dress. We almost look ready for our wedding day, and it makes me sigh for a moment. Then through the magic of the media, Jason comes to life in the picture and is talking loud enough for me to hear, and it almost seems like he is looking up the bluff at me. I know that this is an illusion; he would be looking at you wherever you were standing in relation to the board. But still, it unnerves me.

"Chrissie," Jason pleads with a slightly bruised face, "if you can see this, if you can hear me, please come home. I know you didn't mean the things you said. We all know the stress you have been suffering from your kidnapping. It makes you do funny things. But it is safe, you can come home now. We miss you, Chrissie. We all love you."

Bob Roberts appears and talks with anguish about how my kidnapper beat Jason. About how I was abused and brainwashed until they finally caught and killed the terrible black man. So they are forcing Jason to play along with them. And they are still playing the kidnapping angle. It doesn't surprise me.

Now the image shifts to my parents. My stepmother is holding my sweet cat, Maximus, in her arms and is sobbing uncontrollably into the camera.

"Come home, Chrissie!" my stepmother pleads. "Please, just come home!"

My father has his arm wrapped around my stepmother's waist. A tear is streaming down his left cheek, and he is nodding his head to what my stepmother is saying. Then a "Chrissie alert" pops up on the screen. The reward for my safe return now stands at twenty-five million credits.

Safe return. Right!

I look back down at the stopped truck and see that the man has scooted out from under it to watch and listen to the board messages. He shakes his head, looks around, and pushes himself back under the axle.

Is that a sign? I can't be sure, but I decide to risk moving closer to him. I climb out of my hiding place and inch down the incline of the bluff until I am hidden in the black shadow cast by his truck, close enough to hear him if he says anything out loud. The grass grows tall at the side of the highway, and I slowly crouch all the way down into it.

I am just in time because a police cruiser materializes right behind the truck, and a deep metallic voice commands the truck driver to come out. He pushes himself out from under the truck and stands up facing the cruiser, his arms held out away from his body.

"Loose nut on the brake housing," he explains to the cop. "I got the warning light a mile back and stopped here under the light of the board to check it out."

"Okay," the cop in the cruiser says. "Stay right there. Checking...checking. Sam Marley, license number 860876, Frisco, Northern Province. Look up and hold still for the retina scan. Okay...there! You're clear. Don't take long, Sam, I'll radio it ahead."

"Thank you, sir," the driver says.

"Do you need any further assistance?" the cop asks.

"No, sir," the driver says and waves, "I'll radio my dispatch if it loosens up again."

"Drive carefully," the voice from the cruiser says as it pulls out from behind the truck and continues down the highway. As it accelerates, it vanishes.

The driver just stands there for a few minutes, looking down the highway where the cruiser has gone. Then he sighs heavily, looks up at the board where my face is still gigantically displayed.

"What a jackrabbit!" he says, almost so quietly that I don't pick it up. Then he drops to the ground and pushes himself back under the truck.

Did I hear him correctly? It can't be a mistake; who else would know my nickname? Carefully, I creep to the side of the truck just a few feet from where his heavy, leather boots are sticking out. The man is talking to himself.

"Hiding out here at mile marker 543, nice place for a jackrabbit to hide out…"

I slowly move closer and kick his boot gently. Then I jump back, just in case.

"Shouldn't have left that cab door open," the big man whispers. "A critter like a jackrabbit might jump right up in there."

His meaning is clear. I turn and slowly walk around the truck to the open cab door. It is a big, difficult step up into the cab, but I am able to pull it off. The cab has an old-fashioned steering wheel. I guess some of the truckers still like to use them at times, but everything else I see in this cab is of the latest technology. The dashboard glows with five big displays, instruments, a couple of computer displays, a warning panel where a red flashing code is warning of a brake problem. Ancient country music is blaring out of what sounds like an antique radio, but I know it is actually broad-wave music.

I crawl across his seat and back through an opening to a space that has a bed, a small fridge, and a small viewer. The viewer is active, and I can see Bob Roberts giving the latest "Chrissie update" on *Breaking News*. The bed is unkempt and smells slightly musty, but I stretch out on it anyway.

"Some people are calling it an ancient phenomenon called 'the Stockholm syndrome,'" perfect Bob Roberts is saying on the viewer. "And that Chrissie actually crossed over and became sympathetic with her captor. Just listen to what she says in my interview with her last week."

There I am, looking like a bleached ragamuffin, telling Perfect Bob to get lost. The scene switches to an interview with my stepmother. Bob is handing her a handkerchief.

"That is not my Chrissie saying that," she emphatically tells Bob. "My daughter knows the rules, and she knows how to follow them. Somebody coerced her into doing this."

Bob is facing the camera, a sly grin on his face.

"You heard it here first, folks," he says. "Chrissie's parents are in agreement. She would never willingly skip out on the Parlor. She is a good citizen and would do the right thing. Back to you, Carol!"

The driver chuckles as he jumps up into the cab and slams his door closed.

"That's what they think!" he whispers to me. "Throw that blanket over you, jackrabbit. It will block the cop scanners. And stay quiet, kid. I'll get you out of here."

He pushes buttons displayed on a couple of screens, cancels the red brake warning light, and then throws the truck into gear. Before I know it, we are cruising south down the super highway at over a hundred miles an hour.

CHAPTER FOURTEEN

For the longest time, I huddle under the metallic blanket, staying quiet while the big trucker cruises down the highway. Through the folds of the blanket, I can see the highway boards flashing by, and at least half of them are sporting my face. The trucker is a positively huge man. He must weigh at least three hundred pounds, without an ounce of fat, and his body isn't even halfway contained by his fake leather driver's seat. He is wearing a faded blue baseball cap with really long, graying hair falling out from underneath it, a faded gray work shirt and faded gray trousers. Jimmy Shootin and the Angels are wailing out an old country biker song on the radio, and he whistles along to it.

"Name's Samson, kiddo," he finally says as he taps to the music on his steering wheel. "Runners' transport incorporated! Been working for Moses, transporting runners for near twenty years now."

I shift around under the blanket so that I am propped up on my left elbow.

"Thank you, Samson," I say.

He glances back at me and smiles. His big round face has old scars running down his left cheek. He has piercing gray eyes. He is wearing black leather driving gloves, and with a little effort, he pulls them off. His big hands are deformed, well masked by the gloves, and he only has two fingers and a thumb on each one. He continues to tap on the steering wheel with them.

"No," he says, shifting his eyes back on the highway. "Thank you, actually. You are my kind of people, kid. If it weren't for runners like you and my mom, I wouldn't be here."

Daniel shifts a little in my belly. I wrap my arm around him and hold him tight.

"Here's the deal, Chrissie," Samson continues. "You've got to be hungry, and I've got some top-notch ham sandwiches in the blue wrappers in that fridge there for you and some other stuff too. I've got some nutri-drink in there, should help you get a little stronger. Thing is, you've got to stay under that blanket at all costs. This highway has got roving inspection stations all up and down it. Never know when you'll hit one, and they can detect your body heat if you're out from under that blanket. Capiche?"

"Capiche," I answer.

"Good girl! Now listen. Throw your blanket over that fridge door and get yourself some grub!"

He doesn't have to tell me twice. I open the fridge, grab a ham sandwich that is wrapped in blue heat wrap, pat the wrap, and wait a second as it turns piping hot. Then I tear it open and blow on it until it is cool and absolutely inhale it. It might be just a ham sandwich, but to me, it is a delicacy worth a million credits. I grab a nutri-drink, raspberry flavored, and start to gulp it.

"Tell me about Moses," Samson is saying while he concentrates on the road. "What really happened to him?"

I stop eating and drinking for a moment.

"Stingray happened," I say quietly to him. Stingray, a homicidal maniac who likes to carve pictures into peoples foreheads with his laser knife.

"Damn!" Samson exclaims and slaps his steering wheel hard.

"Moses seemed to know him," I say.

"Well," Samson answers, "I can tell you from my own personal experience, nobody really knows Stingray. He's the worst of the worst. They got to want you bad, kiddo, putting him into the game. You top the news on every viewer and board across the

New Republic. And I ain't never seen a bounty the likes of what they planted on your head! One thing is for sure, the big one is going down!"

"The big what?" I ask.

"You know what's going on," Samson answers. "Daniel is going on. The voice is going on, and somehow the New Republic is on to it. They are bringing out the best they've got to get to you and Daniel. Takes a lot to draw Stingray out of his hole, and that means nothing but trouble ahead for you and me. That's why Moses personally jumped into this one. Takes a lot to bring Moses out of Haven nowadays."

He shakes his big head and pounds his steering wheel again. I wait to see if he will switch the big truck to auto steer, but he seems to prefer driving it himself.

"Eat up and get some rest," he tells me. "We're headed down south, way past the City of Angels. I'm hauling you down Mexico way. I'll fill you in, in a little bit."

I take my last bite of the sandwich, wash it down with a last gulp of nutri-drink, and then lulled by the singing of the big truck's turbine engine, I drift off into a deep, dreamless sleep.

CHAPTER FIFTEEN

It is morning when I wake, and I blink at the bright sunlight that is streaming in through Samson's driver side window.

"Say hello to Mexico!" he exclaims when he hears me stir. "Open up that fridge and get some breakfast. Those sandwiches in the yellow wrappers are sausage and eggs. There are some bottles of orange juice somewhere in there."

"Do you want anything, Samson?" I ask him, stretching and yawning in the process.

"If you don't mind, ma'am," he answers. He looks tired, hunched over his steering wheel and concentrating on the road markers that are flashing by in a blur. We have to be going way past a hundred on the speed.

I hand a yellow-wrapped sandwich and a bottle of orange juice up to him, careful to stay under the blanket, and he gratefully accepts it. I pat my own sandwich, and it is steaming when I unwrap it. It is delicious.

I peer around Samson's massive shoulders at the dashboard in front of him. He has converted one of his big middle screens to a viewer, and a nonstop news broadcast is playing. It is something about a big funeral in Frisco.

"Who died?" I ask.

"Big-time, New Republic boss. Tell you all about it in a few minutes," Samson tells me between bites of his sandwich. I look outside; we are flying across a bare desert that is covered with high sand dunes that fade into the distance along both sides of the highway. The sun is throwing a beautiful pink morning glow across the high sandy crests and making the entire desert shine, something I've never seen before.

"It's beautiful out there," I comment.

"Uh-huh," Samson responds. "It's deadly out there, kiddo. One false step, a sidewinder rattler strikes, and wham, it's bye-bye you!"

That quiets me down, and I continue to watch the viewer. With the last few bites of my sandwich, I feel the telltale signs of morning sickness coming on, and I have another problem. Samson seems to read my mind. I watch his black gloved fingers play over his system warning screen. A red light pops up.

"I'll be!" he exclaims. "Look at that! Looks like I've got that brake problem raring up again, Chrissie. Now listen, I'm going to pull over to the side up there where there's a break in those dunes. I'll leave my door open, and when I hop out and get my toolbox, you come out and scoot up behind a dune and do your business. Capiche?"

"Capiche," I answer. The man must be another mind reader.

"For goodness' sake, stay hidden until I give you the 'all clear' to come back. Not as many cameras down here in Mexico, but you never know. I'll clear my throat like this."

He coughs and hacks so loud, I almost think he is choking to death on his sandwich.

"Like that, okay?"

"I promise," I say. "Thank you, Samson."

"No problem, jackrabbit."

Samson pulls the truck over and grabs his toolbox from under his seat and hops out. I can't help noticing how gracefully he moves for his giant stature. His arms are massive under his work shirt, and I can tell that he is one of those deceptive types like Moses who can move and strike you like a cat if he wants to.

"You be careful out there," he whispers as I climb down and scoot past him. "I'm not kidding about those sidewinders. They like to hide out just below the surface of the sand, particularly this time of morning, so watch your step!"

I head out behind the nearest dune while Samson slides under the back of the trailer. Before I come back out, I freeze and study the highway. The highway is much smaller and simpler here, with only one wide lane running in each direction. I can still feel the electric current flowing along it, the juice that powers the big trucks. Not as many boards either. In fact, I don't see even one in either direction. The Southern Province must be poorer than the Northern Province.

Moses taught me to never be in a hurry. "That gets you killed," he told me. I heed his advice and stay frozen just behind the sand dune, surveying the situation. Samson is clanking around under the axle, hollering and swearing occasionally.

Then I spot it! It moves up slowly, almost imperceptibly, but I can make out the slight distortion of the highway pavement beneath it and beyond it. The cruiser doesn't uncloak; it just sits there behind Samson's truck. I want to warn him, but there's not a thing I can do.

Samson continues to work and swear. I stay frozen, like a jackrabbit hiding under the searching eyes of a desert coyote.

It goes on like this for thirty minutes, and then the cruiser pulls out from behind the truck and continues down the highway. When the coast is clear, Samson starts to cough and hack.

"Strange behavior for a cop," he comments when we are rolling again. "Even for a Mexican cop."

"Are you sure it was a Mexican cop?" I ask. He doesn't answer. When he finally does speak up, he changes the subject.

"Your daddy's been promoted!" he announces to me. "That was the old minister of information who kicked over last week and your daddy not only got his job, he picked up the Southern Province too. That's what the big funeral is all about. If you were to go back to your old home, you'd find it empty. Your folks have moved up to a bigger house!"

I am speechless; I don't know what to say. Samson continues.

"Weird thing is, nobody is saying what killed the old minister. They're just having a big old funeral for him. Usually, the cause of death is all over the news. But one thing's for sure, your daddy is the president's right-hand man now, kiddo."

"He's in the inner circle," I whisper.

"Yep."

I lie on my back in the sleeper and try to think. What does this mean? My father will have a tremendous amount of power now. Is it safe to go back? Does he have enough power to make an exception and keep me out of the Parlor? I know the law: no defective babies, period. But could he have the power?

I guess the more important question is, would he exercise that power? I know that my father loves me. I have no doubt about that. But I must be a huge embarrassment to him. For some reason, Jason flashes across my mind; the way he looked so beaten and abused, the dog collar around his neck. I can see Stingray dragging him across the sand. If I go back, maybe I can get him safely back home too. What does it all mean? Should I go back?

"Don't even consider it, honey," Samson growls. So he is clairvoyant after all. And I realize the terrible danger I've placed him in.

"I'm sorry I got you into this," I tell him quietly. I start to tear up. Samson shakes his head no.

"First of all," he says, tapping his steering wheel for emphasis, "I'm my own man, sweetie. I get my own self into fixes, and believe me, I can get my own self out of them. That's my personal talent. Secondly of all, there is nowhere else I would even consider being except right here, right now, with you. Capiche?"

"Thank you, Samson," I whisper.

Throughout the morning, Samson points out landmarks to me. Just outside of Chihuahua, we pass by a gigantic red arid canyon.

"It's called Copper Canyon," Samson tells me. "An old mining train still runs right down into the middle of it. They struck fresh ore about fifty years ago."

We are cruising so much faster than we were in the Northern Province, at least a hundred and thirty miles an hour, and the scenery is sweeping by. The towns that we pass are really just poor, dust-swept villages that have seemingly been planted in the middle of the desert with no real purpose. The kids playing out in the streets are urchins; they are skin and bones, and they remind me of the skeletons that I ran from in the Frisco underground.

"Not much money down here," Samson comments. "The folks are dirt poor, and it gets worse the farther south you go."

"How far south are we going?" I ask.

"Well," Samson says as he drives, "my job is to get you way down south of Mexico City to a drop-off point where another guide is waiting for you. We'll stay to the east of that city, big inspections through there, and the plan is to drop you off just north of where I deliver my load."

"What are you carrying?" I ask and then immediately regret it. Samson probably doesn't want me to know any more information than I need to know about his business. But he answers anyway.

"Power-packs for the southern refineries," he says. "Made up there in the northern valley. You have to keep them real cold in a refer box like the one we are hauling or *ka-bam*, they blow up. I usually haul power-packs down south, bring mangos and bananas back up north."

It is getting to be lunchtime, and Samson has me pull more sandwiches out of the fridge. I haven't eaten this much food in weeks, but I go ahead and stuff myself. Who knows when I'll be able to feast like this again?

We pass to the east of Mexico City, a gigantic city that sprawls across a vast, high-mountain valley. To the west, I can see a couple of impossibly high volcanoes that are emitting white plumes of smoke straight up into the sky.

"That one over there is almost twenty thousand feet high," Samson points out. I didn't have any idea that volcanoes grew that big. I continue to gaze at it until it disappears behind us.

A few hours later, we are cruising through lush, thick green jungle that spills over to the very edges of the highway. I can see colorful birds dancing around in thick stands of trees. Samson pulls into a truck stop.

"You okay, kiddo?" he asks me before he gets out. I assure him that I am.

"Okay," he says. "Be back in a minute. You stay quiet as a mouse back there."

He climbs out of the truck, carrying his manifest viewer in one hand and disappears inside the office of the big building. When he comes back, he has a worried look on his face as he fires up the truck and pulls out.

"Two cruisers back there," he tells me, "decloaked while I was walking back out."

We head down the highway for a good hour before he speaks up again.

"Listen up, Chrissie," he tells me. He turns around, and for the first time, I see how rough his face really is; his steely eyes locked on mine beneath his long, gray curly hair. His thick gray beard hides most of his face, but to me he looks like a big bear.

"This could all go sour on us," he continues. "And if it does, you be ready! Get into that fridge and put as much food and drink in your backpack as it can hold. Do that now!"

I do as he says and start to stuff my pack. Samson continues.

"If I have to drop you off, do you know how to get away from the highway into the woods and keep heading south?"

"Yes," I say. "Moses taught me how to use the sun and the stars."

"Good," Samson says. "You got that backpack packed?"

"Yes."

"I'm named after a man who killed a thousand warriors with a donkey's jawbone, Chrissie," he tells me with a deadly serious voice. "And I've done my share of killing. But never in anger! I only killed to save the innocents."

He twists around until he is facing me, lifts the blanket away from my face, and traces the sign of the cross on my forehead.

"Do you know why they call you the jackrabbit?" he asks me. I shake my head no.

"Because," Samson says, "a jackrabbit knows when to run. And a jackrabbit knows when to hide."

Samson turns and glances at the road ahead and then turns back to look at me with even more intensity.

"And when it is cornered," he says with a growl, "a jackrabbit stands its ground and fights! Are you all packed, kiddo?"

"Yes," I answer. I've stuffed as many provisions into my pack as I can.

"Good, kiddo," he says as he turns back around. "Because I'm dropping you off...right now!"

Startled, I bolt upright and look out through the front windshield. A mile or so ahead of us, the highway is blocked, both lanes, by at least a dozen cruisers with their bright lights flashing. A half dozen more sit just off both sides of the road.

"Crawl up in that passenger seat, kid," Samson orders. He is slowing the big truck down. I jump to the front of the cab and push my arms through the straps of my backpack. We are less than a mile away from the roadblock now, and I can see one striking figure standing out in front of the cruisers. He wears a shiny silver suit and has his arms folded across his chest. He has blond, slicked-back hair. He wears mirrored sunglasses. Stingray!

"Yep, the gang's all here!" Samson exclaims as he slows the truck to a crawl. "Get ready to jump out, kid. When you hit the ground, head for those trees over there as fast as you can."

"Samson!"

Samson slows the truck a little more and then turns to look at me again. His steel gray eyes are even more intense.

"I'm going to try to run over that devil!" he growls. "When you get to Haven, you be sure to tell those folks how much old Samson loves them!"

"But, Samson!" I plead. I don't know what else to say.

"Go, kid!" he shouts. "Go…go!"

I open the cab door and jump out. The truck is still rolling, and I have to run forward to keep from falling on my face. The area to either side of the highway is dense, subtropical forest, and I quickly duck into a clump of dark green trees. Behind me, Samson guns his truck, fire shoots out from the back of it, and with almost impossible acceleration, the giant rig streaks forward toward the road block. I freeze in the cover of the trees, huddled down, and watch.

The truck becomes a blur and has to be doing well over a hundred miles an hour as it rockets toward the roadblock. A couple of cruisers have time to pull out of the way, but at least ten are trapped. Two of them cloak up, but it's too late for them.

Stingray stands like a statue in front of the roadblock right up to the last instant and then leaps out of the way like a giant leopard. Samson and his truck plow into the cruisers, his trailer-load of power-packs blows up, and everything vaporizes in a huge orange ball of fire. The explosion shakes the ground under my feet, and the roar is deafening. Then I can see nothing but a fiery crater in the highway, black smoke, and melting metal.

Stingray flips across the grass, jumps to his feet, stands up at the side of the highway, and watches everything burn. Then he looks up the road, directly to where I am hiding. He climbs into a waiting cruiser and heads north, right past my hiding place. As his cruiser picks up speed and continues on, it cloaks up and disappears.

I can't hold my tears back.

"I'll tell them, Samson," I whisper through my tears as I watch what is left of his truck burn. "I'll tell them."

PART TWO:

ANGEL

CHAPTER SIXTEEN

It is a curious thing to sit in the weeds and watch your own funeral.

It has been three weeks since Samson's death. Every night, I slowly work my way south through the subtropical jungles of the deep Southern Province. I hunt for a glimpse of the North Star through the dense trees and navigate haphazardly according to its position in the sky.

Tonight, I have reached a very large lake, surrounded by small, thatched villages that are inhabited by colorfully dressed, dark brown people. I get close enough to hear them during daylight hours, talking or singing through the trees as they walk out together to tend their crops in small five- to ten-acre fields that they have hacked out of the jungle. It is so strange; you will be working your way through the dense underbrush and trees, watching out for snakes, and all of a sudden, there is a busy farming village right in front of you.

A small, dirt road stretches through the jungle toward the lake, and strangely enough, I have found a midsized media board, glowing in the dark, floating above it. For the past few hours, I have hidden in the bushes next to it to catch any news. Almost everything is in Spanish, which I stink at, but the coverage about me is mainly in English, especially the interviews.

Apparently, I am dead. Back home, I am receiving a gala state funeral. I am the pitiful, dead, kidnapped daughter of the new minister of information, and the exhaustive tragic news of my violent, untimely death has captivated the citizens of the provinces for days now. Enemies of the state murdered me. They want to send a message to the government, and any member of the family of any high-ranking official is fair game for them. That's how the media is spinning it.

The board tirelessly flashes clips of my perfect childhood. I was a perfect student, destined to climb high in the immaculate hierarchy of the New Republic. There are endless tearful interviews with my teachers, with Madison, with other classmates I barely knew. My stepmother, beautifully dressed in black, and my father give heart-wrenching, sobbing interviews, and I can't help but feel my tears welling up inside as I listen to them. The key person missing is Jason, and no mention is made of him. My father vows to use his new position to catch and kill all dissidents responsible for my kidnapping and murder. He blames it all on a suspected reemergence of a secret organization created by a new breed of terrorist clairvoyants. I shudder at the irony of it all when I think of Moses as a "terrorist clairvoyant." Moses, who took the time to trace the sign of the cross on my forehead when he knew he was about to die. My father goes into great detail about who he thinks they are, how many of them there are, and where he suspects they can be found. "We will leave no stone unturned!" he exclaims with a strange, haunting authority I have never seen in him before.

Throughout the exhaustive funeral coverage, Bob Roberts keeps switching back to the terrific video coverage of Samson's truck slamming into the police cruisers. It is almost unbearable for me to watch, but I have to know how they found out about Samson. The heat from the crash was so intense, it melted everything, including our bodies, including our DNA. So how could they know it involved me?

Finally, I get my answer. There, in the ashes, they found it. It is the nearly indestructible inner filament of my Perma Lighter, its micro serial number flashed up over and over again on the news. The serial number has been traced to a purchase in Frisco at a convenience store by a teenage girl named Chrissie Wright. I gasp when I see it all. It is clearly my Perma Lighter, the one I used to protect myself from Smithy and his pals in the underground that day. I remember Moses's chagrin the day I slipped it into my jacket pocket. It must have slipped out of my pocket when I hid in Samson's sleeper. It rolled under his seat and lodged there.

Footage is shown of Samson stopping at the truck stop. The invisible transportation department scanners at the truck stop do their work. They scan Samson and the truck. They miss me, of course, but they pick up the Perma Lighter. I can see it imaged and magnified, wedged under the metal sliders of Samson's seat. The police are notified, and a roadblock is set up. It all makes sense.

It was my fault. Through my carelessness, I killed Samson. I start to sob. *Samson, please forgive me. I was stupid. I killed you!*

Samson was a runner transporter by trade but also a high-ranking member of the dissident group, the news says, and a partner of my first kidnapper, the black man. They kidnapped me to get to my father, to get to the government. They were demanding a huge ransom for my safe return. No mercy will be shown to them. I have become a martyr and, overnight, a wonderful dead celebrity. As popular as any *One Star* celebrity. Movies will be made about my terrible ordeal so that millions of citizens can learn from it.

The coverage of my state funeral drags on and on. Thousands of people I don't know show up to lay flowers at my graveside. There is, of course, no mention of my pregnancy. No mention of my intent to escape from the Parlor.

My father and stepmother stand to one side of the grave and nod or shake hands with every person who passes by. I can't help it, but I get the strong sense that my stepmother is enjoying herself. She seems to bask in all of the attention.

Big bodyguards surround my parents; men dressed in black suits, wearing dark sunglasses. But the bodyguard standing closest to my father is significantly smaller than the others and wears mirrored sunglasses. He has beautiful, slicked-back blond hair. In the media close-ups, I can see how strikingly handsome he is.

As I recognize him, I reflexively huddle deeper down in the bushes, well covered in the grass.

He nods to a weeping lady who lays a beautiful bouquet of roses on top of the heaps of other flowers, and then, as she moves on by, he looks directly up at the camera and grins that wicked, crooked grin. I jump back. He seems to be staring directly at me. Behind his mirrored sunglasses, I can feel his eyes boring into mine. It takes every ounce of my willpower to look back at him.

I hear his voice in my mind.

Hello, Chrissie, he says.

For just an instant, I feel anger flare up inside of me. I think of Moses, crumpled on the ground. I think of Samson, dying in an inferno. I think of Jason, beaten and dragged on the ground like a cowering dog.

Go crawl back in your hole! I think back. His grin widens.

I will see you again, soon, his voice whispers in my mind.

Then Stingray looks away, turns, and gently pats my father on his shoulder in consolation. Then he continues to study the people who pass by my grave.

I have seen enough. When the board flashes to a commercial, in Spanish, about the virtues of planting and growing coffee, beans, and maize for the hungry people of the Northern Province, I crawl away into the dense foliage. I continue south along the eastern shore of the tropical lake, carefully staying concealed in the dense underbrush.

I have grown stronger even though I know that I must be well into the third trimester of my pregnancy with Daniel. He shifts and kicks me continuously, but I am carrying him well. My feet have toughened up like leather, and even with my pregnancy, I feel lighter.

Here in the tropics, food and water have not been as much of a problem as I thought they would be. Water is actually very plentiful, running in brooks and streams throughout the forest, and if anything, it presents a problem when I continuously have to cross the many streams I find. Fruit is very plentiful, some of which I recognize and some of which I don't. I am particularly fond of the mangos; their sweetness and mild aroma are intoxicating to me. I have also learned to creep up to the small, primitive villages at night and listen for dogs. If there aren't any, and sometimes there aren't, I creep into a hut past its sleeping occupants and steal a few of the flat, round tortillas that they always seem to have stored in round, tightly woven baskets. I take only what I need, and I always quietly thank the people, hoping that someday maybe I can somehow repay them.

Haven is actually starting to seem like a myth to me, a never-never land that I will never reach. No guide has come to find me, to take me farther. I am all alone. I just continue to press south and hope for the best. That is what Moses told me to do.

Snakes freak me out more than anything else in the jungle. I come across them constantly, and luckily, they slither away from me as fast as I frantically scramble away from them. I know that if I could catch and eat one, it would be a good source of protein. So far I haven't had the nerve, or the stomach, to do it.

My other immediate problem is how to deal with the insects, particularly the fat, brown ticks that hide by the thousands in the wild grasses and bushes and persist in constantly crawling up my legs. Every few hours I have to stop and search all over my body for them. Some of them I don't find in time, and it hurts more than you can imagine to yank them out. I am amazed that so many of them exist in the subtropics. The climate here is mostly dry, and I only occasionally need to cover up during brief rain showers that happen every few days, but it is a climate that the ticks seem to thrive in.

After an hour of moving south away from the little dirt road and the media board, I rest on an old fallen log next to a broad, swift-running stream that empties into the big lake. I take a mango and a tortilla out of my backpack and take stock of my situation. *So the government says that I am dead*, I think as I bite into the juicy mango. *Have they written me off? There is no longer any reward hanging over my head?*

Does that mean I can travel faster? Maybe no one is really looking for me any longer. It all sounds wonderfully tempting to just walk into a village and ask for help. But I just don't know.

The sun is rising on the eastern horizon, making the treetops glow a reddish orange that is gorgeous to see. I move a few feet away from the log and find a small clearing downstream from it. It's time to settle down to sleep in the grass. The air is cool but humid, and a thousand birds, insects, and geckos sing deep in the jungle to the rising sun. I have grown used to their music, and it actually reassures me and helps me fall asleep.

As I have done every morning now before drifting off, I whisper to Daniel. "Good night, sweet baby," I whisper to him. "We are still safe. Sleep tight." Daniel stirs in my belly. Then I whisper the other message I have begun to whisper before sleeping. "Thank you, Moses, thank you, Samson. You are my heroes."

Sometime around midday, something wakes me up. As I search my body for ticks, I sense that something is different, and it takes me a moment to realize what it is. The birds have stopped singing. Everything is dead quiet. I look out through the trees across a field full of crops that hugs the lakeshore, and I see them coming.

Dogs! Sniffing the air and the ground and heading straight for me.

CHAPTER SEVENTEEN

There are two of them. They are big, brown, mangy dogs; the kind you don't want to mess with. They are working their way through the crop fields, sniffing the ground and making a beeline toward me. A few dozen yards behind them, I can see that four men are following, carrying clubs and machetes.

The men look as mangy as the dogs. They wear old straw hats, tatters for clothes, and every one of them has long, black, unkempt hair and thick beards.

The dogs must have caught my scent because they are yelping now and quickening their pace. They can't be more than a hundred yards from me, and I have to do something quick.

They bark and howl when they catch the scent that I left when I sat on the log. Slowly and with great care, I move along the stream bank toward the lake. By the time the dogs reach the log, I am thirty feet downstream. They jump and bark, waiting for the men to catch up to them.

The men search the bushes around the log and yell at the dogs. One man hacks at the log with his machete, angry. The dogs run back and forth, and I freeze, thinking that I am safe for now. The men are talking to the dogs, urging them to continue the hunt in a thick Spanish dialect that I can only catch pieces of.

The dogs look confused and start to run upstream along the stream bank, with the men following close behind. I relax.

Slowly but deliberately, I continue to creep along the stream. The stream bank is rocky, helping to cover my trail, but increasing the danger that I could trip. Just as I think that I am getting away, my luck runs out.

The dogs have turned around and are coming back, sniffing the ground and barking excitedly. The men follow right behind, and they will be on me within minutes. I remember my night with the dogs in the vineyards, and I do the only thing I can think of. I hold my breath and slide into the cold water of the stream.

The current is stronger than I could have imagined. I am completely at the mercy of the current and bouncing hard along the stream's bedrocks. *Keep calm, Chrissie,* I tell myself as my arms, legs, and head smack against the smooth, hard rocks again and again. I hold my breath until my lungs are about to burst, and finally, I have to come up for air. I swallow water in gulps as I break the surface of the stream. I pull in a quick breath of air, and then the current pulls me back underwater again.

The water is too deep now, and I think that it is possible that I might drown. But the current is rapidly carrying me to the far side of the stream, and it also weakens as it nears the lake. I take in another breath of air and swim toward a thick stand of bushes that border the washout where the stream widens and finally disappears into the larger body of lake water.

I can hear the dogs, but they are now far upstream and out of sight. I sit low in the bushes, sucking in fresh air and trying not to cough. Then I ease my way up into the jungle. As I make my way through the thick foliage, I can hear the angry shouts of my hunters. The dogs are screaming and yelping. Their masters are beating them.

It is early afternoon, but I am not about to stop and rest now. I have to keep moving to make as much distance as I can between myself and my pursuers.

Head south, I keep telling myself. For two days, I maintain a constant pace without sleeping. The jungle is thicker the farther south I go, and as long as I can move along without coming out into the open, I hazard traveling during the day. The sun helps me keep my bearings, and I am too hyped up from my encounter with the machete men to sleep anyway.

Then as morning breaks after my second night of continuous walking, I emerge out of the trees at the edge of fields that are filled with a variety of crops. My food supply is running low, and I recognize the tall stalks of maize, the avocados, and I sense that potatoes are ripening in the dirt. The farmers here seem to grow everything at once in the same fields.

My stomach is rumbling, and I decide that this is a good place to rest. I will sleep until nightfall and then harvest some food. I pick a spot where I can easily retreat into the forest, settle down, and say good night to Daniel. As I feel a little kick, I drift off to sleep.

CHAPTER EIGHTEEN

Four days later.

Somehow, I have a sense of her before I hear her or see her. I am hiding out in the brush at the edge of another large clearing, a little distance away from a village that I plundered for food last night.

She can't be more than nine or ten years old. She looks like one of the urchins I saw in the desert villages when I rode with Samson, but she is not as skinny. Her clothes are tattered. She is wearing a dirty white shirt, a pleated black skirt decorated with a variety of colorful flowers, and old leather open sandals on her feet. A pink, plastic butterfly clip, looking somewhat out of place, holds one side of her long, jet-black hair out of her dirty face. She is obviously a local, native girl, but she is not out on a casual, midday stroll.

Three big dogs are ranging behind her, hunting her. They look hungry. She looks back at them, screams, and starts to run and hop through the crops toward my hiding place. She has no chance at all; the dogs are going to catch her.

I can't let that happen. I grab hold of the long stick that is propping up my lean-to. As the little girl approaches, I jump up and lunge for the dogs. She stops dead in her tracks, startled that I have appeared out of nowhere, while I swing the stick and fend off the angry dogs. I strike the nearest one hard on the nose, and it yelps in pain. The other dogs jump at me, growling and barking, saliva dripping from their mouths.

I am losing the battle. The dogs keep jumping at me, and I keep swinging my stick at them. If only I still had my Perma Lighter. To my surprise, the little girl does not stay frozen for long. She finds a big stick and joins me, swinging hard at the rabid dogs. Then the ears on one dog prick up, and he turns away from me. He bolts away in a dead run from my hiding place, and the other two dogs join him. Breathing hard, I look up to see what scared them away.

Three Southern Province cops are sitting on air bikes less than twenty feet away, leaning over their handlebars, and watching me. One of them laughs and turns to say something in Spanish to the one sitting next to him, who also laughs. The little girl spots them and screams again. I reach out and pull her close to me.

"Chrissie!" one of the cops calls to me, laughing. They are wearing the typical black uniforms that are almost identical to those worn by the Northern police.

They have obviously set a trap for me, and it worked.

They waste no time dismounting and taking me and the little girl into their custody. They treat me okay, but they treat the little girl roughly, and she is crying.

"Keep your filthy hands off of her!" I growl at them, but they only laugh at me. One of them walks to his bike and talks on the radio. Soon, I know, there will probably be twenty or thirty cops here. And that means that it is over.

They take my backpack away from me, empty it, and start handing the contents back and forth to each other. I watch as they pass the medicines to each other, pocketing the valuable stuff that they probably can't get for themselves down here.

"I can see a time, Chrissie, when you will lose everything," I remember Moses telling me.

The cops sit the little girl down next to me in the grass. Still laughing, they pass the fruit and potatoes in my backpack to each other and argue about the *mas dinero* they are going to receive for my capture. I can actually understand some of their banter. After a minute, the nearest cop looks at me and gestures at my boots.

"Give to me," he commands in broken English. I start to obey, but a thought occurs to me. It is something that Moses told me.

I carefully reach into my pants pocket, and the cops stop what they are doing and watch me carefully.

"Stop!" the nearest one warns me.

I pull my hand back out, but I have what I want. I throw the small fistful of diamonds directly at them.

"There!" I yell. "*Mas dinero!*"

The little girl is huddled tightly against me and, as the cops scramble to snatch the diamonds up, I pull her sideways with me toward the forest. I don't have but seconds, but the glittering diamonds are a powerful draw to the cops, and they have picked up enough of them to figure out that they are probably real.

Before they look up and realize that we have vanished, I make it to the trees and into the underbrush. I have been creeping through this stuff for weeks, I know how to maneuver, and I head for the thickest brush I can find. I motion to the little girl to get down like me and crawl on her hands and knees, and we scoot underneath dense branches, deeper and deeper, until I hear the cops shouting at each other.

"La senorita y la nina, vamos!" one of them screams.

We are deep enough under the brush, and I freeze. I look at the little girl, and she is frightened. I put my index finger to my lips. *We must be quiet,* I am telling her. She nods her head, almost imperceptibly. Yes. She has the biggest brown eyes I have ever seen.

To my utter surprise, the cops keep searching for the diamonds for a long time. What follows next is a very heated argument between them. One of them wins, convinces the other two, and they quickly mount their air bikes and ride away with a whoosh. I let out a sigh of relief. Moses was right, the diamonds are worth more to them than I am. They must be a little skeptical about the reward the Northern Province posted on my head.

I look down at the little girl and nod my head reassuringly. It has been ages since I have been this close to another human, and I want to hug her. She has tears streaming down her cheeks mixing with the dirt on her face. Her eyes are so big, she reminds me of a baby deer. "What is your name," I want to ask her. I search for the words.

"Como te llamas?" I finally whisper to her.

"Lucia," she whispers back. "Eres Chrissie, verdad?"

Yes, I nod my head. *Your name is Lucia, a beautiful name.*

After another half hour has passed, I lead her deeper into the jungle. I head due east where the jungle thickens overhead until I can no longer see the sun. With Lucia's hand in mine, we continue on for another two hours, and then I am just too exhausted to continue any farther. We should be safe enough here.

I make a gesture. I clasp my hands together and put them to the side of my face. I close my eyes and pretend to sleep. When I open them, Lucia is nodding in understanding. We will stay here and hide and try to sleep. At nightfall, we will move out.

CHAPTER NINETEEN

I am dreaming. I am having another nightmare.

I am in the Parlor, in a stark room with bright, white walls. The steel table I am lying on is so cold that it burns me where it touches my naked skin. I am terrified, and I am in terrible pain.

Someone has reached under the white linen sheet that covers my body and is gently squeezing my hand. I turn my head and see that it is Ruthie, my childhood make-believe sister. She is about ten and is watching me with deep concern in her eyes. I try to smile.

I hear voices and look up to see the red-haired lady with green eyes standing in the doorway to the entrance to my room. She is arguing with a white-coated, gray-haired male technician.

"She was carrying two babies!" the red-haired lady is saying with exasperation in her shrill voice. "How on earth could you miss that?"

I look back into the eyes of Ruthie. A tear is running down her right cheek, and she squeezes my hand harder. Slowly, I turn and look at a cold steel tray that has been placed on the other side of the table I lie on.

It is about the size of a dinner tray, and it holds two small bundles that are tightly wrapped in gauze. A little blood oozes through the white wrappings, and each bundle has a nametag pinned to the top of it. One tag says "Daniel." I look at the other tag as I gasp in horror. It says "Lucia."

Ruthie squeezes my hand even harder.

❂ ❂ ❂

I wake up in a cold sweat even though the forest air is warm. Lucia is awake, huddled next to me, squeezing my hand with hers and looking up at me with deep concern in her big brown eyes. I smile at her reassuringly and hug her. I look out through the trees and see that the sun is setting in the west.

I was able retrieve my knapsack when the cops left with the diamonds. They took everything from it, but I can still carry fruit, nuts, and roots in it. Lucia helps me forage for wild fruit, and she comes up with some that I have been afraid to sample. Then I take my big stick to feel ahead for snakes, and after checking the position of the North Star, we turn back south through the jungle.

It is a strange but wonderful feeling to have Lucia's company. I forgot how lonely I had become, and even though she speaks a thick dialect of her Indian/Spanish language, I hang on to every word that I can understand.

"Son muy, muy malas personas la policia," she informs me as she steps lightly across the dry mulch that covers much of the forest floor. "The police are very, very bad men," I kind of understand her to say. She grabs my hand with hers and holds on tightly.

"Tambien esta mal mi papa. Se murio mi mama, pero mi papa me pego` y hizo cosas malas a mi. Mi papa es un hombre muy malo," she continues. (My papa is also very bad. My mama is dead, but my papa beat me and did bad things to me. He is a very bad man.)

I grip her hand back. She is crying. It is terribly dark here. No moon tonight. The trees are alive with the noise of thousands of night creatures, all singing at once.

"Mi papa me vendo` a la policia y me trajeron aqui. Dijeron, 'corrate, Lucia, los perros te van a comer! Tue res la cena para los perros hoy!' Se rieron a mi. Son hombres muy malos," she continues. (My papa sold me to the police, and they brought me here. They said, "Run, Lucia, the dogs are going to eat you! You are dinner for the dogs today!" They laughed at me. They are very bad men.)

"Yes, they are!" I growl. Lucia looks up at me with imploring eyes, and I nod my head and wipe the tears from her face. "You are safe now, Lucia. I will keep you safe."

I have had enough of the brutality of people. I am angry enough to kill the policemen. Given half a chance and a good weapon, I know I would try. I want to kill her father. She can't go back to her village, I know instinctively. If she did, she would die. I grab her hand again and squeeze it.

But killing is not the answer, I say to myself. Stingray kills for fun. I never want to be like him. Not even out of necessity. I don't want to be a killer. I want to get to Haven with Daniel. And now with Lucia.

"I'm taking you with me to Haven," I say.

Lucia looks up at me with wide eyes.

"Haven, en serio?" she asks.

"Yes, Haven," I affirm, "where we will be safe. No bad men."

Lucia's eyes are questioning, but she nods her head yes.

"Si, Haven," she repeats and starts to skip along awkwardly as she moves with me through the forest. "Haven, mi hermana."

She is right. She is my sister now, and I am going to keep her safe.

She points back behind us toward the north.

"Alli esta mi pueblo, pero nunca puedo volver," she tells me. (My village is that way, but I can never go back.)

"Yes," I assure her, "You will never go back."

She is just like me, escaping now from a place that probably means death if she goes back. There is no doubt in my mind that Stingray will kill me if I can't figure out a way to stay ahead of him. I think about the way he looked into that camera at my funeral. The thought of him unnerves me. Another thought also occurs to me. Did he set the police up to trap me with Lucia? Somebody knows I am still alive, and they seem to be playing with me. I don't like their game. I need to learn the rules, and I also need to learn how to play back harder. I am so sick of being helpless.

Now, at least, I have somebody else to protect. I have longed for some companionship, and I look at the little girl walking next to me. Her eyes are alert, and she is listening to every tiny sound in the forest. Someone to protect? Maybe she is here to protect me.

As always, progress through the jungle is agonizingly slow. By now, the season is approaching the fullness of fall, but the temperature does not seem to change much here in the tropical highlands: warm at night, hot during the day. In no time, I am sweating. Lucia is obviously far more acclimated to the heat than I am.

After a few hours, we arrive at a shallow brook and stop to rest. I pull my water straw out of my back pocket and show Lucia how to use it. She tries it and then holds it up in the starlight, studying it with amazement. Something is screaming in the far distance, almost sounding like the roar of a big cat to me. I've heard the cats out here before and have even seen one, but this sound is more like a roaring howl than a screech, and louder. I tense up as it draws nearer and nearer. Soon, it is crashing through the limbs of the upper forest canopy, almost directly above us. I hold Lucia close to me and crouch down in the brush.

Lucia laughs and points up at a thick tree limb. A big black monkey, almost as big as she is, perches there, staring down in our direction with bright, gleaming brown eyes.

"El es el rey aqui," Lucia says to me. "Nos va a cuidar."

"He is the king here," she is saying, I can somehow understand almost every one of her words. "He will watch over us."

She must be right. As we continue on, he follows through the trees high above us.

Occasionally, we stumble upon fields where the local farmers have hacked away the forest and planted their various crops of maize, avocados, and beans.

"Milpas," Lucia calls the small farms that grow such an amazing variety of crops.

"Son hombres de maiz," she exclaims as she points at the small cluster of farmhouses in the distance. (Those are men of maize.)

Men of the corn, I think to myself. *Well, they certainly know how to make great tortillas.*

As I look at the farmhouses in the distance, my mouth waters for the flat corn tortillas that I might be able to steal. But I can't chance being caught now. We will have to make do with what we can find in the jungle, and Lucia seems to know how to find what we need. She pauses occasionally, like Moses, and pulls up handfuls of wild sweet potatoes and other roots. I keep an eye out for mangoes.

We continue this way for nearly a week, picking our way south, and I start to relax with the feeling that maybe the police have not mounted a major search for us. They are probably trying to hock their diamonds somewhere. Out here, so deep in the jungle, there are no media boards. Even dirt roads are surprisingly scarce. And by now, I am sure, the media of the North Province has forgotten all about me and has moved on to the next terribly important *Breaking News* crisis. The people of the north live a fast life and have an extremely short attention span.

Lucia huddles tightly against me as we sleep under our makeshift shelters every day. She constantly calls me her big sister, and it makes me happy. She is the little sister that I always wanted. The black monkey stays with us, and strangely, he drops bananas down to us. Lucia always laughs and thanks him.

Every evening, as soon as the sun sets, we break our little camp after sleeping all day and prepare to move south. I search up through the tree limbs of the forest canopy, the leaves glowing silver from the light of a waxing moon, and try to locate the

North Star. As soon as I gain my bearings, we strike out and cross the small, chilly brooks meandering their way through the ground cover beneath the thickening canopy.

Tonight, we continue picking our way south through the jungle when it occurs to me that the big, black monkey isn't following us. This isn't unusual; he comes and goes as he pleases, but we should see him before morning if he follows his old habits. He will show up and drop something edible down to us.

I am whispering about the monkey to Lucia when we step out of the trees into a broad clearing that marks an area that is being prepared for farming. A village must be nearby. It is possible to step out of the forest and continue south along the empty, rugged ground, and move a little more quickly. I can see in the moonlight that it is an area that is dotted with high piles of recently cut slash.

So that is what we do. Before we reach the southernmost edge of the clearing, a particularly high pile of cut tree limbs and brush stands in our way.

In the bright moonlight, I can distinctly make out the features of the four men as they appear from around the far side of the giant pile. They are the same four mangy, black-bearded men with machetes and clubs who nearly trapped me miles ago at the big lake, and they have their two mangy dogs sniffing the ground out in front of them. Bounty hunters!

I grip Lucia's arm. *Freeze!* They don't seem to see us at first, but somehow they know exactly where we are standing. The dogs must have our scent.

One of the big men is laughing now, and swinging his dull machete in our direction. I become the jackrabbit. I freeze and don't move a muscle.

As the men approach, someone steps out of the woods into the open. I blink my eyes in the silver moonlight and try to comprehend what I am seeing.

It is a woman, perhaps six feet tall. She has long golden hair that is held back from her face by a shining band of silver that circles her head. Even in the moonlight, I can tell that her skin is dark olive, her face beautiful—if a little gaunt—and that there is a ferocious gleam in her eyes. And her eyes! They shine golden in the moonlight.

She takes another big step away from the trees and stands with her hands on her hips. She is wearing tight brown leathers, shirt, and pants that are bound by a dark brown belt that circles her thin waist. She might appear thin, but there is incredible strength in her stance. Strength and attitude.

She claps the silver bands that she wears on her wrists together, and the men turn around to face her. As she claps her wrists, silver shields grow from the wristbands, and cover her hands and forearms. I think of Medea and Ashur, of their arm shields. The men look astonished and stand frozen, staring at her. Then all at once, they spring into action.

The men who hold machetes lead the attack, screaming and swinging their machetes wildly at the woman. She moves like lightning and easily wards off their advance. She fights like Moses, only quicker. A man with a club yells a command, and the startled dogs leap into the fight.

I hear a loud howl in the forest, and out leaps the big black monkey that has been following us for days. He goes straight for the dogs, tossing one of them like a leaf into the pile of brush. That dog yelps in agony and dies quickly, impaled on a sharp, protruding stick. The other dog cries out pitifully and runs, with the monkey close at its heels.

I return my attention to the woman. Lucia grips my hand with all of her might. One man lies on the ground, his machete in his chest. The other three are circling the woman now, gauging her carefully. She frowns and shakes her head in total disdain at them and then reassumes her impatient stance. Then the men all attack at once.

What happens next happens too quickly for my mind to fully register. In a matter of seconds, three of the men are lying dead on the ground, and the fourth is running away, screaming for his life. The woman steps around the dead men, picks up one of their machetes, and throws it at the escaping man. It spins and whistles through the air and finds its target, burying itself into the man's back with such force that it knocks him off his feet. He twists in pain on the ground for a second, and then he lies still. The woman kicks the bodies of the men at her feet. Then satisfied that they are no longer a threat, she walks directly to where we are standing.

Her eyes flash toward me with incredible intensity. She holds up a hand and makes signs with it. I've seen this demonstrated before, in school. She is apparently mute, and she is using sign language. Oddly, as she signs, I can hear her words in my mind.

You are the jackrabbit! she signs. Lucia looks up at me, squeezes my hand, and nods her head. She trusts this lady. I'm not so sure.

Anger flashes in the woman's golden eyes, and she signs again.

Jackrabbit! she repeats. *I am your guide, Chrissie. I am with Moses!*

I nod my head. I am trembling.

"What is your name?" I meekly ask.

She studies me with apparent disdain, and then stares down at Lucia for a long moment.

You should be alone! I hear her voice in my head. She returns her burning stare to me.

Then she shakes her head and sighs.

I am called Angel, she signs.

CHAPTER TWENTY

Angel wastes no time. In seconds, we are running through the dense underbrush of the jungle. I try to weave around and use the natural concealment of the brush and ferns, but Angel glances back and glares at me, shaking her head no.

You are only slowing us down, she signs to me. *We must move quickly!*

Her strides are strong and purposeful, and we have to scramble to keep up with her. I cannot help but play back in my mind the blur of her fight with the men. *This is someone,* I think to myself, *who could kill Stingray.*

Angel glares back at me again. A mind reader. I watch the grace of her movements through the forest, and she reminds me so much of how Moses moved. As I picture Moses in my mind, I can't help but feel a deep pang of sadness. Angel glances back at me one more time. This time, her face is softer.

We continue this way for hours, covering more distance in one night than I have managed to cover in weeks. The pace is much too rapid for me to keep my bearings, and soon I lose all sense of direction. Occasionally, I peer up through the thick branches of the trees that we pass beneath, hoping to catch a glimpse of the North Star. But the tree cover is just too thick here.

After several hours, we finally sit down and rest next to a swiftly running creek, and the black monkey catches up with us. His right side is covered in dried blood, and Angel holds her arms out to him. Almost like a child, he jumps into her outstretched arms and hugs her.

His name is Howler, Angel signs to Lucia and me. *He has watched over you until I could arrive.*

"Howler!" Lucia laughs and strokes the monkey's long, coarse black hair. Then she stands up and walks to the creek several times to carry back handfuls of cool water to wash off the dried blood that covers him. As Lucia washes him, I can see the bite marks where the dog must have bitten him. Howler looks up at me as Lucia washes him, and I sense a kind of sadness in his gleaming eyes.

Angel signs to me. *Howler does not like to kill.*

We continue on. For the next three hours, Angel takes us on a death march. We move through the brush so rapidly, I have to gasp for air. My pregnancy is weighing heavily on me, and I can't catch my breath. Lucia skips along beside me, and Howler jumps from tree limb to tree limb above us; but Angel pushes far out ahead, breaking trail and scouting. Presently, she stops and walks back to me.

Sit down! she signs.

I find a giant fallen tree log half buried in the ground mulch and collapse on to it. Lucia takes a seat beside me. Angel squats down in front of me, still so tall that she towers over me, and reaches out to stroke my belly, feeling for Daniel.

Daniel is well, she signs. Daniel kicks me in the side for good measure.

Angel stands up and places her hands on her hips. It is the same impatient gesture I saw her make to the bounty hunters.

We must go faster, Chrissie! she signs.

I look up at her towering over me as she is, silhouetted against the setting silver moonlight. Her golden eyes sparkle. Is she glaring at me? I cannot tell if she approves of me or holds me in total disdain. Her attitude is a total mystery to me. Lucia seems to sense my distress and confusion and squeezes my hand.

"No te preocupes hermana, estoy contigo," Lucia whispers to me. (Don't worry, big sister, I am with you.)

In school, we learned all about the Greek gods. Angel standing before me strikes a powerful image in my mind. She looks like Athena! She is the personification of that goddess: all powerful, intensely beautiful, and fully equipped for war.

Get up! Angel signs to me and glares. *We must go now. We have to keep moving!*

I lose track of time until I see the first signs of dawn erupting in the eastern sky. The tops of the highest trees glow red, and day birds are waking and starting to sing. Angel hunts around and finally finds a suitable place for us to settle down.

It is a tiny clearing, and once I stand in the center of it, I can see dark blue sky above us, streaked red and orange with the first rays of the rising sun.

Make your shelter, Angel signs to me. *We will rest here.*

I make camp and reach into my backpack. I still have several mangos, and I hand one to Lucia. I offer one to Angel, but she shakes her head no. She reaches into a small leather pouch that she carries on her shoulder and pulls out a handful of roots. As we sit and eat, I become uncomfortably aware that Angel is staring at me.

"I am sorry," I finally say to her. Her expression changes from one of unconcealed disdain. She has a quizzical look in her eyes.

"I am sorry about Moses," I explain quietly. "I am sorry about Samson. It was all my fault. If I hadn't run, they would still be alive now."

Angel shakes her head at me.

No, she signs to me, and I hear her words clearly in my mind. I hear her sincerity.

It was not your fault at all. You chose to save your son. They chose to help you. Do not mourn them, Chrissie, you chose well! And remember this…I also choose."

For the first time, Angel smiles at me. But a tear runs down her cheek.

※ ※ ※

I am dreaming, and it is not a good dream. A quiet voice is speaking to me in my mind, the same voice that told me about Daniel and the lion's den.

You must prepare yourself for what lies ahead, Chrissie, the voice is saying. *Angel will teach you.*

Then suddenly, I am back on the beach where Moses died. I sit frozen in the mangrove bushes. The hot air is stifling. I am carrying Daniel in a way that makes it hard to breathe, and I hurt. Out in the distance, I can see the body of Moses, awkwardly crumpled in the hot sand.

Someone is walking up to me, holding something in his outstretched hand. As he comes closer, I can see clearly that it is Stingray. He is staring directly at me even though I am well hidden. I can't see his eyes, hidden by his mirrored sunglasses, but I can imagine them. In my imagination, they are cold steel gray and merciless. He is grinning his wicked, crooked grin.

He stops ten feet directly in front of me.

"Chrissie," he says as he grins, "someone special wanted to say hello."

He tosses what he is holding, and I can see that it is a severed head. It lands in the sand with a sickening thud and rolls right up to me. When it stops rolling, it is lying in front of me, face up, dead eyes staring into mine. It is Jason. Flies circle his dead eyes, and in the middle of his forehead Stingray has carved a perfect image of a stingray.

I scream.

Lucia is hugging me and holding her small brown hand across my mouth. I am sweating profusely.

Angel sits directly in front of me, legs crossed, studying me. Behind her, the sun is setting.

You were having a bad dream, she signs to me. I nod my head.

"I have them almost every day," I tell her, sobbing.

She shakes her head.

I could see some of your dream, she answers *Who is the boy?*

"Jason, my old boyfriend," I tell her, "Daniel's father. Stingray has him."

Angel sighs and shakes her head again.

They are only using him to get to you. You have to forget about him.

How can I do that? I ask myself. Part of me still loves him; I know it is true. And as I said, he is Daniel's father.

No! Angel glares at me and signs, *You must forget about him!*

I stare back at Angel. We have reached an impasse. I refuse to forget about Jason. I might even do anything I can to rescue him.

That is not a good choice, Angel signs to me, but she sighs and lets it go.

We eat a quick breakfast and move out. True to form, Howler has dropped down half a dozen fruits, some of which I don't recognize. Lucia laughs and thanks him, and he jumps away, howling happily through the trees.

Shortly before midday, Angel runs back to where Lucia and I are attempting to cross a difficult stream. Her eyes are filled with fierce concern.

Hide, she signs to me, *and stay right here. We are being tracked!*

Quickly, Lucia and I huddle down in the brush.

Don't move a muscle! Angel signs to both of us. *Many men followed us. I was taking you to a village high in the mountains. If I should fall today, continue southeast. Another guide will find you and lead you to the village. You must stay at that village, Chrissie. You cannot travel any farther until Daniel is born.*

Before I can respond, Angel has disappeared into the trees. Lucia and I hug each other. Lucia looks up at me with her big brown eyes.

"Chrissie, tengo miedo," she says. (Chrissie, I am afraid.)

I hug her for a minute and listen to the melody of the stream as its water ripples across rocks.

"Don't worry, little sister," I soothe her as we huddle together under the cloak. "I will protect you."

If only it were true.

CHAPTER TWENTY-ONE

Angel returns hours later in the late afternoon. She glances our way as she runs past us and dives like a leopard into a deep pool of water in the middle of the stream. She is covered in blood. She stays in the cool water for several moments, bathing the blood away and dunking her beautiful golden hair underwater over and over again. She seems to be washing away more than blood.

Once she reemerges from the water, I can tell that she is injured in several places—blaster burns that have ripped through her leathers and skin. Both of her legs are burned, her left side, and her left arm. As she approaches the place where we are huddled, she moves painfully. Somewhere far overhead, I can hear Howler thrashing through the high tree limbs.

Wincing, Angel slowly sits down in front of us.

Chrissie, come out, she signs to me as she reaches into her pouch and pulls out a vial of burn balm. Lucia and I approach and silently watch as she gingerly applies the balm to her burns. Then she sits and stares into the distance. Howler perches in a tree just above us and drops down a handful of mangos.

Angel picks up a mango and takes a bite while gesturing for us to do the same. As we eat, I watch the red glow of the setting sun cut across the treetops far above us. Soon, the night birds are singing.

"Who were they?" I finally ask Angel.

She sighs and signs to me. *Soldiers.*

"Were they hunting for me?"

Yes.

Nothing more is said. I can tell that Angel is hurting, and now is not the time. The burn balm works quickly; and I can tell that it already has a healing effect on Angel's wounds, but she stands up stiffly when it is time for us to move. Twice now, I have seen someone hit by a blaster. First Moses and now Angel. Blaster wounds are usually fatal. What kind of people are these guides?

Quickly, Angel leads us across the stream where it is shallow, and then we are moving through thick green ferns under the trees. Howler crashes from tree limb to tree limb high above our heads. For the past few days, I have been able to tell that we are climbing through higher elevations; the foliage around us is slowly changing from subtropical to more of a temperate type of plant growth.

Thick bushes plush with wild red strawberries grow underfoot, and occasionally, Lucia stoops down to pluck and eat a couple. I bite into one and am surprised at how sweet it tastes.

After an hour, with the light of dusk still filtering through the trees, we skirt around a rough open area, and I can see what happened to Angel. At least a dozen bodies of uniformed soldiers lie strewn about, some in awkward positions with obviously broken arms, legs, and necks. Angel does not let us pause to look but hurries us around the area. I have seen similar uniforms in the north. These are obviously soldiers, but from the Southern Province.

Hunting for me.

As we reenter the thick woods and ferns, I take one last glance back at the carnage. One woman did this by herself. How can one woman completely take out a squad of armed soldiers? Angel does not glance back. She just moves ahead through the jungle like a big, lithe feline. She moves like Moses.

As we climb, the streams become creeks and then the creeks become small brooks that we can easily jump across. The woods gradually thin, and we cross more and more natural, grassy meadows that mark the beginnings of highlands. In the meadows, I can see dark mountains looming in the distant moonlight, dominating the far horizon like giant, monolithic sentries.

Just before sunup, we pause next to a brook that dances musically across a descending cascade of smooth rocks. Lucia and I kneel down and take turns sipping the cool water through my straw. Howler joins us, ducks his head in the water, and takes a long drink and then jumps into Angel's arms, nearly knocking her off her feet. She laughs as he hugs her. So the goddess of war laughs.

We will rest here, she signs to Lucia and me. Lucia signs back to her. She is picking it up, and I wonder if she is hearing Angel in Spanish.

I find a pool of water and look at my face reflected in the early morning sunlight. I am thin and haggard. I have lost a lot of weight.

Angel searches around and spots a rotting, hollow log that juts halfway into the babbling brook, and she is harvesting gobs of writhing white larvae. On a wide, flat rock, she pounds the larvae into a paste with a flat stick, reaches into her bag, and pulls out a pouch of what looks like flour. This she adds to the larvae paste and then makes three flat tortillas out of the mix. She covers the tortillas with a thin sheet of heat-wrap and presto! We have hot tortillas.

You need protein, she signs to us as she hands each of us a piping hot tortilla. I try not to think of the larvae as I eat and discover that the tortilla is actually the best-tasting food I have eaten in weeks.

When we are finished with breakfast, Angel sits on the ground, her long legs crossed, and studies me. Her beautiful golden eyes literally glow in the morning light.

She reaches out for a moment and strokes my cheek. I look at her quizzically.

You remind me of my mother, she signs. Then she stretches out and falls asleep.

Lucia is already asleep and huge fatigue is overtaking me. I try to get comfortable, but it is hard to arrange my pregnant body on the ground. My due date has to be arriving soon, and I know that wherever we are going, we must get there as quickly as possible. I finally doze, but I don't sleep.

Later, while the sun is setting in the west, casting a new myriad of color across the treetops above us, we eat a quick dinner of fruit.

"Why would they send so many soldiers to kill me?" I ask Angel as we eat.

She pauses, as if she is carefully considering her response to me. Finally, she signs.

They didn't come just to kill you, Chrissie, she signs. *They really want to kill Daniel.*

Daniel literally rolls in my belly, as if he is reacting to every word that she signs. I feel a terrible nausea creeping up.

"They still want my baby?" I ask. The Parlor wanted to abort him, to kill him. Angel waits, letting the implication of what she is telling me sink in. Then she responds.

He is the greatest threat the New Republic has ever faced, she signs and then changes the subject.

We are only three days away from Santa Maria, she signs. It is the first time that she has actually named our destination.

"So Santa Maria is actually Haven?" I ask. Are we that close?

No. Angel shakes her head. *Haven is too far away for now. Daniel will be born soon, and you have to be in a safe place for that. Santa Maria is safe.*

Angel stands up.

Now, we must move quickly, she signs with a stern look on her face. The old Angel has returned.

I look at Lucia. My boots are still holding up to the wear and tear of the journey, but Lucia's leather sandals are shot. For days,

I have been treating her feet with blister medicine from Angel's bag, but she is starting to hobble badly as she walks.

Angel reads my mind and sweeps Lucia off the ground like a feather as she walks past us. With one blaster burned arm, she swings Lucia around her body to ride on her back and hops across the brook, walking with long, rapid strides. Howler takes off across the tree limbs above our heads, and sighing, I follow.

CHAPTER TWENTY-TWO

We travel increasingly uphill not for three days, but for three exhausting weeks! I am slowing down significantly now, and Angel grows impatient. She said three days! I am angry that she has obviously lied to me.

Every morning, when we settle down, Angel lectures me.

Your thoughts rage across your mind the way Howler flies across the treetops. You have no control at all over them. Watch!

She gestures to Howler, and he grins widely. Then he takes off howling across the trees.

Your thoughts! Angel signs with anger in her eyes. *You must learn to hide your thoughts, Chrissie, the way you hide in the forest.*

Morning after morning, she goes on like this.

Santa Maria is a tiny fishing village, she continues, *far away to the east on the coast. You must convince yourself that Santa Maria is where we are going. Convince yourself that we are already there. You, too, Lucia!*

An enraptured Lucia watches Angel and eagerly nods her head. Angel goes on to describe Santa Maria in exhaustive detail. She describes each tiny village hut, the men taking to their fishing boats, sailing out into the blue ocean to fish; the women, colorfully dressed, working, cleaning the catch and tending to the village chores. She describes the sight of the boats returning at sunset.

When you think of anything at all, think about Santa Maria!

We try our best, but it is not easy. We are clearly climbing up into beautiful, high mountain terrain, and it is hard for me to picture anything else.

Each morning, after Angel gives us this lecture, she tells us to hide and sleep, and then she disappears. Every evening she returns with delicious, hot food. We must be near villages that are tucked away in the green tree-covered hills, but I never see them.

As we journey, Angel continues to carry Lucia on her back until Lucia's feet heal. Then early one week, Angel arrives back at our camp with food and a fresh pair of leather sandals for the little girl. Lucia squeals with delight as she tries them on.

As always, Howler ranges far out ahead of us like a scout. I am growing very fond of him; I love the way he grins at us, the way his big brown eyes gleam at us.

By the third week, I think that Daniel must have doubled in size. I am feeling a lot of pain in my hips and lower back, and Lucia, in an effort to help me keep my mind off of it, teaches me Spanish as we walk. She describes in great detail the huts, the women, the fishing boats.

"Mira," she says, as if we are actually surrounded by the sights that she describes, and then she points at nothing in particular. "Esta!"

I can understand most of her Spanish, but I am far from conversational.

One evening during the third grueling week, Angel returns to us burned and bloody.

Soldiers, is all that she signs to me before she stretches out to sleep. I prop up on an elbow, in moderate pain myself, and watch her sleep. Her wristbands and her silver headband gleam in the waning moonlight. The sun will rise soon.

I fall asleep and dream. I dream that I am lying next to a campfire that is slowly dying out. I watch its red embers spark and flare. Jason is lying on his sleeping bag across from me, asleep. It is our old camping spot in the woods outside of Frisco.

I feel warm and safe with Jason. Camping with him is one of my favorite memories. I feel in love.

Jason opens his eyes and smiles at me across the fire. He gets up and comes over to sit next to me and I smile back at him. As he leans down to kiss me, I see that he is holding something in his right hand. I look down to see what he is holding. A laser knife! Then everything about the dream twists horribly into a nightmare!

Confused, I look back up into Jason's eyes, but I am not looking at Jason anymore! Stingray's mirrored sunglasses stare down at me, reflecting the red embers from the campfire. His face is mere inches from mine and he grins that wicked, crooked grin of his as he brings the knife up to my face.

"Do you really think you can get away, little girl? Where are you?" he rasps. The knife sears me as he carves something into my forehead. I scream and scream and scream!

⊠ ⊠ ⊠

I wake up in a cold sweat. Lucia is eating, but Angel just sits, cross-legged, and studies me carefully. She signs no words to me.

For two days now, we have been following an old goat path that takes us all of the way above the tree line. The way is tricky and the trail is covered with loose rock, and I constantly slip and slide whenever the path takes a downhill turn. The elevation must be high because it is getting harder for me to breathe in my quest to keep up with Angel. Lucia handles the thin air just fine, and Howler jumps across the rocks as fast as he swings through the trees.

We reach the foot of impossibly steep, craggy cliffs that remind me of cliffs I have seen in my dreams. A solid rock wall confronts us and it looks like the end of the line to me, but a boy about twelve-years-old steps out from behind a boulder. A wide rimmed, dirty white hat almost covers his long, black hair and shades his brown eyes. Leather sandals, brown trousers, and a white shirt complete his outfit, along with a fat, round water gourd strapped across his shoulder.

Without speaking a word to us, he leads us to a hidden break in the cliffs. The passageway is little more than shoulder width, with smooth rock walls and no sky above us that I can see. We walk downhill through the tunnel passageway, and after a half mile or so, I can hear the roar of rushing water in the darkness ahead of us.

It is much cooler in the tunnel now. The rock walls literally sweat moisture, and suddenly, we emerge on a rocky ledge perched impossibly high above a white, roaring river that cuts through a deep rock canyon. The rock beneath my feet is slick and wet, and I know that one false step would mean a plunge to instant death in the boiling rapids below.

Hold on to that picture of a seaside fishing village, Chrissie, I think to myself. *Right!*

The boy smiles up at my stricken face and then points to a suspended, fifty-foot long wooden bridge that is strung precariously across a chasm that drops three or four hundred feet down to the river. I freeze; I am terrified of such heights, and Lucia doesn't look too happy at the prospect of crossing the bridge either. But Angel and the boy urge us forward.

One by one, we cross the bridge. As I cross, the wooden planks creak beneath my feet, the hand-ropes move back and forth, and the entire structure swings lazily in the cold breeze created by the rush of the river below. I reach the halfway point on the bridge and realize that something is wrong. I can hardly breathe, and a deep pain is growing in my belly. I pause for a moment and try to catch my breath. I can see Angel waving me forward. I start to creep forward on shaky legs. The deep pain seems to recede a little, but not completely. After what seems like an eternity, I reach the far side of the bridge and Lucia grabs my hand again. My hand is sweaty and slippery, and she looks up at me with a puzzled face.

The path reenters the sheer rock walls, and we enter another dark tunnel. We walk through the damp, musty corridor for what seems like an eternity and finally emerge into bright daylight. As my eyes adjust to the brightness of a morning sun cresting the cliffs above us. I can't believe what I see.

We are standing at the top of a footpath that leads down into a long, narrow valley that is surrounded on all sides by impossibly high cliffs and massive, pinnacle-shaped mountains. The valley is at least three miles long but maybe only a thousand feet or less across. A small village is nestled in the center of the valley with several small streets of red adobe bungalows covered with thatched straw roofs. A small, round stone fountain, maybe ten feet across, sits in a square at the center of the village, flowing with crystal clear water.

At each end of the village, in the distance, I can see small, cultivated fields, which can't possibly get much of the sunlight as the sun crosses the cliffs high overhead. I can also see small herds of cattle and goats. Chickens run freely through the tiny village streets.

Straining to picture instead a seaside village, I turn to Angel. "Where are we?" I whisper to her.

She gives me the same blank-face response that I used to get from my mother, but the boy smiles up at me and motions for us to follow.

A shout goes out across the village, and several people run up the path toward us. We start down the path to meet them, and that is when it hits me. Unbearable, sharp pain in my belly! I gasp, and drop to my knees.

Angel turns around and rushes to me with genuine alarm in her eyes. I feel like I am passing out, with everything turning gray. Hands reach out and hold me. Then…everything goes black.

CHAPTER TWENTY-THREE

It is the voice. The same voice that told me Daniel's name so long ago. The voice that told me that Daniel is in the lion's den. It is speaking to me now in quiet, soothing tones. It comforts me in the darkness.

It is a wonderful thing you have done, Chrissie, the voice tells me. *To risk your life for the life of another. Of all the wonderful things you could possibly do with your life, this is the greatest act of all!*

Somewhere deep, deep in a disembodied existence, I am screaming out in dire pain.

"Empuje, empuje, Mama," some lady with a deep voice is urging me. "Respire, ahora empuje…mas…mas!" (Push, push, Mama, breathe, now push…harder…harder!)

She fades away.

Now, in my mind's eye, I see myself sitting next to my stepmother on the leather couch in the front office of the Parlor.

"Abortion is a simple, painless procedure, Chrissie," the Parlor lady with the green eyes is reassuring me. "You won't even feel a thing."

I can see my stepmother smiling and nodding in agreement with her.

"So everything is set, dear. Your appointment is next Tuesday, at 10:00 a.m. sharp!" the green-eyed lady says.

"Nooo…!" I scream at the top of my lungs. My stepmother frowns.

"Empuje!"

It is a wonderful thing, Chrissie, to save the life of another…, the voice tells me again.

"Empjue, Mama…ahora!"

I scream and push with all my might. Then just before I pass out again, I hear a new sound. Crying. An infant crying.

Later, when I open my eyes, I am lying in a soft bed. The room is slightly dark, but filtered sunlight is streaming in through an open window. Someone is holding my right hand, and I look to see that Ruthie is standing next to the bed, smiling down at me.

No, wait. This isn't Ruthie, my imaginary little sister. My faculties slowly return, and I realize that it is Lucia. She squeezes my hand when I weakly smile back.

Something moves under my left arm, and I look down to see a warm bundle squirming in a colorful blanket. I let go of Lucia's hand, reach down to lift the cover of the blanket, and bright blue eyes on a tiny face open and look straight up at me. Daniel!

"We thought we lost you," the warm voice of an older man says to me. I look up and see that an old, white-haired Hispanic gentleman is seated in a large, wooden chair next to the window. The light streaming in through the window silhouettes the outline of his body.

"How long has it been?" I ask him.

"Nearly a week, Mama," he says and then explains. "In her hurry to bring you to safety, your older *hermana* did not realize how exhausted you had become. You lost too much blood. You nearly died two days ago."

Daniel squirms and whimpers in my arms. I hold him close to me.

The man points to Lucia.

"Your younger *hermana* has never left your side," he continues. "And all of the Mama's have helped with your bambino. Now, you must rest, Mama."

I try to stay focused on the man, but sleep is overtaking me, and I close my eyes. I feel Lucia reach out and take hold of my hand again.

When I open my eyes, the room is darker. Night must be approaching. I am nursing Daniel and I can hear his infant voice as he makes gurgling baby sounds. In the candlelight that filters in from the room beyond my door, I can see Angel standing tall like she is guarding my room. Daniel looks up at me with shining blue eyes and reaches out with his right arm. There is only a nub of flesh where his hand should be, and my heart clenches tight at the sight of it.

I hear Lucia sigh and see that she is sitting in the big wooden chair that the white haired man occupied earlier.

"Te desperto`, Mama," Lucia announces. (You're awake, Mama)

An older, heavyset woman walks in through the doorway, carrying a bowl of hot soup. She smiles at me and hands the soup to Lucia. Carefully, Lucia holds out a spoonful of the warm broth, and I struggle to sit up. I can't believe how weak I feel.

"Esta bonito tu bambino, no?" Lucia asks as I sip the delicious broth.

"Yes, he is beautiful," I agree. I feel the warmth of his tiny body next to mine.

I learn from Lucia that we are in "the village." It has no name. The people in the village also have no names. We now have no names, either. I am merely Mama. Angel and Lucia are my hermanas. The women of the village are mamas, the men papas, except for the old, white-haired gentleman who I saw earlier. He is called Padre. Children are ninos and ninas, older boys and girls are hermanos and hermanas. Daniel, of course, is the bambino.

I understand the significance of all of this. If we go by name, the closers will tune in and find us. The closers are strong clairvoyants. That is why Angel led us on a three-week death march deeper and deeper into the mountains. She had to buy some time for me. That is why we picture this place as a fishing village on the coast. To throw Stingray off!

My hostess Mama is a cheerful, wonderful lady. She has lived alone for a long time and is overjoyed to have company. She is known as Mama number 1 in this community of mamas.

Gradually, my strength returns and I am able to climb out of bed. Before I leave my room, the old white-haired Padre takes a seat at my bedside and warns me.

"You must always guard your thoughts, Mama," he instructs. "Do not dwell too long on any detail of what is outside. Keep the sight of this place out of your mind. Try to picture other places as much as you can."

In the days that follow, I find that it is a difficult exercise to follow. As I slowly begin to walk with Lucia and carry Daniel along the dirt streets of the tiny village, I am overwhelmed at the beauty of my surroundings. It is a majestic setting, like nothing I have ever seen before. Then I forcefully shift my thoughts. I picture myself strolling through a fishing village, greeting the fishermen as they pass me on their way down to their boats. They smile and greet me back.

In the village, I learn to avert my eyes to the ground, as everyone in the village does, as I carry Daniel and walk to the central square to the fountain with the cold, clear water. Padre likes to sit on the edge of the fountain in the mornings and read from an old, black cloth-bound book. When I glance at its pages, I see that its small print is in Spanish, and although I am becoming very fluent in conversational Spanish, I cannot yet read it.

Padre snaps the book shut and smiles up at me one morning.

"I am reading a nice story, Mama, about a den full of big lions," he tells me. "Do you know this story?"

I shake my head no while Daniel squirms in his multicolored blanket. I don't want to talk about the lion's den, but Padre persists.

"This book is full of stories," he says. "And we should discuss them…when the time is right."

I mentally organize the mamas of the village by their number. Mama number 1, my sweet hostess, teaches me how to properly care for Daniel. She wants to teach me how to cook on her wood-stove and make delicious tortillas like the ones that I stole from villages in the past months.

Mama number 2 lives near the village square. She raises chickens and provides eggs for the villagers. So do Mama number 3 and Mama number 4. Mama number 5 herds goats and, with the help of Mama number 6, milks them every morning. Mamas number 7, number 8, and number 9 are farmers, "senoras de maiz." Mama number 10 runs the village mill. And so on.

Old Padre is the leader of the village, and every evening, most of the villagers follow him somewhere to a secret place. Wherever they go, I am not allowed to follow. It remains a big mystery to me.

The boy who led us through the cliffs is called *hermano*, or brother, and he always hangs close to Lucia and me. He has a sweet disposition, and I think he might be sweet on Lucia.

What is missing from the village is any sign of men between the ages of fifteen and fifty. There are absolutely none; and as I take my morning walks with Daniel, Lucia, and brother, I worry and wonder why. I ask brother, but he just looks at the ground as we walk.

At the eastern end of the canyon where the sun first peeks through every morning, I can hear the music of a waterfall that is hidden by a tree grove. One morning, after a month has passed, Angel and Padre walk with me and lead me out of the village across the cultivated fields to the east and into the tree grove. Lucia and brother stay behind and babysit Daniel. My strength is returning, and I easily keep up with Angel's long-legged pace.

Padre is out of breath by the time we reach the grove and sits down on a log that has fallen down next to the deep pool of water beneath the roaring waterfall. He holds his black book in his lap. Because of the noise of the waterfall, Padre has to speak up louder than usual as he talks to me.

"Clear your mind, Mama," he tells me. "Close your eyes and imagine that you are in Santa Maria, far away from here."

I do as he says and imagine the scene.

"Yes," Padre says, "and out of nowhere, you have crossed paths with me, this old man who sits on a bench next to a waterfall that flows out to the sea. Now slowly open your eyes and hold on to that idea."

I open my eyes. Angel is standing next to me with her arms crossed. She is looking deeply into my eyes, and the sunlight is glinting off the silver band that holds back her beautiful hair. Her face, as usual, is serious.

Padre looks up at me inquiringly. I understand the game. Minds outside of ours must be probing, hunting for me right now. Probably Stingray, and who knows who else. I play along and feign surprise at finding Padre here next to the waterfall.

"Where are you from, old man?" I ask in Spanish.

"I come from another fishing village not far from here," Padre answers. "North, up the coast. I could take you there."

Angel shakes her head no and signs.

It is too dangerous, she signs. *And we are traveling south.*

Something drops on the ground next to me. A mango! I look up into the trees and see Howler sitting on a limb, grinning down at me. Where on earth did he find it? There is no telling, but he is screwing up the illusion I am holding on to in my mind, and I try to ignore him.

Padre closes his eyes for two or three minutes. He closes them tightly like he is concentrating on something as hard as he can.

"Good," he says when he opens them again. "I am successfully guarding our thoughts now. We can talk, Chrissie."

Angel bids me to sit next to him and takes a seat on the log next to me.

"I have questions for you," Padre says. "Angel has told me that you know the sign of the cross."

How does she know that? I wonder. We haven't talked about that.

"My mother used to trace it on my forehead when I was little," I explain to him. "She told me it was a very secret sign and to tell no one about it."

"I see." Padre nods. "Angel also told me that men don't see you sometimes, even when you are standing in plain sight."

She has obviously been reading my mind, I think to myself. Moses started to teach me how to do that, but he didn't have time to teach me enough. That I have the ability perplexes me. Maybe I just got lucky. It certainly had no effect on Stingray.

"Ah," Padre says. "I see."

Angel watches me carefully.

"The reason that men do not see you, Chrissie," Padre explains, "is because you are the mother of Daniel. And through Daniel, you are also protected."

I am confused.

"But closers see me," I argue.

"Ah, like Stingray!" Padre says. "Closers are not ordinary people, Chrissie. They also have help from higher powers, and their minds are not easily tricked."

Angel sits quietly, arms folded, and looks from Padre to me. She nods her head in agreement with Padre.

"And now, Chrissie, I must ask...what questions do you have for me?" Padre asks.

Questions? Where do I start?

"Where are we?"

Padre looks at Angel, who nods assent, and then he answers.

"You are deep in the southern mountains, in the village of San Hidalgo, Chrissie," he answers. "The village of the great cliffs."

"I've seen this place before, in my dreams," I say. I remember the dream I had where I was in impossibly high, jagged cliffs, hiding with Daniel behind the rocks, being hunted by that unseen monster.

"Of course you have," Padre agrees. "Because your dreams are telling you that, for now, this is the safest place you can be. This is where you must stay until Daniel is old enough to endure the journey to Haven."

"This place was not safe in my dreams," I argue. "And the risk you are taking to hide me is way too much!"

Padre waves his hand in dismissal.

"It is a risk that we are more than willing to take," he says. "For you, for Daniel. For many years, we have sheltered any brave runner who tries to escape from the terrors of the Parlors."

"There are not enough men here," I continue. "Where did they all go?"

Padre shrugs.

"They have all been taken away to serve in the armies of the New Republic," he explains. "And most of them never return. Those who do return come back old men, like me. Otherwise, the army leaves us alone unless we produce more boys who are old enough to fight. We only have three boys in San Hidalgo now, so we do not attract much attention."

"Fight who?"

Padre looks at Angel, who wears a blank expression on her face, and then he looks back at me.

"What do you know about the world beyond the New Republic?" he asks me.

The world beyond the New Republic? According to what I have been taught, you can't really call it a world.

"Only that it is all a barren, barbaric wasteland where mutants live and kill each other," I answer. "A terrible ruin that no one ventures into. They teach us that in school. They teach us that the New Republic is the only civilization left on the planet, and the true light of the world."

"And do you believe that?" Padre asks.

"I don't know what to believe anymore," I tell him, thinking of the horrors I have seen of the Parlor, the underground, the closers, Stingray.

"Over two centuries ago, there were terrible wars," Padre explains. "The New Republic lost those wars, and before it could be overrun, it used nuclear weapons to seal its borders and close itself off from the rest of the world. In the time since, it has grown to be completely isolated from the rest of the world. Ironically, it still calls itself a New Republic. Actually, it is very old."

The New Republic has imprisoned its own people, Angel signs to me. *And it controls them through fear. It dulls their senses with endless distractions from what is real. Its Parlors kill millions of unborn innocents, it hunts down and murders anyone who believes...*

"Who believes what your mother believed and was going to teach you if she had lived. She started you on the path by giving you the sign of the cross," Padre says. "Like countless other mothers in the New Republic who are secretly rebelling by teaching their children the sign of the cross."

"It is unfortunate," Padre continues, "that she was unable to teach you everything. For now, you cannot control your thoughts, and we must wait until you are out of mind's reach of the closers. We, here in this village, must guard your thoughts for you at all costs. But soon, you will learn everything."

Daniel has been born, Angel signs. *And through him, the voice is speaking. We believe that Daniel is the one we have been waiting for. We believe he is destined to liberate the good people of the New Republic.*

"Not an easy task," Padre says. "Because it is nearly impossible to penetrate the New Republic. It uses its armies to keep its borders sealed, to keep its own people from leaving, and it protects those borders with its nuclear weapons. Weapons that we have long abandoned, weapons that we abhor. Weapons that are too terrible to imagine. The New Republic is trapped in a horror of its own making, Chrissie, and it clings to a terrible old technology. But the New Republic is not the light of the world! It is the darkest place on Earth. The time of the New Republic is coming to an end, and soon, it must join the real world."

The real world?

My mind is reeling. The New Republic is not the light of the world? All of this time, have I been lied to by my parents, my teachers, the government?

"Your parents and your teachers probably live in as much ignorance about the true state of the world as you do," Padre interrupts my thought. "But the president and his government certainly do not. They work hard to keep your people living in ignorance. What do you know of the moon, Chrissie?"

I know that it is a big, cold rock in space that orbits the world. I know that it has helped me find my way south at night with its ethereal glow. That is about all I know.

There are cities on the moon! Angel signs to me, and I can tell by her smile that she is proud of the fact. *There are cities on Mars, Chrissie. We barbarians have even reached the near stars. This is what men were destined to do.*

"With a new way, Chrissie," Padre tells me. "And at the same time, a quiet, gentle way. A new path that has not been strangled by the evil of godless men. A new path revealed to our people who still listen to God!

"The great minds who built the great ships that are now reaching for the stars were the babies of runners who escaped from the Parlors of the New Republic," Padre continues. "Runners, like you, Chrissie."

And like my mother, Angel signs and then taps her throat for emphasis. *The Parlor wanted to kill me for my disability too.*

"Runners are celebrated as great heroes in the world beyond the New Republic," Padre says. "As you are. And you, Chrissie, are also the mother of Daniel!"

Howler drops down from his tree and jumps into my lap, hugs me like a child. His gleaming black eyes smile up into mine.

I smile down at him, but I think of Daniel. What would I do without him? I cannot imagine life without him.

"Yes," Padre continues. "And through Daniel, the voice not only spoke to you. The voice has spoken to us all."

You wondered why the officials of the New Republic want to kill him at all costs? Angel signs to me. *It is because the voice spoke to them too, to their minds. To us, he gave a message of hope, to them, a nightmare! They realize how powerful Daniel will grow to be. They want to kill him, and you, because of that.*

I think of the voice that comforted me, that told me of the lion's den. I have not heard it since Daniel's birth.

"Yes, you are right," Padre agrees, reading my mind. "None of us have heard the voice since his birth. Daniel has been born, and he must grow now. In time, he will regain his awareness. He will remember who he is! He will remember what he must do!

"And now," he continues, "we must decide what you will do, Chrissie. We will try our best to keep you and Daniel safe here for the next year. It is far too dangerous for you to travel with an infant in your arms."

Angel agrees.

Stingray is confused, she signs, cocking her head to the side as if she is listening to something that I can't hear. *He leads the police south to the coast.*

"Good," Padre says, and sighs. "Our plan is working. Everyone works here in the village, Chrissie. You, of course, must care for Daniel. But is there anything else you want to learn while you are here? What is it that you want to do? Any of the mamas can teach you their skills."

I think about that as I listen to the hypnotic roar of the waterfall. I think of Moses, of how he gave his life for me. And of Samson. I think of Jason, shackled and beaten by that horrible monster, Stingray. I must try to help him somehow. Part of me still loves him, and even if I didn't, he doesn't deserve the treatment he is getting because of my decision to run. I think of Angel, sitting next to me, her life always in terrible danger because of me. But first, before I give them an answer, there is something that I really need to know.

"Where is Haven?" I ask.

Padre smiles.

"Chrissie," he says gently, "Haven is located somewhere safe. Exactly where it is located isn't important to you right now. But you will eventually know its exact location."

Of course! And it is a safe place precisely because people like me don't know where it is. It is safe from people who can't fight the government or protect themselves or really guard their thoughts. It is safe from people who can be used by the government, by the closers.

Then I remember another dream I once had. The voice told me something important in that dream.

You must prepare yourself, Chrissie, the voice said to me in that dream. *Angel will teach you!*

"When they are cornered, jackrabbits fight!" Samson told me with the last words he uttered before dying.

I know what I must do. I must do something that will help redeem me for my mistakes. For my carelessness with the Perma Lighter that led to Samson's death. For my helplessness that continues to put everyone around me in mortal danger. I need to do something that will help me cope with the deaths that, through my weakness, I have helped cause.

"I want to learn how to fight, how to protect my baby, and how to protect myself," I tell them without hesitation. "I want to learn to be a guide."

Padre sighs and nods his head.

"You have courage. And you possess a gift that runs strong in your family, Chrissie," he says. "In your mother and in your aunt, in you, and of course, strongest of all in your son, Daniel."

He turns to Angel, who is watching me with an intensity I have never seen before.

"It is decided then. Start her on the path, Angel," Padre says, and then he stands up from his seat on the log.

Angel's eyes flare with anger.

No, Padre! she signs. *That is my decision. My decision alone!*

"You must!" Padre insists and turns to walk back to the village. Angel turns and glares at me.

If I decide to train you, you will suffer, she signs to me. *There will be pain!*

CHAPTER TWENTY-FOUR

With the voice gone, I have only Stingray to torment me in my dreams now. Almost every night, his face appears so close to mine that I can feel his breath on my cheek. I can see my own eyes reflected in his sunglasses.

"Where are you, little girl?" he rasps.

I try to run, but I am frozen like a jackrabbit. He seems to hold a power over me, freezing me in place. When I don't answer him, he grins that crooked grin of his and snarls.

"I'll find you soon enough."

I try to look away from him, to look down at the ground like I have been taught to do in the village.

"Just give me the kid, Chrissie," Stingray rasps, "and this all goes away."

I try to shake my head no, but I can't even do that.

Then I wake up in a cold sweat. Daniel sleeps in a wooden crib next to my bed, and I pick him up and hug him. Most nights, Lucia sits up when I do, from her small bed in the corner of the room, hugs her knees to her chest, and watches me.

Daytime life is no better. Whenever I think about what Padre and Angel told me, I feel betrayed. So the New Republic is actually a prison. The real world has left it far behind, and it keeps its people living in total ignorance. There are cities on Mars! I try to imagine what it must be like to live on Mars. I can't.

Reason takes hold of me as I try to work out my anger. I ran away with Daniel. That is enough. There are no Parlors in Haven.

It soon becomes apparent that Angel and Padre are engaged in an epic battle of wills. She has decided not to train me. Padre insists. A week has passed, and I spend the time nursing Daniel, walking with brother and Lucia, and helping Mama number 1 in the kitchen. I ask Mama number 1 why my big sister will not teach me. Mama number 1 just shakes her head and hands me a broom to sweep the kitchen floor.

Every evening, the villagers continue to follow Padre to his secret place, leaving me and a few others behind. They do allow Lucia to go with them. When I press Padre for information, he continues to politely refuse.

"For now, Mama," he says, "it is something that you must not know."

One day, I corner Angel.

"Why won't you teach me?" I insist. She glares at me.

Guides die! she signs and walks away.

I decide to give in. What was I thinking, anyway? I could never possibly be like Angel or Moses. Angel fights entire squads of soldiers by herself. She is impossibly strong. I am just a seventeen-year-old girl. My journey has toughened me, but I can never be like her.

I resign myself to learning how to cook from Mama number 1. She cooks meals for the women who tend the fields of corn and grain, the women who raise the livestock, the milk ladies, and the butchers. I become her apprentice and immerse myself in the work in the kitchen and in the open hut behind her house where she pounds out the tortillas on flat, hot stones over a slow, steady fire.

"We have cooked this way for thousands of years," Mama number 1 tells me with pride. Slowly but surely, I catch on, and soon I am pounding out the corn paste right beside her. Then Lucia can't stand it any longer and pitches in to help. We become a tortilla factory.

One day, after I have delivered tortillas to several homes, I take a narrow backstreet back to my house when it happens. Out of nowhere, something sharp and painful strikes me across the back. I cry out and tumble through the dirt. When I look up, Angel is standing above me, holding a long, thin switch and patting it against her hand.

Your training begins today, she signs to me.

CHAPTER TWENTY-FIVE

My life has turned into one giant ball of pain. For a month, as soon as I have nursed Daniel and handed him to Lucia, Angel takes me on a long run through the canyon. It is always still dark, and I have a habit of tripping over things sticking up out of the ground. To make matters worse, running in my boots gives me terrible blisters on my feet.

After breakfast, we run back to the grove of trees by the waterfall. Angel has built a practice area here, complete with obstacles for me to leap across and climb. Most of the time, I fail. She teaches me incredible, stylized fighting movements. I have seen those movements before when I saw Moses fight. The movements are beautiful, but doing them for hours on end is exhausting.

You have to get stronger! Angel lectures me daily.

All day long, at any time, she comes out of nowhere and hits me hard with the switch. She steps out from behind a tree and—*whack!* She comes from around a corner in the village or even in our house and—*smack!* Sometimes, she seems to appear out of thin air. As often as not, she attacks me from behind, and the first thing I am aware of is the fact that I am rolling on the ground, howling in pain. The mamas glance down at me as they pass by, shake their heads, and go on about their business.

My body is one big welt. I am bruised all over, and at night Lucia patiently rubs healing balm into my wounds. She calls me her *hermana loca*, her crazy big sister.

Angel is a tyrant! She is merciless! In the afternoons, we fight. She teaches me how to use the stylized movements to strike and to block. I feel like I move like an elephant in a tutu. But Angel never breaks a smile. Her face is always deadly serious.

You must get stronger, you must be quicker. You would be dead. A closer would finish you before you could even think to do that! You are too clumsy. You are too slow!

And on it goes, and after another month, I begin to question my sanity.

Life in the village drones on. The mamas keep the place running like a clock, and every evening, almost everyone disappears with Padre. I sense a certain tension in everyone, however, and I ask Padre about it.

"Our three boys are reaching the age. The mamas fear that soldiers will arrive before long and take those boys," he tells me. "And that they will discover you and your bambino. But don't worry, Mama, I would never let that happen."

Daniel is nearly three months old now, and he smiles at me with sparkling blue eyes. Even at this early age, he is trying to form words with his mouth. Lucia holds him and talks to him constantly. It is obvious to me that he will become much more fluent in Spanish than English. The lady at the Parlor was right; he is missing his right hand and foot. But to me, he is perfect.

As the third month of my training commences, Angel's attacks with the switch increase in frequency and intensity. My life has morphed into the "pain of the switch." But something else is also happening. I am beginning to sense Angel's presence just before she strikes. I am starting to automatically dodge and block the switch as it whistles toward me with lightning speed. My arms are taking the brunt of the punishment now. They are constantly swollen, black and blue.

In the fourth month, Angel makes me run barefoot every morning. The pain is excruciating, but my feet eventually become as hard as leather, like hers. I am starting to flow through the morning ritual of the stylized fighting forms. We fight each other, striking and blocking with our arms, kicking with our feet. Angel's arms and legs are as hard as steel, and she punishes me with every blow.

At night, the switch, the fighting and running, the obstacles all dominate my dreams. Occasionally, Stingray's face appears, but I ignore it. I am too exhausted to worry about him. My sleep is nearly as exhausting as my daytime experience. Before I know it, I am up awake again, nursing Daniel. The switch whistles at my head as I am nursing, and without looking, I reach up and block it with my forearm.

I can feel myself becoming quicker, harder. My training intensifies. Angel teaches me how to fight with sticks, how to fight with knives, how to accurately throw knives. Always, she criticizes me. I am too slow. I am too clumsy.

Padre sits next to me one day at the fountain as I scarf down my lunch. I am one big bruise, but I am a hard bruise. He watches me eat, shakes his head, and smiles.

"It is a hard path that you have chosen, Mama," he says to me. "Do you regret it?"

"Regret what?" I ask through a mouthful of tortilla. I have to hurry. Angel is waiting for me at the waterfall."

In the fifth month, she builds a wooden dummy with stout arms for me to practice my movements on. It is an ancient device, she tells me. I immediately see how useful it is. I use my stylized blocks and strikes on it, and day by day, I get faster. My arms and legs harden, and blocking Angel's strikes do not hurt nearly as much. I actually enjoy the physical contact, and I hit back harder.

By the sixth month of training, Angel is teaching me stealth. I learn how to camouflage myself, blend in with my surroundings, how to hide for hours, and then sneak up on Howler. Every time I succeed, he runs screaming into the trees.

My movements on the wooden dummy are smooth, quick, and automatic.

And then another surprise. I am beginning to read Angel's thoughts. *Quicker*, she thinks as we fight. *Good*, she appraises in her mind, even if her face betrays nothing. I try out my developing mental skill on others in the village. Lucia wants to grow up and marry brother who led us through the tunnel; she thinks about it all of the time. Padre whispers silently to his God and to other names I have never heard of before. He calls it prayer, like the prayers of Moses. Mama number 1 worries. In fact, worry is the predominant thought that courses through the entire village.

One evening, after dinner, I finish nursing Daniel and hand him to Mama number 1. He smiles and grabs at me as she takes him in her arms.

"Don't worry," I soothe him, "Mommy will be right back. I promise."

There is a mystery I have to solve, and I now have the skills to do it.

I stick to the deepening shadows as the majority of the villagers follow Padre south away from the village. Lucia and brother hold hands as they follow him. I keep a comfortable distance behind them all, and I blend in with the outlying huts, the stacks of wheat. I move gracefully, silently.

They walk to the base of the south cliffs where giant rocks and piles of rubble lie heaped on the ground below the towering behemoths. Big dry bushes of thistle grow along the cliff walls, and one by one, the villagers disappear behind them. I kneel down on the ground and watch as they go. There must be a cave, I decide, well hidden from sight.

I also decide not to pry any further for now.

⬦ ⬦ ⬦

"What about blasters?" I ask Angel one day when we have finished our sparring match for the afternoon. For the first time, she smiles just slightly and sits down cross-legged on the ground.

A blaster is a useful weapon, she signs as I sit down across from her. *But you always have to carry it, and it has its limitations. A good guide can defeat any opponent who uses one.*

She lifts her leather shirt and shows me the many scars across her midriff. I wince at the sight. Blaster burns.

A good guide will sense the shooter's timing, his aim, and will deflect his shot, making it a nearly harmless burn, she continues. *And yes, I have been shot many times. And I have killed every single shooter that shot me.*

I nod and wonder how I could possibly do the same.

The biggest problem with a blaster is that it can be taken away from you, Angel continues. *And it makes you lazy, and it can be tracked. And that is why guides do not use blasters. Remember this always, Mama, you are the weapon, not the blaster.*

But it is an excellent question, I hear Angel think in her mind. She is watching me intently as I read her thoughts. She knows that I am reading her thoughts.

"How many runners have you saved?" I ask her as I try to count her burns.

How many burns do I have on my body? she asks by way of an answer.

And all of those years I had always heard that only a handful of runners ran and that no one succeeded in making it all the way to Haven. Actually, hundreds or even thousands have made it. More propaganda from the government!

She stands up, and a sharp knife appears from nowhere in her right hand.

Take it away from me! she signs to me in command.

Padre soon makes it a point to join me at the fountain every day, usually during lunch. Today, Angel is off somewhere doing who knows what, and I sit at the fountain, listening to its musical, cascading water, holding Daniel, and talking to him. He is eight months old now and saying his first words. *Mama…hermana… padre…monkey.*

I glance down into the fountain and look at myself. A dark, hardened face reflected in the clear water stares back at me. I have changed. I am nearly as dark as the villagers, and my naturally brown hair has grown back in. My eyes hold an intensity that I have never noticed before. Gently, I hold Daniel up and show him his own reflection. He squeals with delight.

"And how is my young warrior today?" Padre asks as he takes a seat next to me.

"Sore," I answer, "as usual."

Padre chuckles. Daniel reaches out with his good hand and tugs on Padre's beard.

"You have come far, Mama," Padre continues. "You have grown. Soon, you and your bambino must travel on and complete your journey."

"You once spoke of a gift that is strong in my family," I inquire. "What did you mean by that?"

"You already know what your gift is, Mama," Padre says to me and smiles. He squeezes Daniels arm.

"You use it all of the time."

Without another word, Padre stands and walks away, waving at Mama number 14, the butcher, as he goes.

I start to stand up, but my mind jumps alert. I can almost see through her eyes as she quietly sneaks up behind me. I sense her movement. The switch whistles through the air, and without even looking, I catch it firmly in my fist. With a strong, twisting wrench, I pull it from her grasp and break it in half.

Slowly, I turn and look up into Angel's golden eyes. She stands there, arms folded, and studies me intently.

CHAPTER TWENTY-SIX

Almost a year has passed since we first arrived at the village. I am sitting cross-legged across from Angel. The waterfall roars behind her as she instructs me.

Imagine a cloak, she signs. *Use the cloak to cover your thoughts.*

We are still working on this. I close my eyes and try to imagine a dark cloak. I wrap it around my thoughts. It works at first, and I feel like I am doing it, guarding my thoughts against any unwanted intrusion. Angel watches me.

Then it happens. What always happens! My thoughts spring out and run amok like a raging monkey. The harder I try to guard them, the harder they work to break free. My thoughts bounce around in my head the way Howler jumps from tree to tree.

I am thinking about Jason. I can go back and rescue him.

Angel sighs.

That is the one thought that will get you killed, she signs.

This is a real problem. I have learned that every single person in the village guards their thoughts as they see fit. They only let out the most insignificant information. They even let out misinformation that the clairvoyants of the New Republic might pick up and run with. And they all work together to guard my thoughts.

The mamas of the village are masters at this. That is why the village has remained largely unmolested by the New Republic for so many years. That is why Angel brought me here. The village is an essential stopover for guides with runners in tow. This has been going on for decades. And after nearly a year of Angel's intense training, I am still bungling it all. I could actually get them all killed.

Angel wears a look of resignation. She has done her best, and it will have to do.

In three days, Mama, we will resume our journey south, she informs me.

She pulls her silver headband from her head and snaps it in half. She holds each half of the headband in the open palms of her hands and I gasp as the silver metal closes and forms two smaller bands. Wristbands, identical to the ones that she wears.

Put them on, she signs.

She watches as I push my hands through them. The bands feel strangely alive and immediately snug right up to the skin on my wrists.

Clap them against each other, like this, she signs. With her palms facing away from each other, she claps her wristbands together and they grow to cover her hands all the way up to her elbows.

I copy her movements and the wristbands morph into armguards that cover my hands and lower arms. They feel completely pliable, but I know that they are harder than steel.

Angel holds up her arms in an on-guard position as she rises up in front of me. I stand to face her.

Now, she signs, *fight for your life!*

She attacks me with a ferocity I have never experienced from her before. As the waterfall roars behind us, we strike and block, kick, parry, and dodge each other's advances. I am holding my own, but I still can't match Angel's incredible quickness and strength. To make any progress at all, I try to work my way inside of her long reach.

I block three of her lightning strikes and then rush in, connecting with a strong punch to her midsection. I hear her gasp, and I know that it is effective. I know from experience how much it hurts. Anger flares in Angel's golden eyes. She reverses the direction of her attack to cut off my advance. The next thing I know, I am on my back, looking up at Howler who is staring down at me from a tree limb. He grins and drops a mango down on top of me.

That was good, Angel signs to me as I stand back up. *But it would never work against Stingray. If you ever have to fight him, he will kill you.*

I don't want to fight Stingray. I never want to see his face again. But something in my mind tells me that another meeting with him is inevitable.

And I may not be there to help you, Angel signs. I cringe at the thought. After a year of hard training, I still feel like I am struggling to grasp everything that Angel is trying to teach me.

"When will I be ready?" I ask her with exasperation in my voice.

It takes many years to learn to be a guide, she answers. *I have only started you down the path.*

It has been a terribly hard path.

I have been teaching you how to protect your bambino, Angel continues. *And how to protect yourself. You are already a capable fighter, but you must continue to work hard.*

"What about Stingray?" I ask.

He is a unique problem, Angel signs. *But there might be a way to surprise him, if you are very lucky.*

She assumes a fighting stance again.

Attack me, slowly, she commands. I move into her the way she has taught me to do.

This is the way Stingray counters, I hear her thought in my mind as she moves. *And then he reverses like this and strikes here and here.*

The movements are unconventional, but brilliant. How does Angel know these things?

To surprise him, you must counter with this twisting move and reach behind his neck, here.

I do as Angel instructs and grip her neck in an unusual hold. It is a deadly hold; I can tell just from the leverage that it gives me.

"Then what?" I ask.

Then, you apply pressure and do your best to kill him!

"Kill him?" I ask, remembering what my mother taught me, what Moses said about how precious life is.

Yes! Angel answers with an intensity that startles me. *If you have the chance, kill him without any hesitation!*

If I am lucky enough.

Chrissie! Angel signs, and I look up at her in surprise. She has not used my real name in nearly a year.

I am so proud of you. You have done well!

Angel claps her wrists together and her arm guards become wristbands again. I do the same as she gathers her pouch. Lunchtime is approaching, and we usually run back to the village at this point. I start to remove my wristbands, but Angel stops me.

Leave them on! she signs. She stares down at the ground, deep in concentration. She cocks her head to one side, as if she is listening to something. Then she looks up at me in alarm.

We must hurry! she signs and then takes off running toward the village.

We reach the edge of the tree grove, and I gasp at what lies on the ground in front of me. Three uniformed policemen lie on their backs, dead. We move closer, examine them, and I recognize their faces. It is the three Southern Province cops who used Lucia for bait so long ago, who took my diamonds and fled on their air bikes.

Now they are dead and staring lifelessly straight up at the deep blue sky. Their eyes are missing, gouged out; diamonds have been carefully placed where their eyes once were. The figure of the stingray has been carved into their foreheads with a laser knife.

Their bodies are carefully arranged on the path that leads out of the woods, and they form an arrow that points straight toward the village!

We'll approach from the south, Angel signs to me. *Find your bambino and remember, Mama, cloak your thoughts!*

It is possible to approach the village from the south by working along the base of the cliffs, using the giant boulders at the bottom of the cliffs as cover. The village is disturbingly quiet; but as we draw closer, I can see at least a dozen police air bikes parked along its western perimeter.

We reach a point where Angel will continue through the boulders and I will proceed directly into the back streets of the village. I turn to go.

Wait!

Angel reaches out, traces the sign of the cross on my forehead, and hugs me hard. Tears stream down her cheeks.

The enemy is always stronger than you think, Chrissie, she signs to me. *Never, ever underestimate the enemy. This is a lesson!*

Then she turns and runs toward the boulders.

Stealth has become second nature to me. I reach the back row of red adobe and stone houses and work my way in the shadows of an alley toward my house. As I proceed, I work as hard as I can at keeping my mind clear of any thoughts that will give my position away. I know who is here in the village. I know he can read my mind if I let him.

My bedroom is empty. Daniel's crib is empty. I creep quietly into the kitchen and there, on the kitchen floor, Mama number 1 lies dead, a big butcher knife gripped in her right fist. There is blood on the knife, and I sense that she at least made somebody pay dearly for her death. I kneel next to her and quietly close her lifeless eyes.

I hear Stingray's voice booming up and down the village streets, echoing off of adobe walls. From the kitchen window, I can see part of the village square and fountain. A dead policeman lies on his stomach a few yards down our street, blood staining the dirt around him.

The villagers stand side by side, tethered hand to hand by coarse rope and facing outward in a circle around the fountain. From my vantage point, I can't see Lucia or Daniel. I try to stay calm. I guard my thoughts.

Police surround the villagers and are armed with blaster rifles. Stingray, outfitted in a shiny golden jumpsuit, paces back and forth in front of the group. Behind his mirror glasses, his face twists with agitation.

"Chrissie!" he shouts, "I know you can hear me! How many of these people do you want me to kill today?"

For emphasis, he turns and knifes Mama number 6 through the heart with his laser knife. She crumples to the ground. I guard my thoughts. I try to stay calm.

"This is a tiny village. There aren't that many of them, dear!" he shouts. "You need to come out before I kill all of them."

A policeman walks up to Papa, the shoemaker. He hits Papa hard in the face with the butt of his blaster rifle, and Papa crumples. Stingray looks at the policeman and shakes his head.

"I'm having a hard time controlling my animals, Chrissie," he continues. "This is going to get ugly if you don't come out!"

He turns around in a circle and studies the streets and houses of the village. He is obviously confused. He really can't locate me!

"Okay," he says, "we'll play it your way! Who do I kill next?"

I need a plan, but I am afraid that if I think too hard about anything, Stingray will sense it. He walks up to Padre, who is bleeding and has obviously been beaten up.

"I think this old man is next!"

He grabs Padre by the throat and starts to squeeze.

"Show yourself, Chrissie," he yells. "And bring your kid with you, or I will choke the life out of this old man!"

I still myself. Lucia must be hiding Daniel, and Stingray doesn't know where he is. Daniel still has a chance! I can't wait for Angel; hopefully she is close by. I have to attack now. Attack Stingray and at least a dozen armed policemen. Angel demolishes entire squads of soldiers. I have never taken out anyone. I know in my heart that I don't possibly stand a chance, but maybe I can distract Stingray, buy time for Angel, and she can save Daniel. I jump up and Stingray seems to sense it. He starts to turn in my direction.

Out of nowhere, Angel plows into him like a rabid tigress. The sun gleams off her silver armguards as she trounces Stingray and hits him again and again. He rolls away on the ground, and a policeman raises his blaster rifle to shoot her.

"No!" Stingray screams at the cop. "She's mine!"

Slowly, he climbs to his feet. Angel has drawn blood, and I can see it streaming down Stingray's right cheek. He wipes it off and looks at it. Then he looks up at Angel, and through those mirrored sunglasses of his, he grins that strange, crooked grin.

"Hello, beautiful," he says conversationally. "It's been way too long. I was hoping you would join the party."

He snaps his fingers, and silver armguards appear from beneath his jumpsuit sleeves and cover his forearms and hands.

Angel attacks again, and I have never seen her move so fast, hit and block so hard.

"You've really been practicing!" Stingray says with surprise as he hits the ground again. "Who's your partner?"

Then he leaps. He takes the fight to another level. My fight-trained eye follows his unconventional moves, and it looks like Angel is in trouble. She pulls away from him and he laughs.

"A little more practice. You are almost there, Angel," he mocks.

He moves rapidly toward her, and I see it develop. It happens exactly the way she demonstrated at the waterfall. He moves to counter her strike, and she twists. Angel steps in, and she has him in the neck lock. The hold that can kill him! Stingray looks surprised, and for the first time, I see what looks like fear cross his face.

"Come on," I whisper to myself. "Come on!"

It has all happened so quickly, I haven't been able to tear myself away from the window. But now, I have to help her. I turn to charge out the door.

No! Angel's voice screams in my mind. *No matter what happens, stay hidden! You must save Daniel!*

She is killing Stingray! I can see it. Her hold has him paralyzed, and he can't breathe. His legs start to go limp.

Then the nightmare begins. A bright, blue-white flash darts out of nowhere. Angel releases Stingray and stumbles backward. A policeman shoots her again and she goes to her knees. At least eight blaster rifles flash and hit her at the same time.

"No!" I scream in my mind.

"No!" Stingray screams at the top of his lungs. Angel falls backward and lies in the street, dying.

Stingray flies into a rage. Like lightning, he attacks the police and starts killing them with strong, deadly strikes. Two of them shoot at him as he attacks, and he easily deflects their shots away from his body with his armguards. Before I can take another breath, all the policemen lie dead in the village square.

Stingray is literally frothing at the mouth. He goes to Angel, kneels, and holds her head in his arms. With his sleeve, he wipes the froth away from his mouth and then bends down and touches his forehead to hers. Angel moves slightly, and then her eyes close as she dies. My Angel whom I have grown to love like the big sister I never had.

There is not a doubt in my mind that Stingray is grieving. He holds her tightly for several minutes. When he stands up, he paces back and forth again with his hands clasped behind his back. I stay put. I can't beat him, and I know it. Not after what I have just witnessed. He is a true master! He would play with me and then kill me and then what?

"Here is how it is going to play, Chrissie!" he shouts as he paces and stares at the ground. "You come out and bring the kid with you. I let the villagers go and we all get to go home!"

And you get the money, I think to myself. Stingray's head snaps up, and he looks toward the houses.

"The reward?" He shouts. "Do you really think I do this for the money? Don't insult me, Chrissie! I do not do this for money!"

I double my efforts to cloak my thoughts and Stingray's eyes sweep to the other side of the village. Then he looks back down at Angel's body and shakes his head.

"Ok, Chrissie, you win!" he shouts out finally. "If you can survive this, we'll play the game a while longer! Your choice, not mine!"

He has an airbike parked near the fountain and he walks over to it, picks up a small transmitter.

"It's Stingray," he says into the microphone. "Call in the bombers. Nuke this place. Nuke it all."

"They want you dead or alive, Chrissie!" He shouts as he climbs on the bike. "Do you hear me? Dead or alive!"

Then he is gone. I run to a side window and watch as he disappears through the tunnel that originally led us into the valley. It is the tunnel that leads to the treacherous swinging bridge, and it is the only way in or out of the valley as far as I know. There is a flash in the tunnel and a roar, and I watch in horror as the tunnel collapses. Stingray has sealed us in. Then, I hear the drone of high-altitude bombers as they approach from the north.

I look at the villagers, roped together around the fountain. They are all struggling to get free. I run back to the kitchen and pry the butcher knife from Mama number 1's cold hand. I will run out and cut the ropes, free the villagers, try to find Daniel and Lucia.

But we have no time! And nowhere to go.

PART THREE:
DRAGON

CHAPTER TWENTY-SEVEN

Padre is bleeding from a deep cut on his head and can hardly stand up.

"Padre, I'm here," I tell him as I try to steady him. I use my shirt to wipe the blood away from his eyes, and he blinks at me. I can tell that he is in a lot of pain as he sways back and forth. I cut the rope that binds him to Mama number 3 and quickly then move to his other wrist. "Can you walk?"

"Yes," he says with a shaky voice. "They hit me hard, but the stars I am seeing are fading away now."

"Where is Daniel?"

"He is safe with Lucia, Chrissie," Padre answers breathlessly as I move through the villagers, freeing them from their bindings. Padre pulls a laser knife from a dead policeman's belt and helps.

"We have no time!" I shout as we struggle to free everyone. The roar of the engines of the approaching bombers is echoing off of the cliff walls.

"Quickly, follow me!" Padre calls and runs south out of the village square. I follow, and out of the corner of my eye, I see mamas bending down and wrenching blaster rifles out of the hands of dead policemen.

We are headed for the cave. As we reach the cliff wall and the cave opening, I can see the shadow of a bomber circling overhead.

"Howler!" I scream at the top of my lungs. I am frantic now. I have to find Daniel. Padre is assuring me that Daniel and Lucia are in the cave. How can I be certain? When the bombs fall, there will be no room for error.

One by one, we rustle through the dry bushes that hide the cave opening. It takes my eyes a moment to adjust to the darkness, but I detect a hint of candlelight reflecting off the smooth walls of the passage inside. Immediately, I follow Padre down steps that have been carved out of the rock floor and into a chamber about the size of one of the village houses.

"We must keep moving!" Padre calls back to me and leads us down through two more chambers, each one at least a story lower than the last. We are halfway through the third chamber when the first bomb hits with a thunderous *whomp!* and the cavern floor literally drops at least a foot from beneath my feet and sends me sprawling. Rocks and stalactites drop down on top of us from the cave ceiling, and several of the mamas scream. Through the roar of the blast, I can hear the first and maybe the second cave chamber collapsing behind us. Our chamber holds together.

"Hurry!" Padre shouts out and leads the way down more rock steps. I quickly regain my feet and follow, searching frantically everywhere in the candlelit corridors to find Daniel and Lucia.

Another bomb hits and knocks us off our feet again. I hear more cave walls collapsing, and I know that we are most certainly sealed in from behind. At least thirty villagers were behind me. I can't tell in the dim light if they are still safe or if the falling rocks have buried some of them.

One final bomb hits. We are at least a hundred feet below the entrance of the cave, and this impact does not do as much damage to our immediate surroundings. I am able to stay on my feet, and Padre leads me into a huge subterranean chamber that is well lit with dozens of candles. This chamber is at least ten times larger than the ones we have just passed through. It is different from the other chambers in other ways also. I cannot help but gasp at the grandeur of what I see here. The walls of the huge chamber are ornately carved out in relief with countless sculptures and statues of people I don't recognize. They are dressed in strange, flowing robes. The chamber is big enough to hold hundreds of people, and its vaulted ceiling towers almost a hundred feet above our heads. Beautiful, crystalline stalactites hang down from the ceiling and, like the chamber walls, sparkle and glimmer in the flickering light of the candles.

At the far end of the chamber stands a large ornate marble table on a raised stone floor. A large, golden cross stands upright on the center of it.

"There, Chrissie, beneath the altar!" Padre points to the table, and I rush across the chamber floor up to and around the table. There is a space behind its solid front face and beneath its thick tabletop. Lucia huddles there and looks up at me with frightened eyes. She holds Daniel tightly in her arms, and his blue eyes are as big as saucers. He says, "Mama?" as he reaches out toward me, and I cry as I sweep him up into my arms. As I hug and kiss him, I reach out to hug Lucia, who is also crying.

"Thank you," I sob to her. "Thank you."

A black, furry arm reaches around my shoulder. Howler's head is next to mine, and he hands Daniel a half-eaten mango. He made it out of the woods in time.

Padre is busy checking the other villagers, counting heads, and even though he is still bleeding profusely, worried about their injuries. There are a lot of injuries, mainly from the falling rocks from the bomb blasts, and several unhurt mamas are already nursing the wounds of the villagers who are suffering the most.

Padre finally looks at me through glistening, teary eyes.

"There are twenty-six of us, Chrissie," he says quietly. "We left over a dozen behind."

The news shatters me. More than a dozen dead! And Angel... gone!

"As soon as everyone is tended to, we must keep moving!" Padre exclaims. "There is a secret way out of here as we go deeper into this cave, and we must hurry to get to it. I don't want to take the chance of anyone finding it and sealing us in."

I hand Daniel back to Lucia and hurry to help the mamas with the wounded villagers. Daniel cries and reaches out for me with his deformed hand.

"Don't worry," I assure him. "Mommy will be right here."

To help soothe him, Lucia carries him alongside me. Most of the villagers' wounds are superficial head cuts from the falling rock, but one older papa has a bad concussion. He should lie down and rest, but Padre insists that we continue to move and orders a mama to lead him by the hand.

"We can drop any pretenses now, Chrissie," Padre tells me as we exit the big chamber through another descending, candlelit stairway. "My name is Padre Garza."

He turns to look directly at me.

"And I come from a village," he says, "which no longer exists."

I can't look back at him. I look down at the rocky floor and tears drop from my eyes.

"I am so sorry, Padre," I answer quietly.

Padre takes me by the shoulders and makes me look at him.

"Mama," he says, "do not be sorry! Never be sorry! It has been our honor to hide and protect you. We would all willingly die to do so for any runner, but especially for you. You are the mother of Daniel!"

Then Padre announces loudly, "Friends, let us pray!"

He leads us in the first prayer I have ever heard uttered aloud. He prays for the villagers we have lost, and he prays for Angel. He prays for our safety.

Then after taking one last look at the cathedral, bowing his head and making the sign of the cross, he turns and leads us down a cascading series of stairs that descend deeper and deeper into the underground labyrinth. We pass through what seems to be an endless series of smaller chambers. Brother, whose actual name is Juan, runs ahead of us, carrying a torch, and lights candle lanterns along the way to help illuminate our path. Padre talks as we descend.

"The government uses low yield TacNukes to wipe out any village it suspects might be a rebel stronghold," he explains. "That is its standard policy. In the past century, hundreds of villages have been wiped away in this manner."

"I have never heard of such a thing," I gasp. I think of the irony of such a policy. In the Northern Province, so many laws have been established for our safety. We can't even buy kitchen knives. The government goes overboard to keep us safe. Here, they nuke people?

"Of course you haven't, Chrissie." Padre shrugs his shoulders. "You come from the Northern Province. This all happens in the south, where we are taken by force from our villages, where we are made soldiers for the New Republic, or slaves for the mines and factories and work farms. Even our village, as remote as it was, was raided in the past and our young people taken away. Now, its canyon will be like all of the bombed-out land that stretches along the southern border. It is a wasteland that no one crosses. No one will be able to go near it for hundreds of years. This is how the New Republic seals the southern border from invasion, and how it sends a message to would-be rebels.

"Soon," he continues, "every public board across the Southern Province will flash images of the glowing ruins of our canyon to the people of other towns and villages. A warning! You, of course, will not be mentioned, Chrissie, because you are already supposed to be dead."

Yes, I am already dead. I saw my own funeral.

"And the government wants to continue to convince them that you are dead so that their hope dies also. You see, Chrissie, every single person in the Southern Province knows about you and Daniel. The voice spoke to all of them in their dreams before Daniel was born."

I nod my head. I know. *The voice.*

"And now," Padre continues, "we must stay with you and help you and Daniel find your way to Haven!

"Besides"—Padre shrugs his shoulders—"where else can any of us go now?"

We continue to descend and reach a slightly larger chamber that Padre calls the supply room. It is an amazing storehouse. The villagers immediately go to work gathering food that is packed in ready-made backpacks, water gourds, and weapons. Mama number 6, whose name is Rosa, finds a strong backpack and rigs it so that I can carry Daniel in it. Mama number 3, whose real name is Marcia, picks out an ancient-looking short sword and secures it in her belt. Some of the villagers are already carrying the recently pilfered police blaster rifles. The rest quickly arm themselves with the few other blasters they have cached along with spears and long knives.

The old mamas and papas look all business now. Throughout the past year, I have sensed their toughness as a people. Now seeing the way they expertly handle their weapons, checking the actions, swinging the swords and checking their balance, strapping on knives, I can tell that they are warriors. Angel knew what she was doing by picking their village as a refuge.

Padre watches me and approaches me with an explanation.

"Every mama and papa here has been trained by a guide at one point in their life, Chrissie."

Now amply supplied, we continue to descend. For three hours, we descend through a cool, damp tunnel probably several thousand feet. Finally, I can see a tiny shaft of light ahead, cutting through the dark. I help as we push aside three heavy boulders and then we are standing outside on a high rock ledge in a waning evening light. Below us, as far as the eye can see, extends an unaltered, thick flowing tropical forest canopy that ripples across an endless, undulating sea of mountains and hills.

"Behold, the real Southern Province!" Padre exclaims. "Quickly, follow me along this path."

We carefully descend down a steep path that switches back and forth through rock and scree across the face of the mountain we have just emerged from. Within minutes, we reach the jungle below.

Howler screeches and jumps on to the nearest tree. He disappears ahead of us as he swings from tree limb to tree limb. I know that he will be our forward lookout. And it feels good to be in the thick forest once again.

CHAPTER TWENTY-EIGHT

As nightfall approaches, we stop to rest and organize in a small clearing beneath the stars. Sitting in his backpack, Daniel pulls at the back of my hair as I look up at a full moon. People live up there on that shiny sphere. I try to find the tiny red dot in the night sky that is Mars, but it is not visible.

"Chrissie, do you want a weapon?" Padre asks me as he takes inventory of our supplies.

"No," I answer, remembering Angel's warning about carrying weapons. I feel more comfortable without one. I do wear the bracelets on my wrists, the ones that turn into shields. Padre nods.

"Fourteen mamas, not including you," Padre counts. "Six old papas, including me. Daniel, Lucia, Juan, and two other boys. Eight blaster rifles, four laser pistols, six knives, five swords. Juan and Papa Rodrigo carry bows and arrows for hunting."

Stunned, I sit down on the soft, fern-covered ground. Tears come to my eyes. I had been too busy escaping to give anything much thought, but now I think of Angel. I can still see the look in her golden eyes as she clutched her heart and fell to the ground. Another sacrifice for me, for Daniel. Moses, Samson, and now Angel. And Mama number 1 who was so kind to me. The villagers who perished in the bombings. How many more?

Padre takes a seat next to me and puts his arm around my shoulder.

"So much death," I say to him as the tears roll down my face.

"There will be more, Chrissie," he says. "But we do not want to kill anyone. The New republic forces us to fight."

"Moses said that every life is precious."

"Yes," Padre agrees, "which makes it so much more terrible when a life is taken. But we have been forced into vicious battle against a terrible evil. Anytime you fight an evil like this, Chrissie, lives will be sacrificed."

I sigh and shrug my shoulders.

"All of you have sacrificed too much, Padre."

"Strong worlds are built by people who are willing to sacrifice everything," he says quietly. Starlight shines in his eyes as he looks at me. "People like you, Chrissie."

The villagers rest. Some of them apply healing balms to their wounds, replace dressings on cuts. They try not to watch Padre and me as we talk, but I know that they are listening intently.

"So what is the plan?" I ask.

"The old papas have all served in the New Republic military," Padre says. "We have all served and fought along the republic borders. It is a twenty-year duty and that is why most men never return. We were the lucky ones."

"Who did you fight against?"

"Sadly," Padre explains, and there is a hint of shame in his voice, "we mostly fought our own people, the rebels of the Southern Province. We had no choice. There was always a gun to our heads if we refused. As a young soldier, I did many terrible things that I regret, memories that I will have to live with for the rest of my life. When I returned to San Hidalgo, I vowed never to help the New Republic again. For twenty years, I have been a rebel. I have helped hide runners like you, Chrissie."

Padre pulls tortillas out of his pack and hands me one. Daniel is sound asleep on my back, but soon he will be awake and will need to nurse.

"I learned many things in the military," Padre continues as we eat. "How to fight, how to organize men and move quietly through the forests, and how to stay alive. We will organize."

Padre wastes no time calling to three old papas, Luis, Cezar, and Manuel. They carry their blaster rifles with time-worn familiarity as they walk up.

"Split the villagers into three squads," Padre tells them. "We will travel in a loose *V* formation with you, Cezar, at the point, Luis to the left, and Manuel to the right. I will follow behind you with Chrissie and Daniel."

The papas look at me and nod reassuringly.

"I am sorry, Chrissie," Padre tells me. "But we will have to do as your guides for now. Angel would want us to head southeast, to the coast. That is where she planned to take you. We will need to move quickly. Hopefully, the government will not discover that we are still alive for a while. Even if they do, this is our forest. We know this country better than they ever will."

I look at the people settled around me. One mama is sharpening her knife with a whetstone and checking its edge. Another is working on her blaster. I think I am in good hands.

The papas set off to work, gathering their squads. Lucia will stay by me, it is decided, but each of the boys will be assigned to a different squad. Juan will work with Cezar at point position in our traveling formation.

"Sleep," I tell Lucia just as I feel Daniel stirring in his backpack. She sighs and lies down on a blanket in the soft mulch on the ground. The forest is alive with night sounds, and I listen to the singing night birds and insects. Somewhere out there, I hear a familiar howl. It might be Howler, but the forest is probably full of his cousins.

As I nurse Daniel, I wonder about the day's events. How did Stingray find us? Where was Jason? Do they think we all are dead now? I would not believe that for a minute. Stingray knew. He knew about the cave. He knew that we would escape. The game is still being played.

What really bothers me is the way Stingray reacted to Angel's death. He flew into a rage and killed every single one of those cops. Then he let me go. I don't understand him. I certainly don't understand his actions. None of it makes any sense to me. One thing is certain, though. Stingray and Angel had crossed paths before.

Daniel finishes nursing, and I doze for a few minutes; but mercifully, I don't dream.

When it is time to move through the jungle, I realize how strong and light on my feet I've become. Angel's relentless training has paid big dividends for me. Even Padre notices my ease of movement and comments.

"You move like a cat in the jungle, Mama," he says to me.

The villagers travel fast. I am amazed at how well they adapt to the changing terrain and how silent they are as they work together. Each squad sends scouts far ahead to make certain that the way is clear for us. Overhead, a dozen black monkeys swing through the trees, friends of Howlers.

It will take at least three weeks to reach the coast, Padre tells me. That is our goal, to stay just north of the many garrisons of New Republic soldiers that stretch along the southern border and angle toward the coast. The triple-canopy jungle should help to hide us until we reach the coastal plains. Then the way is very dangerous because of a lack of vegetation.

"It is the best plan I can come up with, Chrissie," Padre tells me as we work our way south. "Hopefully, real help and guidance will be waiting for us as we near the ocean. Word of what happened to us should reach Haven. Someone should come."

What if they don't? I think to myself.

Padre shrugs as he reads my thoughts.

"Then we hide and wait. And we fight if we have to," he says.

We fall into a rhythm. We walk for six hours and rest for six hours, regardless of whether it is night or day. Padre knows the Southern Province intimately; he patrolled it for twenty years.

"I was a sergeant," he tells me. "And I commanded more men than this."

Padre knows where the safe villages are as we progress and sends scouts ahead to contact them. As thick as the jungle is, villages just seem to spring up out of nowhere. One minute we are hacking our way with machetes through thick ground cover, fording cool streams in waist deep water; and the next moment, people and huts materialize where nothing should be. They farm small cleared-out fields, milpas, like the ones I saw farther north.

This is the way a majority of people live in this province, I learn. It makes it harder for the soldiers to find them, for the government to control them. This is a land of rebels.

Villagers bring us gifts of food and supplies. Some of them know about Daniel and me and make special trips just to see us. Like Padre told me, runners are celebrated by the rebels. And Daniel is special. Some of the old papas who come out say that they want to see "el profeta." They gaze at Daniel when they see him. Old mamas who emerge from the thick woods bring toys and baby blankets for him and beautiful, colorful embroidered dolls, baby clothes, and caps. We accept what we can and politely refuse the rest.

Daniel travels well. He twists my hair into tight knots as he straddles my back, points at birds and monkeys, and jabbers to Lucia, who is never more than five feet away from me. He has learned to sleep when we stop to rest and eat, which gives me the break I need. But always, before our six hours of rest is up, I rise early and practice the fighting forms Angel taught me. I have to stay hard. The time is soon approaching, I sense, when I will have to fight.

CHAPTER TWENTY-NINE

In the middle of the second week, our path takes us out of the forest hills and downhill toward the coast. We are completely exhausted. One night, just as we set up the perimeter guard for our rest break, she walks right into the middle of our camp. I have a sense of her before I see her, and I quickly hand Daniel to Lucia.

"Hide!" I whisper to Lucia. Without a question, she takes Daniel, scurries into some nearby bushes, and disappears.

The woman is a sight to behold. She wears a green satin bodysuit that blends in so well with her surroundings that it nearly cloaks her. But she obviously couldn't care less about being seen. Her stride is strong and confident.

Her movements make her appear younger than she actually must be because her hair is bright silver white and stands straight out around her hard, chiseled face. Two mamas lunge at her as she approaches the center of our camp, and they fall to the ground as soon as she turns to stare at each of them. She heads straight for me, and I jump to my feet.

"Don't look into her eyes!" Padre screams out from behind me. "She is a hypno-clairvoyant!"

I have no earthly idea what a hypno-clairvoyant is, but it can't be good. I avert my eyes just in time. Even so, I can physically feel the power of her awful stare. With a loud shriek, she attacks.

She possesses a slight height and weight advantage on me, but she has no idea of what I am capable of. She thinks that I am just a helpless teen girl.

Her initial attack is so ferocious that she overreaches, and that is the mistake I am hoping for. I duck, strike a hard blow to her ribs, and then slam her to the ground. As she regains her feet, I spin around and kick her hard in her exposed side. She takes a step back. I keep my eyes averted from her face, but I can sense her surprise.

"My, my," she exclaims, and then she laughs as I activate my arm shields. "We have a fighter!"

She holds out her wrists and shows me her silver armbands. Then she claps her wrists together and shields up.

Now the fight is for real. She will not underestimate me again. We strike and parry, block each other, and kick. She is good, but not nearly as good as Angel. I see an opening develop in her style and rush her with a flurry of strikes. She backs away from me, and I hear a loud *thwack!* She goes down. Padre is standing behind her, holding up a big, broad stick.

"Thanks, Padre," I mutter breathlessly as he and Papa Cezar jump in and hold her body down. For a brief moment, she struggles against them. Then she relaxes into a dead calm.

"What are you called?" I ask her as I catch my breath, keeping my eyes averted from hers.

"Medusa," she answers. Her voice is like the hiss of a snake.

"Where is Stingray?" I ask. She laughs a raspy, hissing laugh.

"Stingray failed us, so he is being punished. He works with the army now. Where did you learn to fight like that, little girl?"

"Angel."

She laughs again. I can still physically feel her powerful, steady stare, and it is sickening. She sits like a coiled cobra, just inches from my face, ready to strike.

"Ah, Angel," she says, "teaching her tricks to undeserving little children!

"Games are over, little girl," she continues. "And now the president sends real closers for you to play with. And he knows which villages help you run. He has decided to make them pay for their disloyalty to him!"

I almost look up.

"Chrissie!" Padre warns. "Don't look into her eyes!"

Medusa laughs.

"Every day that you refuse to turn yourself in," she hisses, "along with that little brat of yours, Stingray has orders to destroy one village…like…"

She lowers her head and her voice turns into a whisper.

"Like now!"

In the next instant, nighttime turns to day. Brighter than day. Then the trees bend sideways as the air buckles, thunders, and the ground shakes. Birds and monkeys tumble out of trees, screaming in terror.

"Beautiful, isn't it?" Medusa comments to me as the bright white light on the horizon fades into a deadly red glow. "The pure, white radiance of a nuke?"

I hear Daniel whimpering in the bushes. Instinctively, I look up at Medusa to see if she hears him, and that is the mistake she has been waiting for. She locks me in her gaze. Her eyes are huge and piercing green. They burn right to the center of my mind.

And then…I am in another place.

I am lying on my back, strapped down on a big steel table. The table sits in the middle of a field surrounded by a giant stadium. A man is standing over me, raising something above his head. A bright, white light flashes like a strobe light behind his head, and I squint to make out his features. All that I can tell is that he has graying hair and wears a pair of mirrored sunglasses. Stingray? I can see a crest that is embroidered in gold on the front pocket of his dark jacket. I recognize it; it is the crest of the president of the New Republic.

Somewhere in the distance, a loudspeaker is blaring out the words:

"What is your name?"

"My name is Christina Wright."

"What do you want, Christina?"

"I want to be a productive, law-abiding citizen of the New Republic."

The loudspeaker repeats these words over and over again.

The man grins down at me with a wicked, crooked grin, and his arm swings down in an arc toward my exposed neck. I am vaguely aware that a huge crowd fills the stadium to the brim and is watching and cheering him on. Then I see what it is that he is swinging toward me, and I gasp in horror. It is a huge, steel meat cleaver, gleaming in the bright light, and he is about to behead me with it.

I fight. I force myself out of the vision, back to Medusa's deadly eyes. She tries to force me back into the vision, back to the meat cleaver. To kill me?

I fight harder and pull myself back again, but the effort is so hard, so exhausting. Then in a last ditch effort to resist her, I visualize Daniel. I hold his face in my mind, focus on his sparkling blue eyes. He smiles at me.

Medusa scowls, and with a loud screech, she pushes Padre and Papa Cezar aside. She lunges at me, ready to physically kill me, and I am paralyzed helpless. Then out of nowhere, Mama number 3 rushes in and stabs her through her chest with a short sword.

My head is pounding and I am trapped in a deep fog. I am vaguely aware of watching Medusa shriek in pain and fall over on her side.

"She is dead," I hear Padre announce, but in my mind, I can still see her terrible green eyes staring into mine. Then…everything starts to fade to black.

"Chrissie." Someone is holding me by the shoulders, shaking me. "Chrissie!"

It is Padre, and he is speaking rapidly to me. But in my fog, I only catch bits of what he is saying.

"Must run...a quicker pace...will nuke a village a day... no time..."

He helps me struggle to my feet, and I am terribly dizzy. Mama number 5 gives me a small vial of liquid to drink. It is vile tasting.

"Radiation poisoning..." I hear her explaining to me. I am dimly aware of Lucia standing next to me, holding Daniel, and staring down at Medusa.

"Don't look, child," Padre is telling her, but she is looking anyway. Then we are moving. I feel like I am floating above the grass, and I also feel like I am going to throw up. We find our forward lookouts. Papa Luis and two of the boys are dead. One of them is Juan. They are lying on their backs, staring wide-eyed up into nothingness. Medusa spent some time on them before she walked into our camp.

I hear Lucia scream and cry when she sees Juan. Padre holds her hand tightly and moves her away from the scene. We find Howler lying in the bushes as we continue forward. He is alive but stunned. Papa Cezar and Mama number 5 build a sling for him out of a blanket...I see them carrying him between them.

We are running now, and I keep tripping over things. I am dizzy and the fog will not lift out of my head.

Daniel and Lucia are crying. Mama number 3 is carrying Daniel in her arms.

Where is my backpack?

The jungle is dark, but I am vaguely aware of other people nearby, running alongside of us. It has to be our three squads, staying close beside us so we can move quicker.

We splash through a stream, and I feel cool water on my feet. Then on the opposite bank, I trip again and go down even though Padre has a strong grasp on my arm.

As I climb back to my feet, I lean forward and throw up violently.

"I am sorry, Chrissie," Padre is breathlessly saying to me. "Must go quicker...villages...no time..."

The fog closes in on me. I am dimly aware of a teen girl running through the jungle with a group of people, but I am somewhere else, watching from a distance.

Night becomes day, and the people keep running. They stop only briefly. Day turns to night, and as I detachedly watch them run, a brilliant white light flashes in the distance and the jungle erupts. The people scream and cry. *What could that be?* I wonder, as I watch the white light fade to red.

It goes on like this and on. I have no idea how long.

Then it is night again. The people are running slower now, but still running. Ahead of them, the jungle explodes with a volley of dozens of streaks of blue-white light. Some of the people who are running scream and fall while others shoot back with their blasters.

The teen girl stops running. And then I am not watching her from a distance anymore. I am her.

We are being ambushed. Lucia and Daniel are nowhere in sight. Padre is shouting out commands, and the villagers are fighting like maniacs against soldiers who are emerging out of the woods.

I activate my arm shields and wade into them. My mind is still wounded and foggy, but I can fight. A soldier takes aim at me with his blaster rifle and fires as I charge at him. I automatically deflect the laser blast with my arm shield. How did I do that?

Then I reach him and kill him. I am moving fast now. Reaching soldiers and taking them out before they even have a chance to react. There is fighting all around me, but I have to ignore it. More soldiers come. And then more.

How many have I killed? I lose count, and still they keep coming. Two are jumping at me with knives, and I take them on. I disarm one of them as I kill him, and then I throw the knife hard through the chest of the other soldier who is charging at me.

Then searing heat pierces my left side. And everything goes black again.

CHAPTER THIRTY

I am seated at a beautiful wooden table that has been placed in a vast field of colorful flowers where the sky above me is a deep crystal blue and a sweet, fragrant breeze gently caresses my face. My mother sits across the table from me, peeling an orange with her delicate hands. She looks up from the orange and smiles at me. It is a sweet but sad smile. Ruthie, my imaginary little sister, stands just behind her with her hand resting on my mother's shoulder. She smiles at me too.

My mother finishes peeling the orange and, without a word, hands it to me. I am famished, and I bite into it. I have never tasted anything so delicious.

Ruthie and my mother are dressed in exquisite white dresses, and both of them glow with a gentle, golden radiance. I sigh and breathe in the wonderful air.

Now another woman takes a seat next to my mother. She looks so much like my mother that I know in my heart; she must be my Aunt Rachel. She smiles at my mother and then turns to smile to me.

I look up and see Angel and Samson walking across the flowers toward us, holding hands and laughing about something. When they see me, they stop laughing and wave emphatically at me. When they come close enough and take their place behind my mother, Angel speaks to me.

"Hello, Chrissie," she says cheerfully. "I have missed you so much!"

It is the first time I have ever heard her light and beautiful voice. Samson waves at me with a perfect, undeformed hand. Like my mother, my aunt, and Ruthie, they too radiate with a golden glow. And in the distance, more people are crossing the vast field of flowers toward us. Thousands upon thousands of people. Some of them I recognize: Mama number 1, brother Juan, and others whom I have just recently lost in the battles with the soldiers. And a man walks among them. At least I think it is a man. He shines with a radiance that is brighter than the sun, and it is hard for me to make out his features. He stops at a distance and waves directly to me.

"Yes, that is him, Chrissie," my mother tells me. "The One I told you about when you were just a child. Although you were too young to remember him now. Now you must rest for a moment."

I immediately feel drowsy.

"Am I in Haven?" I ask, struggling to keep my eyes open.

Aunt Rachel laughs, and her laugh has a sweet, musical quality to it.

"No dear," she says. "The name of this place sounds like Haven, but it is an altogether different place."

"We are all here, darling," my mother says. "And we always watch over you. You are never alone."

"You have endured too much already," little Ruthie says to me with her sweet voice. "And we love you so much. But you cannot stay here with us. It is not yet your time."

I feel so at peace in this place, so refreshed even though I am drowsy. I want to stay here with my mother, my sister, all of them.

A tear runs down my mother's cheek, but she is still smiling.

"Your job is unfinished, dear," she says to me, and Ruthie nods in agreement.

"You have to go back."

Thousands of people who were crossing the field stand behind my mother now although I cannot focus on them enough to make out their faces.

"You have to go back, Chrissie," they are all saying. "You have to go back."

Then the shining man speaks up from across the field of flowers. His voice is familiar to me, though I can't quite place it."

"There is more for you to do," he says.

❖ ❖ ❖

I open my eyes to a bright, hot sunny morning. I am covered in sweat and half sitting, half lying on the ground, propped up against a giant block of stone. Daniel is cradled in my arms, nursing. Lucia is leaning against my right shoulder, sound asleep. Mama number 5 is sharpening her knife and carefully watching me from where she sits a couple of feet away. She is wounded and covered in caked blood in a dozen places, but she still looks strong. She smiles a sad smile at me.

Howler crouches at my outstretched feet, looking into my eyes with concern. He has made a little pile of mangoes and bananas next to my leg. He picks up a mango and holds it out to me. I take a bite of it, and nausea overwhelms me. The pain in my left side is excruciating. I pass out again…

❖ ❖ ❖

"You were amazing, Mama."

It is Padre's voice. I open my eyes, and he is kneeling next to me where I still lie in the same position against the stone. Lucia holds Daniel now and is playing stick dolls with him and talking to him.

I wince as Padre rubs balm into the laser burn that pierced a hole completely through my side. He doesn't look much better than I feel. A laser burn cuts across his right cheek, and there is a large dried bloodstain on the front of his shirt. His face is tired and gaunt.

"I have never seen anyone fight the way you fought," Padre continues. "And all the while we thought that we had lost you."

The balm soothes, and I feel a little of my strength returning to me. I glance down at Howler's gifts and pick up a banana. I feel like I haven't eaten in years.

"How long have I been out?" I ask.

I take a bite of the banana and notice that my arms are still shielded. I clap my wrists together and unshield. I wince again as I do so. I have more wounds than just the one in my left side. My right shoulder has a dressing applied to it. Another burn? Dried blood stains both of my pant legs.

"It has been days, Chrissie. And every single night, they have destroyed another village. And we have fought them every single night. Do you remember the giant?

I don't remember anything. It is like my mind was wiped clean.

"He was a closer called Goliath," Padre tells me. "He walked out of the woods alone and killed six of us while he called out your name. Our rifles were useless against him. Papa Manuel and Mama Elena attacked him from behind with spears, but he threw them aside like dolls and snapped their spears in two. I attacked from the front with a blaster, and Mama number 3 attacked with her sword. He tossed us aside and kept calling for you.

"All hope was lost, Chrissie. All of that day, we had carried you unconscious in a sling. And then a miracle! As Goliath shouted out your name, you leapt at him from nowhere. You held a broken spear in your hand and you ran it through his throat. He fell like a big tree in the jungle. Then you passed out again. But too many of us died that night. At least you, Daniel, and Lucia are still safe."

So many people have died. Tears run down Padre's face as he continues.

"The next night, Chrissie, they carried Mama Marcia away."

Mama number 3. So fierce with her short sword.

"Where are we?" My head pounds with pain as I speak.

"We are near the coast," Padre tells me. "But more soldiers have surrounded us, and we were forced to take refuge in these ruins."

Painfully, I twist my head around and look. We are seated at the base of a huge, crumbling pyramid that is half buried in creeping green vines and surrounded by a number of smaller crumbling stone structures. I can see the edge of the jungle, but it is distant, and we are surrounded on all sides by large fields of vine-strangled bushes and tall grass.

"How did you get me here, Padre?" I ask as I survey our surroundings.

"Chrissie," Padre answers, "part of the time, you ran. But your eyes were blank, your mind was never present, and frequently you would pass out and collapse. Then we would carry you."

Padre has placed the remainder of our party in defensive positions at the top of the pyramid. I wince in pain as I struggle to my feet to get a better look. My legs are weak and wobbly. I nearly pass out from the pain in my side as I stretch to see past the tumbled stone blocks that lie all around us.

"Keep your head low," Padre warns me. "The soldiers surround us on all sides. They have us trapped, Chrissie."

"How many soldiers?" I ask as I look out across the fields.

"Hundreds, Chrissie," Padre sadly says. "Hundreds. And Stingray leads them. I am so sorry, Mama. We have failed you and Daniel."

"How many of us are left, Padre?"

"Nine."

Nine?

I look down at Lucia, who is quiet now. She and Daniel both watch me intently. I catch a glimpse of black fur crossing between two fallen stone blocks that lie behind them. Howler. We are surrounded by hundreds of soldiers, but I have never been in a quieter place. Then I sense something—a quiet whisper in my head. Stingray's whisper!

Climb to the top of the pyramid, the whisper says. *I have something to show you.*

"Hide Daniel," I tell Lucia, and then I turn to Padre. "I'll be right back."

The steps that lead to the top of the big pyramid are steep. Some of them are crumbling. My head is still pounding, and I am still dizzy as I start to climb them.

"Chrissie, I don't think…," Padre starts to warn, but I shake my head no and continue up.

"Padre," I call back down to him, "protect Lucia and Daniel. I won't be long."

Papa Cezar, Papa Rodrigo, Mama number 2 and Mama number 14 are posted behind crumbling walls at the pyramid's top level, their blaster rifles trained at the distant woods that surround us on all sides. Right at the edge of the trees, I can see multitudes of soldiers. They aren't even trying to hide.

"Why aren't they attacking?" I ask Papa Cezar.

"I don't know, Mama," he says. "Perhaps Stingray is waiting for something. Maybe he is waiting for you. Look."

He hands me his blaster rifle, and I sweep the edge of the woods with the rifle's scope. I can see Stingray standing in the sun, wearing sandals and shorts, a beach shirt and a straw hat that shades his mirrored sunglasses. As I train my gun sight on him, he grins at me and picks up a megaphone.

"Hi, Chrissie!" he calls out. "It's about time! I was getting worried about you. Medusa must have done a real number on you."

"She's dead!" I scream out.

"Good work!" Stingray shouts. "I hated her anyway. She was pretty freaky."

Not as freaky as you are, pal.

I can see him laughing.

"I'm going to miss you, Chrissie," he continues. "I'm going to miss the thrill of the game. But business calls. And I have surprise for you!"

I follow him through my sight as he walks across the field to a bare spot in the grass where two big stakes have been driven into the ground. Chained to one stake, with a metal collar around her neck, is Mama number 3. She sits, leaning against the stake, and I can see that she has been severely beaten. So has Jason, who is chained to the other stake.

"Did you miss your boyfriend?" Stingray shouts. "He missed you, sweetheart!"

Stingray hits Jason hard, and Jason tumbles to the ground.

"Come out right now, Chrissie," Stingray continues as Jason falls. "And I promise I won't kill Daniel."

"He has us where he wants us," I say to Papa Cezar. "Why doesn't he just rush in and finish it?"

Papa Cezar shrugs his shoulders.

"He is like a big cat," he answers. "And he likes to play with mice."

"Come in, Chrissie. Bring me Daniel or I start with these two!"

We are finished. Stingray has won, and I am out of options. I face the president's meat cleaver, and Daniel gets a one way trip to the Parlor.

"You're taking way too long, Chrissie!" I hear Stingray call. I train my rifle sight back on him.

"Let's see," he says, "who do I kill first?"

He looks from Jay to Mama number 3 and drops his megaphone. Then he has his laser knife in his hand and Mama number 3 by the throat. Before he can do anything, Mama number 3 reaches out, grabs his laser knife with both of her strong hands, and pierces her own heart with it. Stingray scowls and kicks the dirt into a dust cloud as she falls over. Then he picks the megaphone back up.

"This wouldn't be necessary, Chrissie, if you would just do what I say!"

As he turns to Jason, I take careful aim and fire a laser shot at his head. Without even looking up, he deflects it with his armguard. I fire three more shots, and Stingray deflects them just as easily, and then straightens up and grins at me.

"Nice shooting, Chrissie!' he calls through the megaphone. "And now, please, look up at the sky."

I can hear them before I can see them. Dozens and dozens of bombers cross overhead, blotting out the light of the sun.

"Beautiful, aren't they?" Stingray calls over the high-pitched din of the planes. "They carry nukes, Chrissie. Every single one has a different village as a target. Now, do you want to come out, or do you want thousands of innocent people to die? It's up to you."

My friends look up at me questioningly from their places on the pyramid.

"Stay here," I tell Papa Cezar. I make my way back down the steps to Padre. He stands there, his arms folded. Lucia stands next to him, holding Daniel. She is crying. I break out into tears.

"Padre, I don't know what to do," I confess. The bombers circle overhead.

"I'm waiting, Chrissie!" I hear Stingray call out in the background.

"Mama," Padre says, "for some reason, he wants you alive. He could have killed us all anytime he wanted."

"Mama!" It is Daniel, reaching up to me. I take him out of Lucia's hands and hold him.

"I just don't know," I say again. "He's won."

Daniel twists around in my arms, reaches out, and holds my chin. He makes me look into his intense little blue eyes, and then he points toward Stingray with his left hand.

No, I shake my head. I can't do that.

He looks at me with an intensity I have never seen in him before.

"Mama!" he says in his baby voice, holding my chin with his deformed arm. Slowly he closes his eyes, leans forward and touches my forehead with his. I feel a mild shock as his forehead touches mine.

And then I hear the *voice* in my mind. The *voice* that told me that Daniel is in the lion's den.

"It is time, Chrissie," the *voice* says. "Time for you to choose."

I know what I have to do. I can't allow thousands of innocent people to die. There is really only one choice now. I have to carry my baby into the middle of the lion's den. I hold Daniel in one arm and hug Padre with the other. Then I hug Mama number 5 and kneel down to hug Lucia. She resists.

"I'm going with you!" she insists with folded arms.

"No, little sister!" I say firmly. "You can't."

Padre takes Lucia by the shoulders, and she screams and cries, but he holds her firmly. Sadly, I kiss her on the forehead. Then I turn with Daniel to leave.

"I love all of you!" I tell Lucia and Padre.

"We will pray for you, Chrissie!" Padre tells me. "Be strong and have faith, Mama...God is your guide!"

I start out across the grassy field toward Stingray. I am doing what I vowed never to do. I am carrying Daniel right into the heart of danger. When I am halfway across the open field, I hear Lucia cry out behind me, "I love you, big sister!"

Stingray and the soldiers are approaching. Stingray is grinning his wicked grin, and he reaches out for Daniel. Instinctively, I pull Daniel back away from him. A soldier next to Stingray steps forward and hits me in the side of my head with the butt of his laser rifle. Then...blackness.

CHAPTER THIRTY-ONE

"What is your name?"
"My name is Christina Wright."
"What do you want, Christina?"
"I want to be a productive, law-abiding citizen of the New Republic."

I did not say that. I am trapped in a room with bright white walls, strapped down on a cold steel table. I am listening to a recording that is blaring out over and over again from a loudspeaker somebody placed just inches from my head. It has been repeating those same words for hours and hours. Directly above my face, a bright white strobe light flashes rapidly, making me blink.

My mind is foggy; everything is unclear to me, and all I can do is concentrate on the words that keep repeating, again and again.

"What is your name?"
"My name is Christina Wright."
"What do you want, Christina?"
"I want to be a productive, law-abiding citizen of the New Republic."

It is impossible to tune it out. The words sear their way into my brain like white hot embers, and my body shakes and writhes in total agony. How long has this been going on? Centuries, I say to myself; I have been enduring this torture for centuries. Where am I? What am I? What could I possibly have done to be here in this place, at this point in time?

I don't know. I don't remember anything. I don't remember anything at all.

After another hour passes, the recording stops, and a woman dressed in a white hospital outfit opens a door and walks into the room. She is tall and graceful, with long silver-white hair that she braids down the middle of her back. She picks up a round, metal stool and sets it down next to the table that I am strapped to. She sits down and smiles at me. She has the biggest green eyes I have ever seen.

Her eyes seem to pierce right through to the heart of my soul. I try to turn away from her, but I can't. As I look into her eyes, I can feel her powerful hold on me.

"What is your name, dear?" she asks with a pleasant voice.

"My name is Chrissie Wright," I say to her.

"What do you want, Christina?"

"I want you to let me go!" I scream at her.

The woman's smile is replaced with a frown, and she shakes her head.

"Christina, do you remember where you are?" she asks with a gentle voice.

Do I know where I am? My mind is completely blank. I'm not even really sure who I am. The loudspeaker calls me Christina Wright, but I am not one hundred percent sure who Christina Wright is. *Chrissie*, I tell myself. *I know my name is Chrissie. That is all that I really know.*

And this woman! She can't possibly be normal. I am not even sure she is human. Something about her is terribly wrong. Her green eyes hold me completely captive in her terrible stare. It makes me sick, and I feel like I need to throw up.

"You are where you always are, in Haven Hospital Prison," the woman tells me. "Where you have been a prisoner for the last two years, Christina. Do you remember now?"

"No!" I scream. I pull at my straps.

"Doctor?"

It is a man's voice from the door.

"Yes?" the woman with the green eyes asks as she turns around.

"A word with you, please?"

"Of course, Warden. In the other room, please."

She stands and walks through the doorway, closing it behind her. But it swings back slightly open. I can hear them as they talk.

"She is experiencing another major episode," the woman is explaining. "She has become completely trapped in her make-believe world. Some days, she seems to remember everything. But yesterday, she told me again that you are some sort of monster called 'Stingray.'"

"She has to break free," the man says. "There isn't much time left."

"I am going to need to increase her medication again, Warden," the woman says with an exasperated voice.

"You're the doctor."

"Thank you, Warden."

Minutes later, a giant of a man dressed in a gray jumpsuit rushes in, grabs my right arm in his steel grip, and injects me with a syringe. I scream out as I feel liquid fire entering my veins. Then everything in my mind goes blank, and I feel like I am floating in an ocean of vomit.

The loudspeaker begins to blare again. The strobe light flashes.

"What is your name?"

"My name is Christina Wright."

"What do you want, Christina?"

"I want to be a productive, law-abiding citizen of the New Republic."

CHAPTER THIRTY-TWO

My mind is completely lost. Every day, I find myself strapped to the steel table with the strobe light flashing overhead and the endless recording that burns itself into my mind. What is true, what is fantasy? Faces emerge out of the fog at times, and their names flash through my head. Someone called Daniel or Padre, Angel, Moses, and others. Terrible faces too. Stingray, Medusa. Was any of it real? I can't be certain.

Sometimes, I think that I might get a grip. Then the giant shows up with a syringe, and the woman doctor with the huge green eyes stares me down. She takes notes on a viewer without even looking down at it. For hours, she just stares at me. And without even looking at her, I can feel her awful power in my mind.

"Last year you were making real progress, Christina, and then you relapsed, hard. You are not responding to your therapy as well as we would have liked."

It is the man they call Warden. He is sitting casually in a chair that he has placed in my cold cell across from my prison bed. I try to cut through the haze in my mind. I look up and see that it is daylight outside of my steel-barred window.

He is dressed in a gray business suit. His blond hair is combed carefully back away from his forehead. His mirrored sunglasses gleam at me. His sunglasses!

"Go to hell, Stingray!" I scream. I try to lunge at him, but I discover that I am chained to my bed. The giant man who stands guard at my door rushes in, but the warden waves him off.

"I am Warden Donovan, Christina," he tells me when the big man leaves. "Stingray…that is such an interesting name. Tell me, what does it mean to you?"

"It means you are the monster!" I persist, straining at my chains. "I dream about you! You killed everybody!"

"There is not much time left, Christina," the warden continues. "But I have not given up hope on you. Not by a long shot. So we will go slowly, like we always do. Let's start again from the very beginning. Where are we, Christina?"

I have no idea.

"We are where we have been for the past two years, dear," he says. "In the Haven Hospital Prison, the finest reeducation facility in the New Republic. You are lucky to be here, in the heart of the beautiful Southern Province."

"Beautiful?" I ask, remembering fragments from a disjointed dreamscape. "After you bombed it to pieces?"

"No one has ever bombed the Southern Province," the warden answers gently. His voice holds genuine concern for me, but I just don't know. It's something about those sunglasses!

"I know that you are confused, dear. We all know. So let's go over it again, one more time."

"Who is Daniel?" I demand.

"There is no one named Daniel," he answers. "That is a part of the fantasy you created after your abortion at the Parlor, after we rescued you from the underground when you ran away from home. You have an incredible imagination, Christina. We actually saved your life from the murderers in the underground. Including their leader, Moses. Do you remember?"

My head is spinning. I am confused.

"I don't want you to be here," he continues. "Nobody wants you to be here. We all understand the hysteria that pregnancy can bring into the mix. But you had to pay the price, Christina. You knew the penalty for running! A minimum of two years, solitary confinement. But your father is the minister of information now.

He had you and Jason transferred south to us, where you can really be helped. But you have to want to be helped, dear."

Jason? I see a face emerging out of the fog. Jason, a tall blond boy.

"Who is Jason?" I ask.

"Your boyfriend, living three cells down from you, honey," the warden tells me. "For the past two years. He helped you plan everything, remember? Now listen, your first shot at parole is coming up in less than a month, and your father wants you back home with him. But if you insist on living in your fantasy world, if we fail to bring you back, you could stay here indefinitely."

I say nothing. There is nothing for me to say. I don't know what is real. Have I dreamed about things that never happened? Sometimes, I remember running through jungles. Fighting... killing! I remember people who were trying to help me. I remember a baby.

"If we can't help you," the warden continues, "you are a real danger to yourself and to everyone else. You will be fully institutionalized here. Try, Christina. Try hard to come back to us. We only want what is best for you."

He rises to leave.

"Thanks for the conversation, you murderer!" I growl at him. He turns to look at me, and I can see my reflection in his mirror glasses.

"No problem, Ms. Wright," he says with sadness. "We have this same conversation, every single day."

The giant man wheels me on a cold gurney down to the white room, injects my arm with medicine, and straps me to the cold steel table. The white strobe lights start to flash. The recording plays loudly. And the thick fog flows back into my brain.

"What is your name?"

"My name is Christina Wright."

"What do you want, Christina?"

"I want to be a productive, law-abiding citizen of the New Republic."

CHAPTER THIRTY-THREE

I really doubt my sanity. Did I make it all up? In my chronic sleeplessness, I can hear the echo of a child crying outside in the hallway sometimes, laughing at other times. I crawl out of bed and stretch up to look out the tiny glass portal of my cell door. Once, I think I catch a quick glimpse of him, scurrying down the hallway in some kind of a baby walker. Real? Or a hallucination? I don't know.

CHAPTER THIRTY-FOUR

If there is a hell, I am sitting right in the middle of it. How much time has passed? How can I possibly know? I barely remember yesterday.

The loudspeaker burns into my brain:

"What is your name?"

"My name is Christina Wright."

"What do you want, Christina?"

"I want to be a productive, law-abiding citizen of the New Republic."

The lady with the green bug eyes stares me down. The warden pays me his daily visit. The giant rumbles in, straps me to the steel table, and drugs me.

There has to be a way to end this.

Is this all there is? What if I give in to them? What if I just repeat the words that have been seared into my mind? Will it all stop then? Will it all be over?

A voice in my mind screams, *no!*

And there you have it. I have to endure. I have to keep breathing. I really have no other choice. I hate these people, and I know that I cannot give in. So nothing changes, day after day.

One day, a woman peeks in through the portal on my cell door and leers at me. She is a living horror. Half of her face is jet-black and the opposite half is bone-white. I have these hallucinations sometimes, and I remember them when my memory is halfway working. Another woman with bright yellow eyes peers in; a man grins at me with shiny black teeth. They are monsters, and I scream when I see them. All in my imagination? Then the giant rushes in with his big syringe.

Sometimes I remember that the warden told me a boy named Jason is living three cells down from me, but I never see him. Never even hear his voice. Is he really even there?

I don't know what to believe.

Then one morning, I see something new.

It happens at dawn. I hear a noise. I crawl out of my bed and look through my cell window down into the grassy central courtyard outside. A man is there, dressed in strange, colorful, flowing gown. He kneels serenely on his knees, his face calm. In his belt, he carries two swords, one long and one short. He bows slowly as the sun rises. Then he begins to perform a ritual series of movements with his sword. I watch in fascination as the sword flashes and glows in the red rising sun. For more than an hour, he performs patterns of movement, with and without his swords. He moves with a grace, a style, and a quickness that stokes dying embers in my memory, of something I must have seen before. But what? And where have I seen it? I don't know.

He is clearly Asian, that much my dull mind surmises; and later, on another day, I spot him in the hallway as the giant wheels me down to the white room with the loudspeaker and the bug lady and the flashing light. The Asian man glances down at me with an impassive face, but he is dressed in an official uniform, just another prison guard on his way somewhere.

The strobe light starts to flash. The recording plays.

"What is your name?"

"My name is Christina Wright."

"What do you want, Christina?"

"I want to be a productive, law-abiding citizen of the New Republic."

It goes on like this.

Every morning, I crawl up to look outside of my window at dawn. Every morning, he is there in the courtyard, performing his ritual. How long does this go on? I have no idea. It could be for weeks, or it could be for years.

Then one morning, I am astonished to see the warden there in the courtyard, kneeling and facing the Asian man. He wears flowing gowns just like the Asian, complete with the swords. Slowly, they stand and bow to each other. Then they draw their long swords. The swordfight is brutal and short in duration, and I am astonished to see both men still standing at the end of it. They bow again, and the warden leaves the courtyard.

The Asian man kneels and sits in total stillness and concentration. He is a young man, not more than twenty years old, and strikingly handsome as the glow of the red rising sun reflects off his exotic attire.

And it seems like years pass by.

Daily, I endure the giant and his syringe. The strobe and the loudspeaker. The warden. The bug-eyed lady. The sounds of a child in the hallway.

One morning, as I am eating the gruel the big guard has shoved through my door, I hear a slight scratching noise at my window. I stand up and find a skillfully folded paper animal that has been carefully placed on my windowsill. It is a paper monkey. There is a hint of writing exposed in its folds, and I open it to read what is written inside.

Don't listen to them! the written words say.

As quickly as I can, I hide it under my mattress.

Before long, the giant opens my door and wheels me down to my therapy session.

CHAPTER THIRTY-FIVE

It happens every morning now. After the Asian man performs his morning ritual, he always leaves a gift on my windowsill. Always a different animal, ingeniously folded from thin white paper. With something written inside.

A folded paper bear opens to read, *Do not be afraid!*

A swan unfolds. *This will all pass!*

And now, every few mornings, the warden arrives in the grassy court and kneels across from the Asian man. His mirrored sunglasses glow red with the rising sun, and they fight each other ferociously. The warden bows and departs; the Asian man sits calmly, and after a little while, I receive another gift.

A lion with a huge mane. *God is always with you!*

And then an elephant. *Patience!*

This goes on for what seems like ages. Then one morning, just before dawn, he places a fierce-looking dragon on my sill. I grab it quickly and look out at him. He is already kneeling serenely in his meditative position. As always, he slowly bows to the rising sun. Then slowly, ever so slowly, he looks up at me. Then even more slowly, he raises his hand to his mouth and makes a slight chewing motion.

I think I understand. I slouch down below the window with my back to the cell door and study the dragon. I immediately see the writing partially visible within its folds.

I am called Dragon. I am your guide, the writing says.

Guide? What is a guide? I don't know, but it is clear that the Asian man wants me to eat the paper. It is sweet as it rapidly dissolves on my tongue. I stretch back up to the window to look out at the Asian man, but he is gone. Soon, all his gifts that I hid under my mattress have vanished as well, dissolved in my mouth.

CHAPTER THIRTY-SIX

Time drags on, but I feel like my head is clearing a little. Every morning, I watch the Asian man meditate in the courtyard; and every morning, he leaves me a folded paper gift with another saying written in it. One morning, he has written something in the folds of a paper cat.

Medicine," the message reads. I promptly eat it. Then I can feel my head clear a little more. A cat. I seem to remember a cat from somewhere, long ago. It is just a fleeting thought.

Maybe a week later, my head is really clearing. The paper animals have a stronger effect on me. I can even feel some strength returning to my body. At night, when my cell is dark, I stand up and try to copy the flowing movements that the Asian man practices every morning. I do this for hours, and I feel that somehow, my body already knows the patterns of movement.

It all helps. My constant state of nausea is receding.

I grow more defiant during my daily sessions under the strobe light. I glare at the woman doctor and struggle hard against my table straps. That is probably a mistake. They respond by increasing my medication.

One morning, the Asian man places a beautifully folded eagle on my windowsill. It contains writing in its folds.

Give them what they want, it reads.

I am confused. Give them what they want?

But the Asian man's gifts have helped me tremendously. For the first time that I can remember, I can piece together strings of days. I am not forgetting as much. I trust him.

The giant wheels me down to my therapy session, and I lie there on that cold table, blinking at the strobe light, listening to that horrible recording over and over again. Staring back at the green-eyed doctor. Every afternoon, the warden has his cozy little conversation with me.

"Try to remember, Chrissie," the woman doctor implores me as I watch her from the cold steel table I am strapped to. Her big green eyes bore inexorably into mine. The giant guard gave me a huge burning injection before he wheeled me in and my mind is tumbling into dark space.

"You are reading my mind," I mutter to her. The doctor gasps and shakes her head.

"No! We already discussed this! Remember your school history, Chrissie," she lectures. "Clairvoyance is old history. It is strictly prohibited! You know that! The last of the clairvoyants were executed over one hundred years ago."

"Now think back!" she continues. "You ran instead of reporting in for your appointment with the Parlor. With Jason Morson's help, you bought a weapon, a Perma Lighter, from a convenience store. Then you hid in the underground. But you did not know how dangerous the underground was for a young girl like you. They nearly killed you down there. Their leader caught you and held you for ransom. His name was Moses. We killed him and rescued you just in time! At the Parlor, the abortion proceeded as planned, and then you and Jason were sterilized. You were tried in a court of law, found guilty, and sent here. You have been here for two years. Do you remember?"

She stares at me with those huge green eyes. It is time. I can see no point in resisting any longer.

"Yes," I answer. "I remember."

I really still don't remember much. I don't remember being here for the past two years. I barely remember last week. But if that is what she wants to hear from me, fine.

The doctor smiles and stands up from the round steel stool. She walks into the other room and returns holding a different viewer. Her fingers start to play across its glowing screen, pulling up page after page of notes.

"I must say, dear," she laughs, "with your hyper imagination, you certainly gave us a run for our money. Such stories! Cities on the moon! And on Mars, of all places! Guides and closers. This old religion nonsense about a baby named Daniel who talks to everybody in their heads. And this Stingray character!"

She laughs again.

"I will admit, the warden can be intimidating at times, but you really ran him through the coals!"

I watch her silently as she continues to play her fingers across the screen.

"This is such a good read," she says as she does so. "And this Angel, a woman who wipes out entire squads of soldiers?"

She looks up to stare at me with her big green eyes.

"You probably think I am this character, Medusa."

She goes on like this for I don't know how long because I continue to drift in and out of my heavy fog. Then she drops the viewer on to a steel tray next to the table. I cringe. She is going to turn on the strobe light, start the recording. But she doesn't.

"Today is going to be easy," she says warmly. "What is your name, dear?"

"My name is Christina Wright," I answer quietly.

"What do you want, Christina?"

"I want to be a productive, law-abiding citizen of the New Republic."

"Congratulations, dear," she announces with a big smile. "You made it!"

Later, I am sitting on my cell bunk, still floating from the giant's last injection. I am Christina Wright, I tell myself, a productive citizen of the New Republic. I am sterile; I will never have children. That boy named Jason is sterile too. That Asian man is nice and he wants to help me, but I realize that he is only a guard who has been showing me compassion with gifts of cute, edible paper animals. Maybe that is a part of his culture. And really, it was all a dream, just a dream. All my fantasies were part of my hyper imagination.

For the next three days, they leave me alone in my cell. No visits to the white room. No conversations with the warden. Three times a day, the giant shoves a tray of food through my door. Every night, I practice my movements in the dark. Every morning, I watch the Asian man practice in the courtyard. He leaves his paper gifts.

Then on the morning of the third day, he leaves a special gift. It is an animal, a jackrabbit, and it is twice the size of any of the other gifts he has left sitting on my windowsill. It contains writing: *remember who you are!*

I eat the paper,, and I feel a tremendous surge of clarity wash through my mind. All the fog clears away in an instant.

I remember who I am! I am Chrissie Wright, the daughter of Mary Wright. I am the mother of Daniel. Daniel in the lion's den!

I remember what I am. I am the jackrabbit.

I remember who they are. I remember everything!

CHAPTER THIRTY-SEVEN

"Christina, may I say, you look fabulous!"

That is the warden. I am sitting at a long table in a brightly decorated dining room. The table is exquisitely laid out with the finest white linen tablecloth and a banquet's feast of food served on the finest silver. Fine porcelain china is arranged in front of me along with expensive silverware and a lead crystal wineglass filled to the brim with red wine.

I am dressed up in a priceless red dinner gown complete with a fine pearl necklace and ruby red high heels. My golden brown hair is pulled back away from my face with a silver hair clasp. The warden sits directly across the table from me.

To the warden's right, a heavyset older Hispanic man who wears a heavily decorated army uniform presides at the head of the table. The warden simply calls him the general.

"You're a lucky man, Jason," the warden continues as he looks through his mirrored sunglasses at the boy who is seated next to me. "You and Christina are going to be the talk of the New Republic!"

The other guests, who line both sides of the dining table, laugh. There is my terrible green-eyed lady doctor, my giant cell guard, and other prison guards, male and female, whom I have seen from time to time.

"These two will make a wonderful little family, don't you agree, General?" the warden asks in perfect Spanish.

"Yes, indeed!" the general agrees, smiling widely at me.

The warden, like Jason and the other guests, is dressed to the hilt. He wears a gold tuxedo that compliments his dark tan complexion. Jason is dressed in a black dinner suit.

"Christina, you are not going to believe this food!" the warden exclaims as servers dressed in white coats swarm around us, offering trays of just about everything imaginable.

He is right, the food is literally intoxicating. The medicines they have been treating me with have always sapped my appetite, but these wonderful smells, so different from the gruel I've become used to, make me hungry. I allow the servants to pile on seafood and beef, fruits and vegetables I haven't seen in ages. I glance at Jason who is already quietly eating, and then I dig in.

"That's a girl," the warden says approvingly as I eat.

"It is good food," the man seated to the warden's left remarks. He is the young Asian man I have watched in the courtyard every morning, the one who has given me the paper animals. Up close, I see how strong he looks, how handsome he is. He is wearing a dark tuxedo. He smiles at me.

"Oh, Christina," the warden says as he straightens back up. "I have forgotten my manners! We have started eating, and I haven't even introduced everyone to you."

He sweeps his hand around the table and I glance from face to face at the gathering.

"This is my assistant warden, Mr. Sasaki." He gestures to my guide, the Asian man. The Asian man smiles and bows politely to me.

"And farther down my side of the table, you have the lovely Doctor Mendenhall."

The doctor lady with the huge green eyes and silver-white hair smiles and nods at me.

"I credit her with curing you," the warden continues. He continues down the table naming different guards. The giant who guarded my cell door. Other faces look familiar, but when I saw them looking in through my cell door portal, they looked like demons. Now they look like normal people.

"And finally," the warden concludes, gesturing to the uniformed man seated at the head of the table, "our beloved General Garza, leader of the Southern Province Armies. He is responsible for this gala feast, in honor of you both."

I nod to the general who smiles a wide smile at me and then beams at Jason. Jason smiles back.

"Thank you, General," Jason responds. "And thank you, Warden Donovan. This dinner is very kind of both of you."

I suppose that I should be just as beholden as the handsome blond boy sitting next to me, but somehow I don't feel an ounce of gratitude surging through me. I stay quiet.

The warden stands and raises his wineglass.

"Ladies and gentlemen," he says, "a toast to Jason and Christina, our guests of honor. I received the confirmation just this afternoon. The president plans to grant them both a full pardon. He is personally flying down to our coast tomorrow to escort them home."

The dinner guests rise and raise their glasses.

"Hear, hear," they toast us. "To Jason and Christina!"

The food and wine is beyond belief, and I have no qualms enjoying it. Then over a dessert of cake that melts in my mouth, the Asian man makes conversation for the first time. First, he looks at me, and maybe I imagine it. An image of a jackrabbit races across my mind. Then it is gone. He smiles slightly, looks away from me, and turns to Jason.

"What is your name?" he asks Jason in Spanish, and I detect just a hint of a different, exotic accent.

Jason looks up and smiles at both the warden and the Asian man.

"My name is Jason Morson."

"What do you want, Jason?"

"I want to be a productive, law-abiding citizen of the New Republic."

"Excellent!" the warden breaks in, beaming at Jason. He ignores Mr. Sasaki and turns to me.

"What is your name, dear?" the warden asks me. I see my own reflection in his mirrored sunglasses.

Take off those damn sunglasses, and I'll tell you, Stingray! my mind shouts out. But I smile and answer aloud.

"My name is Christina Wright."

"And what do you want, Christina?"

I want Daniel! my mind screams again. I can't help myself; I can't control my anger! So much for guarding my thoughts. *And I want to kill you! I really want to kill you! For Moses, for Samson, for Angel, for all of the villages you bombed, but especially for San Hidalgo!*

Then I answer aloud, sweetly.

"I want to be a productive, law-abiding citizen of the New Republic."

I turn and glare at the woman doctor. I want to make her pay! For some reason unknown to me, I picture Medusa in my mind, covered in blood, and dying with a sword stuck through the middle of her stomach. The doctor gasps out loud, and her big green eyes grow even bigger. Then she glares back at me, and I feel like I have been hit in the stomach with a sledgehammer.

I turn quickly and look directly into Stingray's mirrored sunglasses. *Take this,* I think to him! I picture Angel, beautiful Angel, dying in his arms. I picture him stomping around the fountain in San Hidalgo square, froth dripping from his mouth.

Stingray, you stupid insect, I think to him. *You killed the only person you ever really loved!*

Stingray sits straight up, and I can see the shock on his face. Then he relaxes and grins back at me with that strange, crooked grin of his. He takes a deep breath. Then finally, he turns and leans toward the Asian man.

"Tomorrow is going to be quite a day," he says, still grinning that strange grin.

"Yes, indeed," the Asian man agrees. "Quite a day!"

As I finish the last bite of my dessert, I become aware that Mr. Sasaki is watching me, studying me intently.

CHAPTER THIRTY-EIGHT

The gala dinner party is over, and I am back in my cell, back on my hard bunk, back in my orange prison jumpsuit. Tomorrow, I've been told, they will give me new travelling clothes.

I am mad at myself. That familiar fog has seeped back into my mind, and I am confused. Did I suffer another relapse? My mind screamed out terrible things at the warden and the doctor. Because of my fantasy! Thankfully, no one can really read my mind.

I am Christina Wright, a productive and law-abiding citizen of the New Republic. Tomorrow, I will be reunited with my father and stepmother. And Jason? Who knows. He just seems so strange to me. But they say that he was once my boyfriend. Maybe I do have a future with him.

Competing memories and fantasies march back and forth across my consciousness, winning and losing little battles to control my mind. I want to remember everything that I knew before the banquet, but those memories are fading fast. The old nausea is creeping back in, and my banquet meal does not sit well in my stomach.

It is late. Bright moonlight flows in through the bars of my cell window. I am not sleepy. Like the warden said, tomorrow is a big day. I am going to be pardoned. I am going to go back to my old life in the New Republic and learn how to be Christina Wright, a productive and law-abiding citizen of the New Republic.

I am thankful that my father has agreed to take me back after all the trouble I have caused him. He is a big man in the republic now, appointed minister of information by the president himself, and I must be a terrible embarrassment to him. I vow to make it up to him.

But somewhere deep in my mind, I am extremely sad. It must have something to do with my medications. What is it about that Asian man? I can't remember now.

I lie back on my bunk and try to sleep, but my mind is racing. Fantasy images keep breaking through into my consciousness, faces from my fantasy world, faces that I made up. Moses, Angel, Padre, Daniel.

It has to be midnight. I hear a slight scratching noise at my window, and I get up to investigate. The Asian man has left another folded paper animal on the windowsill. I look out into the courtyard, but he is gone. I pick up the animal and study it. Another jackrabbit.

I carefully unfold it to read the message inside.

Prepare yourself! Practice!

I cram the paper into my mouth and feel it dissolve on my tongue. This time, it is not sweet, and I reflexively wrinkle my nose. It tastes acrid and metallic.

Ever so gradually, my mind clears, and all my memories come flooding back. My real memories! The ones that I know are true. I guess that is how it is. I still need strong doses of his medicine to fend off what they have done to me. Will it always be this way?

My cell is dark. Slowly, quietly, I start to work through the fighting forms that Angel taught me.

Punch, kick, reverse, jump and spin kick, recover, punch, disperse, recover and spin attack, inside and twist, punch, recover, counter and finish…

Faster!

I hear Angel's voice in my mind.

Punch, jump and spin, back fist attack and recover, flow into reverse and rapid attack, twist and up-under punch and disperse, recover, spin, back kick and finish…

Too slow!

It is as if she is standing right there in the dark cell, watching me, teaching and critiquing.

Center…breathe…focus…gather and attack…build the power…turn…block and punch and jump up into a spinning kick…recover…center…breathe…relax…

Good!

I feel strength and energy flowing back into my arms and legs. Into my very center! I assume my position again on the floor of the prison cell. I no longer see the walls that confine me. I only see a distant horizon where a bright, shining light is just beginning to break. And I practice.

I practice all night long.

CHAPTER THIRTY-NINE

Midmorning. I should be exhausted, but I am running on pure adrenaline. I am sitting in a prison transport that is flying low across the coastal grasslands of the Southern Province. My head is clear. And I still remember everything.

Next to me sits the horrible green-eyed lady doctor. Mendenhall? Who knows if that is her real name? Mr. Sasaki—or Dragon, I suppose—sits facing me. The seats are arranged flush against the sidewalls of the transport, facing each other. Dragon wears his ritualistic flowing garments complete with his swords. It is his formal attire, he tells me, for meeting the president. Other guards are also present in the transport with us, but they are hard to see. The windows are blacked out, and everything is dark.

True to their word, they have given me a set of khaki traveling clothes to wear, complete with socks and tennis shoes. I am glad to be free of the stinking orange prison jumpsuit. Jason is not with us, and I am told that he is riding with the warden in a black prison limo following directly behind us.

We travel for what seems like an hour when the doctor takes my hand in hers. She is wearing a strange, green satin jumpsuit that probably matches her eyes, but I avoid looking into her terrible eyes. Even so, as soon as I feel her hand touch mine, I can feel her powerful psychic energy probing my mind.

Look at me! her voice erupts into my head. I can feel her staring at me; the feeling is familiar, and so I imagine a cloak and drape it across my thoughts.

You little witch! That is her voice in my mind again. An exasperated voice. I clamp down on her hand with both of mine, find her nerves, and twist and squeeze as hard as I can.

"Look at me!" she screams aloud as she snatches her hand away and shakes it in pain. I refuse to comply; I stare instead into Dragon's eyes. He watches me impassively.

"Please, Chrissie, please look at me…"

A little girl's hand slides gently into mine. Out of the corner of my eye, I see Ruthie sitting next to me where the doctor was sitting. I see her white dress and her long, blond hair. But I don't look into her eyes. I snatch my hand away, clasp my hands together, and stare at Dragon.

"That's it!" the doctor screams. "Clear the windows! Let Chrissie enjoy the view of the beautiful Southern Province!"

The transport windows clear and allow bright, outside morning light to flood in. The landscape outside is rushing by; we are really moving, but I gasp at the sight outside. I see nothing but a totally bombed-out wasteland. Not a desert, but worse. The land is raped, cratered, and completely burnt out. Not a living thing exists as far as I can see. Padre and I would have never been able to cross a place like this.

"Enjoy the scenery, Chrissie," she spits out at me. "On your last day of life!"

I continue to focus on Dragon.

"Tell me, closer, what are you really called?" I ask her.

"Hydra," she hisses. "You helped kill my sister Medusa, remember?"

For an instant, I uncloak my thoughts and imagine the sight of Medusa being run through with Mama number 3's sword. I vividly picture the way she screams and falls over dead. Hydra shakes all over and shrieks out loud. She sees my thoughts, so I picture her instead of Medusa complete with the sword through her midsection.

"It was my pleasure to kill her," I whisper.

Hydra screams even louder, and slaps me hard across the face.

"Look. At. Me!"

I detect just a hint of a smile cross Dragon's face. I stay focused on his dark brown eyes. Hydra starts to rant.

"You little worm!" she goes on. "We are heading down to the coast. The president made a special trip down here just for you. Do you want to know why he is really here? He wants to personally execute you! He likes to perform executions himself. He performs them like…this!"

Suddenly, I am in another place. I see myself again in the giant stadium, lying on a steel table with a man looming over me. The bright sun is at his back, and he is swinging his large, gleaming meat cleaver in an arc toward my exposed throat. A huge crowd cheers.

I struggle back out of the vision. I clear my head and concentrate on Dragon's eyes. He is impassive, like a rock.

"Yes," Hydra says smugly. "So you have seen the President in your visions. You've seen his favorite method of execution. He loves to see heads drop in the dirt! He can't wait to see your pretty little head drop!"

"So," I mutter, "I get it. You're a hypno-clairvoyant. You are a stupid freak! I thought all of the clairvoyants were outlawed by the New Republic centuries ago? How did they miss you and your stupid freak sister?"

"We only kill the ones who are not useful," Hydra answers with a harsh growl. "And you might have proved useful to us if I had been able to turn you. But you are as strongwilled as your mother was, and just as impossible!"

My jaw drops. I almost turn to look at her. She laughs, and her laugh sounds like rusty metal door hinges creaking in the middle of the night.

"Oh, you didn't know, did you, dear little girl?"

Her voice is so much like Medusa's. That sweet doctor voice that I heard in the white room is completely gone.

"I was the one who was in charge of your mother's reeducation. She had the gift, Chrissie. We wanted to turn her. But she refused to cooperate. She was too difficult and, I'm so sorry dear, we finally had to kill her."

So it is true. They killed my mother, all those years ago. Hydra is getting to me. I have to shake her off. But her voice contains a sadistic tone now.

"Your mother could have run, like your aunt," she continues. "But she didn't run, did she, Chrissie? Do you want to know why your mother didn't run?"

I quietly shake my head no. But in my heart, I know why my mother didn't run.

"Because of you, Chrissie," she hisses. "She didn't run because of you. You were the reason she stayed. She couldn't leave you behind. You caused her death!"

It's true. I think back. I picture my mother coming home from reeducation. She must have spent the day strapped to a table under a strobe light, a loudspeaker blaring:

"What is your name?"

"My name is Mary Wright."

"What do you want, Mary?"

"I want to be a productive, law-abiding citizen of the New Republic."

And all the while, Hydra's green bug eyes must have been staring her down.

Then she would come home with her blank stare, hug me, sit me down, and quietly brush my hair.

I start to cry as I remember, and Hydra laughs.

"Poor little baby!" she cackles. Her pure hatred for me shakes me out of my despair.

"What about Daniel?" I ask defiantly. "What have you done with my baby?"

"Ah," Hydra laughs. "Daniel is in good hands. We decided not to kill him! Tell me, what do you do with a wonderful, raw talent like Daniel? You seize it, Chrissie, and you turn it. You force it to serve you, and you use it as a weapon against your enemies. Daniel is a very, very powerful weapon!"

Hydra's doctor voice returns, with an extra helping of sweetness.

"Don't worry, dear," she soothes me. "Daniel will do extremely well in the New Republic."

Dragon watches me impassively. Hydra stands up and gestures to the other guards.

"Allow me to introduce your escorts by their real names," she says.

The giant who has guarded my cell door for so long, who has given me all of those injections, is a closer called Titan. I killed his brother, Goliath, in the woods. A woman removes her sunglasses, and her eyes are an impossible, insect yellow. Yellowjacket. Another woman rips a mask off her head, and her face is split unnaturally, one side jet black, the other side bone-white. Melinoe. They are the ones who leered at me through the little window of my prison cell door. They are all closers. All killers!

"And last of all, this is Dragon," she continues, gesturing to my guide. "A pure killer and the finest swordsman in the New Republic. Although Stingray might disagree with that. Dragon would love to take his sword and separate your head from your body!"

Dragon smiles at me and bows his head. He remains silent.

"Any one of us would love to kill you," Hydra exclaims with a hiss that sounds like Medusa's. "But you are our special gift to the president. So as you can see, dear girl, you are surrounded by the best. Don't even try to do anything foolish. We wouldn't want to disappoint the big man who holds the meat cleaver!"

Hydra sits down and jabs me hard in my ribs. As I gasp for air, I can see the barren land outside gradually sloping down toward a coastline. Soon, a ribbon of blue appears on the far horizon. The ocean.

As the transport nears the beach, which is destitute of any growth or buildings, except for a layer of scraggly bushes that lie just off the border of the sand, I spot hundreds of dark shapes floating far out in the water.

"The president's personal fleet," Hydra exclaims with obvious pride. "And look, his personal transport is approaching!"

I can see it. At first, it is just a tiny dark speck that lifts off the deck of an impossibly big ship; a ship positioned directly in the center of all of the other ships. Warplanes roar and circle above the transport as it turns and flies a few hundred feet above the ocean toward the beach.

By the time our transport slows down, the presidential transport has already touched down in the sand, just a few feet inland from the ocean surf. The crest of the president is emblazoned on the side of the gleaming black vehicle in bright gilt, and a man with shining white hair, wearing the golden presidential crest on his dark jacket, steps out of its hatch, along with at least two dozen bodyguards.

A sleek, black air-limo sweeps around us and parks a hundred feet down the beach. A door opens, and Stingray steps out. He literally gleams in the sun. He wears a shiny golden bodysuit, and his tan face and mirrored sunglasses are plainly visible to me even though we are still a distance away. As we draw near, and our prison transport lands gently on the beach, I can see that Stingray is wearing his long sword at his side. For ceremonial purposes like Dragon? I wonder.

Then I look back at Dragon, who has seen Stingray's sword. And Dragon is smiling.

CHAPTER FORTY

It happens so fast. The rear hatch of our transport drops with a sick thud directly into the sand, and bright sunlight floods in, blinding me momentarily. The closers jump up from their seats and file outside. Hydra leads me out, and Dragon follows. As we approach the hatch, she turns around to face me one last time and roars, "LOOK AT ME!"

She catches me off guard, and I look up at her face. But I can't see her eyes. I am still blinded by the sunlight. At the same time, Dragon nudges me from behind and presses two objects into my hands. As I feel them, I recognize them at once. Wristbands! Armshields! I push them over my hands while Hydra turns away from me in a huff and leads me out on to the beach.

The other closers stand facing the presidential transport, which is parked a short distance from us. The president and his entourage are waiting for us. The president is smiling.

"Hydra!" Dragon suddenly calls out.

She turns to face him, and his long sword flashes out of its scabbard, sweeps through the air, and her head is rolling in the sand. Instinctively, I clap my wrists together and shield up.

The other closers stare in astonishment at Hydra's lifeless head. Dragon takes quick advantage of their hesitation and tosses his short sword to me.

"Defend yourself!" he shouts and then leaps and runs Titan through with his long sword. As the giant falls forward,

Yellowjacket turns around to face me. She looks at the sword in my hand and laughs.

"My sting is worse than the sting of your sword, little girl," she chides as we circle each other. She is a small woman, with bundled dark brown hair that accentuates her unnaturally yellow eyes. Where is her stinger, I wonder? Then she shows me as she pulls a long, dartlike hairpin out of her hair. Dragon's sword is no good to me, I realize, and I toss it aside.

You are the weapon! I hear Angel's voice in my mind.

Yellowjacket grins as she watches the short sword skip across the sand. Then she lunges and throws three hairpins at me in rapid succession. I deflect them and their obvious poison tips with my arm shields. And then she is on me.

She does not lack for close-in fighting skills, and I am still pretty weak and not yet fully practiced. But Angel taught me well. And Yellowjacket is not Angel! With a flurry of rapid strikes, I surprise her and make her back up. Before she can jump back at me, Dragon's long sword flashes past me and finishes her off.

I look at Dragon, and he is breathing hard, looking back at me. Dead closers lie scattered in the sand all around us. He spots his short sword where I threw it and, glancing back at me with a huffy expression, picks it up and shoves it back in his belt.

I look up and down the beach. A thousand soldiers have appeared and are charging at us from both directions. They will be on us in minutes.

So I whisper to myself, "This is where it ends. This is where we die." There are just way too many of them. I think about it. I am not afraid to die. Dragon is at my side, and between us, we will fight as hard as we can before they finish us off.

"With his back against the rock wall, he killed a thousand warriors with the jawbone of a donkey," Samson told me of his namesake.

Dragon reads my thoughts, and he smiles and nods to me in agreement.

"Fight hard, jackrabbit!" he says as the slaughter approaches.

I glance back at the presidential transport and see that the president and his bodyguards are scurrying back up into the transport hatch. As the hatch closes, Stingray turns away from it and walks toward us.

At the same time, the beach starts to explode in a hundred different places. The black ships at sea are shooting at us. The concussions nearly knock me off my feet. But wait, the explosions are going off in the middle of the charging soldiers. The black ships out at sea are targeting them!

"Look up, Chrissie!" Dragon yells at me above the noise. I look up and gasp. The sky above us, as far up into the heavens as I can see, is filled with gigantic, glowing, flying discs. More discs than I can count. There has to be a hundred of them, at least, and they all outshine the midmorning sun.

"The starships of the Free Nations!" Dragon yells. "We have a chance after all!"

He reaches out to me and traces the sign of the cross on my forehead.

"Be brave, Chrissie! Now hurry. Run to Stingray's limo. Daniel is strapped down in the backseat!"

Daniel! I turn, and as I run to the limo, Stingray casually walks up. He grins at me but he lets me pass right by him. He turns his head and locks his eyes on Dragon. I hear some of his words as I pass.

"I always knew it had to be you," he says to Dragon. "And now, I'm going to kill you."

They face each other and draw their swords. The blades gleam in the morning sun.

"You always wanted to know who is better," Dragon answers fiercely, holding his sword high above his head. "Time to find out!"

Then I am out of earshot. I glance back once as I run to the limo. The scene is amazing. The presidential transport has lifted off and is floating a couple of hundred feet in the air. A missile has hit it in its side, and it is listing poorly to the left with black smoke pouring out of a gaping hole. Men are falling to their deaths out of that hole. Stingray and Dragon are engaged in a vicious sword fight to the death. Blood already covers Stingray's left side. The soldiers charging us from up and down the beach are halfway here, and the sand around them continues to heave up from explosions. Their bodies are flying hundreds of feet into the air.

I reach the black limo and throw open the rear door. I expect to see Jason, maybe holding and protecting our baby, but I only see a cage. Inside of it, Daniel sits on a pad, looking up at me with his big blue eyes.

"Mama!" he cries out. He has grown. He has grown a lot! I tear at the cage hatch like a madwoman. I am overcome with rage. My child, caged like an animal! I can't get it open. Frantically, I try and try. Then I search for something in the limo to pry it open with. I can hear the screams of the soldiers as they close in on me. The explosions in the sand are also closing in. I have no time!

Then I spot something on the front seat. A laser knife! I grab it, and in an instant, the cage hatch is open and I have Daniel in my arms.

"It will be okay, baby," I assure him and kiss him as I pull him out of the car. "It will be okay."

But now, the battlefield surrounds me.

I see three laser cannon shots hit the presidential transport simultaneously as it limps out to sea, and it explodes into a thousand glowing pieces. Thousands of soldiers are less than a hundred feet away now, running at me and screaming at the top of their lungs. Dragon makes a sweeping, diagonal cut across Stingray's chest with his long sword, and Stingray drops to his knees. Then they both disappear in the blinding flash of an explosion followed by thick black smoke.

I turn to face the soldiers. Daniel squeezes my neck as they approach. It is over.

Then when they are just about to engulf me, lasers cut through their entire front ranks, and they go down in the sand. Who is shooting at them?

I turn around just in time to see two transport-sized silver discs uncloak on the beach, almost directly on the same spot where the presidential transport landed. Their hatches open, and dozens of men with laser rifles pour out, forming a line. Big turret guns flash thick laser beams from the top of the transport discs, mowing down every wave of soldiers as they approach. Then I spot someone tall and lanky standing in the front of the men, wearing the same silver uniform that they wear. He is a black man, and he is frantically waving at me.

Moses!

I run toward him, and vaguely I am aware of a large explosion that hits directly behind me. It nearly knocks me off my feet. I turn around and watch as Stingray's limo flips high into the air. I gather myself and struggle forward with Daniel crying in my arms. Then I am in Moses's arms.

"It's good to see you, child!" he yells above the noise as he hugs me and kisses me on the cheek. Then he hugs Daniel.

"Climb aboard!" he shouts.

"Dragon!" I yell back.

"Don't worry!" Moses yells. "If he is still alive, we'll find him!"

Helping hands pull Daniel and me aboard the disc. A dozen silver-uniformed men guard us, but Moses stands tall on the beach, his hands shielding his eyes looking for Dragon.

The hatch of the disc closes, and I feel a sweeping rush in my chest as it silently lifts off and dashes straight up into the sky.

CHAPTER FORTY-ONE

I am standing next to Captain Perez on the bridge of the FNS *Indomitable*, a floating disc-shaped starship the size of a city. He is a tall, handsome man in his midforties, with a full black beard and gleaming dark brown eyes. I have just met him, yet already I can sense that he radiates kindness and warmth. He wears the same one-piece silver uniform that everyone aboard the ship wears. The difference is the gold insignia of a captain displayed on his shoulders. He is speaking out loud to a microphone that I can't see.

"What's your position, away boat number 2?" he asks.

"Two thousands meters out and closing," a deep voice answers on the radio.

"Is Moses aboard?" Captain Perez asks.

"Yes, sir," the man on the away boat answers. "And we have Dragon. We need immediate medical attention for Dragon and for three other casualties."

"Alert sick bay," Captain Perez orders an officer standing nearby.

The bridge of the FNS *Indomitable* is built completely out of a strange material that shows up as silver on the outside, but is almost completely transparent from within. I feel mild vertigo setting in as I look below my feet and can see the vast black New Republic fleet of ships floating in the ocean far below us. Every one of the ships below is shooting up toward us with their laser cannons with no effect. The Free Nations fleet seems to utilize some kind of protective force field. Above us, layer after layer of gigantic Free Nation starships float as far up into the sky as I can focus. Not a single one of them is shooting back at the president's fleet. Daniel, resting in my arms, points at every ship that he can see.

"Look at that one, Mama!" he says to me. "Look at that one... look at that!"

I hug him again and again. I am amazed at how well he can talk. Captain Perez smiles at him and gently squeezes his arm.

"A future starship captain, no doubt," the captain says. Then he spots something.

"There, Chrissie!" he says and points to the glowing silver disc that is rushing up toward us.

"Prepare to bring aboard away boat number 2," he orders.

"Aye, aye, Captain," a voice answers. Daniel looks around to find out who is talking.

"How do these giant ships stay in the air like this?" I ask the captain. I have seen air cars, jets, and low-altitude transports in the New Republic, but never round, floating cities!

"Welcome to the real world, Chrissie," Captain Perez answers.

A hatch slides open, and Moses walks in, grinning from ear to ear.

"Chrissie!" he shouts as he runs across the bridge deck. He grabs me in his big arms and hugs both me and Daniel at the same time.

"The Lord be praised, I am so proud of you!" he exclaims, and I see tears streaming down his face and soaking his beard. I can't hold back my tears either.

"I thought you were dead!" I whisper, remembering the way Stingray tossed his limp body into the trunk of the police cruiser so long ago.

"I'm not that easy to kill, child!" he tells me. Captain Perez gently interrupts us.

"We have company," he says and points at what looks like a dark cloud growing on the horizon.

"Incoming high-altitude warbirds," the officer on the deck announces. "What are your orders, sir?"

Captain Perez looks at Moses and me then down at Daniel, who is hugging my neck.

"Too many people have died today," he tells the officer. "Open our hail frequency to all ships."

"Aye, aye, sir," the officer answers. "Hail frequency, stand by!"

"This is Captain Perez of the FNS *Indomitable*," the captain announces. "All ships, stand by!"

He turns and smiles at me.

"Watch carefully, Chrissie," he says to me. "You are going to like this."

"All ships," he continues on the hail frequency, "you are free to depart! Take up your positions in earth orbit."

Daniel and I watch as the huge glowing discs that surround us shoot straight up into the sky one by one until they are tiny dots that disappear from sight. Daniel points and grabs like he is trying to catch each one of them, and says 'Ooh!' as they vanish.

"Set course one one zero, full speed, engage!" Captain Perez orders.

"One one zero, full speed engaged, sir!"

I watch as the ocean below us starts to move, but I hear no sound and feel no motion. It is as if the world is moving away from us. Then the black presidential fleet and the warplanes are gone, left far behind us.

"What about Dragon?" I ask Moses. I remember the way he and Stingray disappeared in the explosion on the beach.

Moses shakes his head.

"He is down in sick bay," he tells me gently. "He is in pretty bad shape, Chrissie!"

"He saved my life."

"I know, child," Moses says. "I know."

"And Stingray?" I ask.

"We found Dragon lying across the top of Stingray," Moses says. "Stingray was cut through the middle and burned badly. He wasn't breathing, Chrissie, but we had no time. He looked dead to me, but like I said, we had no time. We left his body on the beach."

I nod my head. I saw so many bodies lying dead on the beach. Such a terrible sight.

"Moses, I want to see Dragon now."

Moses looks at me with big, sad eyes for a moment.

"Okay, Chrissie," he says quietly. "You go see him. You're not the same little girl I left on the beach so long ago, are you?"

I shake my head no. Moses reaches out.

"Do you want me to watch Daniel for you," he asks. I hold Daniel tightly to me.

"No, but thank you, Moses," I answer. "I'm never letting Daniel out of my sight again."

An officer leads me down to the medical area. Dragon lies unconscious in a room. His limp body floats in midair by some means that I can't detect, engulfed in a soft, warm light. Nurses apply wet membranes to the bad burns on his face and arms. Some of the silk fabric of his outfit has melted directly into his skin, and I cringe as I see it. Maybe it wasn't such a good idea to bring Daniel down here; but when I look at Daniel's face, I see that he is worrying over Dragon like he is a dear, old friend. And he is whispering to him.

"Dwagon," he whispers. "Dwagon, wake up...wake up!"

I feel the light that surrounds Dragon's body as we reach his side. It seems to have a healing power, and I feel the pain of my own injuries easing. I feel my body relaxing.

Dragon stirs and opens his eyes. He smiles weakly at Daniel and then at me. Slowly, his hand reaches out, and I take it in mine and hold it gently. With my other hand, I reach out, and trace the sign of the cross on his forehead. Daniel reaches out with his deformed right arm and copies me. A nurse brings me a chair, and I sit down with Daniel. Together, we reach out and hold Dragon's hand again.

Later, a doctor approaches me and looks at Daniel.

"May I examine him?" he asks me. He carefully examines Daniel's deformed hand and gently works the joints back and forth. Then he takes Daniel's footless leg and examines it.

The doctor playfully pinches Daniel on the chin and winks at me.

"We can fix all of this," he tells me.

CHAPTER FORTY-TWO

Mercifully, I have slept a dreamless sleep. Daniel is nestled next to me in a warm bed when Moses knocks and cracks open the door to our berth.

"Rise and shine, sleepyheads!" Moses announces cheerfully. I yawn and stretch, and Daniel stretches too.

"How long did we sleep?" I ask Moses.

"Ten hours, Chrissie," Moses tells me. "Both of you were tired."

I was devastatingly tired. I sit up and feel totally refreshed. It is the best night of sleep I have had in I don't know how long. Yesterday, after looking at Daniel, the doctor shined a warm light in my eyes that would, he promised me, completely counter the effects of the powerful drugs that the giant injected me with in prison. It seems to have worked. My mind is crystal clear.

"Last night," Moses continues, "we positioned ourselves at our destination. We are sitting just off the coast of Africa."

I studied Africa in school. It is supposed to be a dark continent overrun by wicked barbarians. I tell that to Moses who laughs heartily.

"Well, I happen to be one of those barbarians!" he tells me. "The captain requests that you and Daniel join us for breakfast, and then we will proceed to Port Liberty, where a grand reception has been planned for you."

"Thank you, Moses."

"Oh, and Chrissie," Moses adds before he closes the door. "Check out your closet as you are getting ready. Breakfast is at 0800, thirty minutes."

I find a beautiful blue jumpsuit hanging in the closet. It fits perfectly and goes well with my sneakers. A little silver uniform hangs next to it, with "Admiral Daniel" embroidered in gold on the breast pocket. I hold it up for Daniel, and he laughs out in delight.

Soaps, bath oils, and makeup line the bathroom countertop. I study myself in the mirror as I wash my face. A gaunt, hard-eyed warrior stares back at me. I am not certain that the makeup can do anything for her.

Breakfast is a semiformal, sumptuous affair. Captain Perez and his officers spare no expense in making Daniel and me feel as welcome as a guest could possibly feel. The food is outrageously wonderful. I cannot remember the last time I saw such a rich bounty of eggs and bacon, sausages, biscuits and gravy, every fruit imaginable. The coffee is so rich, it makes me dizzy. When was the last time I even tasted coffee?

After Moses leads us in a prayer of thanks for our safe return, we dig in. As I eat, I marvel at the simple but elegant beauty of the ship. I see no hint of any technology I can recognize. Only the soft glow of warm light that seems to infuse everything around me and...a quietness. The breakfast table glows, the walls glow. I see no viewers of any kind, no devices or gadgets. Everything inside the ship seems to blend in seamlessly with everything else.

"Do you like our ship?" Captain Perez asks me when he notices the puzzled look on my face.

"I love it," I answer, "but I don't understand it. None of it makes any sense to me. In such a short time, you have built things I can't even imagine. You have cities on the moon, on Mars."

"Even on other worlds," Captain Perez says.

"Chrissie, there is so much for you to learn," Moses adds.

I shake my head.

"But it hasn't been that long since the wars," I argue. "Less than two hundred years. I am seeing things that I can't even comprehend."

I grew up believing that the New Republic possessed the highest technology ever known to man. What I see here has to be thousands of years more advanced. How did it happen?

"It happened because of people like you, Chrissie," Moses answers. "Because of brave runners who defied the law of the Parlors and brought their babies out to safety.

"Three wonderful minds emerged in the past century and a half. First, there was Joseph Damir, the man who discovered the presence of soft energy. It is the energy of the universe, the energy that powers this great starship and the cities of the Free Nations. It is the soft glow that you see now on this ship, Chrissie. It is the energy that heals and sustains life for us. Right now, it is at work, healing Dragon."

"Yes," Captain Perez nods in agreement. "And fifty years later, Rebecca Swift, a student of Dr. Damir, a vastly brilliant student, unraveled the mystery of the 'tunnels in space' that have allowed us to journey to other worlds, to other galaxies. She developed the principle of 'resonant communication' that allows us to communicate with the wonderful people of those worlds. And thirty years later, the great scientist Michael Marshall realized that gravity is a field that can be completely countered, and when he designed our cities and these great ships, Chrissie, we were simply off to the races."

"Three incredible minds," Moses says, "who were, at first, three unborn babies scheduled for termination in the Parlors. You see, dear, we still listen to God. He answered our prayers and revealed to us the need to create a system of guides to help these runners safely escape, to give them and their unborn innocents a chance to survive."

"And thrive!" Captain Perez exclaims. "We have sacrificed so much. So many of our wonderful guides paid the ultimate price and died at the hands of closers. But their sacrifices were not in vain! God rewards those who strive to protect the innocents who cannot yet protect themselves!"

"You will see," Moses smiles, with a sparkle in his eyes.

"And now," Captain Perez says, "we are eager for our brothers and sisters in the New Republic to finally join us, to learn what we have learned. But the New Republic isolates itself with nuclear weapons that no other world in God's universe would even contemplate possessing."

"And that is the problem," Moses explains. "The New Republic is a terrible danger not only to themselves, but even to us. They have spies, and they are slowly but surely catching up to us. And if they can fully grasp our advances in technology and put those advances to use, all will be lost. The New Republic does not hesitate to use any weapon in its possession."

I nod. *Tell me about it,* I say to myself. I remember the blinding white flashes of the nukes in the jungle. And villages of innocent people perished in those flashes.

"It is our hope that the dictatorship of the New Republic will crumble from within," Moses continues, looking directly at Daniel. "And that its people will decide to join us."

"Well," I say between bites of sausage, "I saw you blow up the president's transport, so he is dead. That's a start, isn't it?"

Captain Perez smiles and shakes his head.

"No, Chrissie. The president's transport was destroyed by his own ships. It was part of a coup that we have been watching develop."

I stop eating and look across the table at Moses.

"That's right, child," he concurs with Captain Perez. "Promotion by assassination. Today, a new president will seize control of the New Republic. He arranged to have the old president killed. Those were his ships that destroyed the president's transport. And those were his troops on the beach. They were not only attacking you, Chrissie. They were there to make sure that the old president did not survive the morning."

"And to make it look like we were to blame," Captain Perez adds.

"And it is no coincidence that this all happened when it did," Moses continues. "You see, Daniel is undoubtedly the greatest mind of this present age. His birth has been prophesized for over a hundred years, and now, he is here. He is the prophet, Chrissie. We know this to be true, and they also know it. When the president of the New Republic realized who Daniel was, he ordered Daniel's death at all costs, and your death as well. Daniel brought the voice, and the voice terrified the president. But in the prison, the clairvoyants studied Daniel. They learned about him and what he can do. He could be useful, they reported. But the president would not budge. He still ordered death! Others, however, disagreed.

"Someone high up in the government realized what a powerful weapon Daniel could be against us. He hatched a plot, organized a coup, and killed the president. Now he is president, and he is the most ruthless man ever to have held the position. He plans to capture Daniel, to turn him and use him against us."

It makes sense. They all heard the voice, and it scared them. Then they wanted to learn how to use it. I shudder as I picture Daniel in prison in the hands of hypno-clairvoyants like Hydra and Medusa. Then I really shudder when I realize that they did have him, while I was strapped to a cold steel table under a strobe light. What did they do to him?

"What about me?" I ask Moses. "Does the new president plan to take me back, too?"

A sad look crosses Moses's face, and he shakes his head.

"No, Chrissie," he answers. "He very much wants to kill you."

That figures, I think, *but he will have to take a number and wait in line.* I turn back to Captain Perez.

"I have seen the power of your fleet," I say him. "Why don't you just sweep in and take control of the New Republic?"

"It would result in a terrible cost in lives," Captain Perez explains to me. "Because of their hoard of nuclear weapons, which would ultimately kill all of their people. Your people, Chrissie!"

"God had a better idea," Moses says. "He decided to send a powerful messenger instead. He decided to send a messenger who can convince the people of the New Republic that there is a better world that awaits them."

With that said, Moses, Captain Perez, and every officer seated at the breakfast table look at Daniel, who is busy playing with his cereal. I nod in understanding. Daniel the prophet, and with him, the voice.

After breakfast, I stand on the bridge of the FNS *Indomitable*, staring at a view that I can't believe. An ethereal glow fills the entire sky above the coast. In the glow, I can make out structures that seem to float in the air. Far below it all, a beautiful white coastline gives way to vast, manicured gardens of flowers, plants, and orchards. The garden is dotted here and there with a few tiny structures, but nothing intrusive to the beauty of the grounds.

"Most of us live in the sky," Moses explains to me. "And we tend to our gardens below. And like I promised, Chrissie, there is peace here, no distractions. We lead quiet lives. We like to meditate, pray, and think."

Daniel points to everything and says, "Ooh, Mama, ooh!"

I feel exactly the same way. It is like sensory overload, looking at such a vast, magnificent sight.

"Why would you ever even want to leave a place like this?" I ask Moses.

He looks down at me, and a tear drops down his cheek.

"For people like you, Chrissie," he answers quietly. "I will always go back into that terrible wilderness to help people like you."

An hour later, I am back with Daniel at Dragon's side, holding his hand. His eyes flutter open, and he smiles at me.

"Dwagon," Daniels says. Moses pops his head in.

"The away boat departs in thirty minutes, Chrissie," he informs me.

I look down at Dragon. He squeezes my hand and smiles.

"I will see you in the gardens," he whispers weakly.

After long thank-yous and good-byes on the bridge of the FNS *Indomitable* and a huge hug from Captain Perez, we are away.

As I sit next to Moses on the away boat, he explains the government of the Free Nations.

Every nation is governed by a Council of Twelve," he tells me. "Twelve citizens who are chosen by lottery to serve for a four-year term. Every two years, six of those council members rotate back out to their regular lives, so there are always fresh faces serving. And citizens of the Free Nations feel that it is a great honor to serve. I myself once served on a council, when I was still a young man."

"You aren't that old!" I tease him with a smile. "Still, I don't see how a country can have so many leaders instead of just one. How do they ever agree on anything?"

"That's the beauty of our system, Chrissie," Moses explains. "Sometimes they don't. But because they are selected by pure chance, and because they only serve for four years, they as individuals do not try to enrich themselves or cling to power. They serve, and then they go back home. We have learned that power is such a corruptive force, it can't be trusted in the hands of only one man, or even a few men, for very long. Power takes hold. It takes over and eventually destroys anyone who tries to possess it. Even if they start out with good intentions. And then everyone suffers. And we may not yet have the best system of government here in the Free Nations, but it works for us."

Moses glances down at the silver wristbands I still wear on my wrists.

"You won't need those where we are going, Chrissie," he assures me.

I smile and nod. But I am not ready to give them up yet.

CHAPTER FORTY-THREE

A huge crowd waits for us on the beach. Thousands of them stand in the white sand dressed in bright, colorful garments. I look up and down the beach, and the crowd fills the beach as far as I can see in either direction. They wave and cheer as I step out of the hatch of the away boat with Daniel in my arms. Then an even bigger surprise!

Standing at the very front of the crowd are the familiar faces I have missed for so long. Lucia, dressed in a beautiful white lace dress and holding a bundle of colorful flowers, stands next to Padre, who wears a black suit with a white collar that circles around his neck. Next to them, I see Papa Cezar and Mama number 5, Papa Rodrigo and Mamas number 2 and number 14—all of them crying, smiling, calling to me, and frantically waving.

The crowd roars as Lucia runs to me, hands Daniel her flowers, hugs me, and kisses me on the cheek. She starts to cry as I hug her back. Then she slaps my arm.

"Don't ever leave me behind again, big sister!" she cries. Then she hugs me even harder.

"I won't, little sister," I shout to her above the noise of the crowd. "Never, I promise."

"How did you make it out?" I ask Padre as he steps forward and hugs me.

"Moses found us, Chrissie," Padre tells me. "He saved us all!"

"How long has it been, Padre?" I ask him. "How long did Stingray have me?"

"One year, Chrissie," Padre tells me. "You and Daniel were in that prison for one year."

A year! A full year living in a continuous fog that could have lasted for ten years or ten days. That is how little of time or reality I grasped in that horrible place. No wonder Daniel is so big now. No wonder he is walking and talking. Then the horrible thought settles in. Daniel was with those monsters for a full year. With Stingray and Hydra! I hold him tighter and look down at him. But he only beams up at me with his big blue eyes.

And Jason. Is he still sitting in his prison cell? Will I ever know?

The crowd parts, and Moses leads us through the throngs of smiling people, up several rows of white marble steps and into the richest gardens I have ever seen in my life. A stone pathway winds through a maze of lush plants, flowers, and trees.

"We are almost there, Chrissie," Moses tells me, and shortly we reach the entrance to a huge white marble amphitheater that is situated in the middle of the gardens. It has been designed to hold several hundred thousand people and is filled up completely with the cheering people of Port Liberty. We walk down the center steps of the amphitheater and climb the steps to its large stage where I see twelve men and women waiting for us in flowing white robes.

"The Council of Twelve," Moses explains to me as we descend toward them, "of Africa."

Everyone wants to touch us. Everyone wants to hug us. It is overwhelming.

The members of the Council of Twelve greet us warmly as we reach the stage. I look at them, and I am astonished to see how young some of them are. There is an Asian man, a black woman, a girl not much older than me with long, jet-black hair, brown eyes, and brown skin. One elderly man is white with silver hair and a long white beard. They are a very diverse group, and they all smile at Daniel and me with genuine warmth.

The youngest girl on the council raises her hands and hushes the huge crowd that fills every space in the amphitheater.

"It is the day that we have long awaited," the girl announces to the crowd. "Chrissie and Daniel are with us now!"

She turns to me, reaches out, and takes my hand.

"Chrissie, we, the people of the Free Nations, have watched you, we have followed your journey. We honor your bravery, and we celebrate your decision to run to save Daniel. In the Free Nations, every life is celebrated, every life is precious!"

The crowd roars in agreement, and after a moment, she raises her hands again to quiet them.

"And because of your courage," she continues, "because of your proven valor in your battle against the forces of evil, we, the Council of Twelve of the Africa, in accordance with God's will and in accordance with all of the Councils of Twelve everywhere, extend our hand in welcome to you and to Daniel and offer you full citizenship among us."

I can't help it. Tears flow out of my eyes as she takes my hand in hers. Daniel sees my tears and kisses me on the cheek. It has been a hard journey. So many friends have been lost along the way.

As I accept the offer of the Council of Twelve, the crowd goes wild. Flower petals float down on us like snow, and bundle after bundle of flowers are thrown to the stage. Padre leans over and whispers to me.

"We hacked into the networks of the New Republic, Chrissie," he whispers. "So smile and show them that you are alive and well. This is being broadcast live on every board and viewer they own."

Then Padre steps forward and quiets the crowd once more.

"Let us pray," he says out loud. And thousands upon thousands pray together for me, for Daniel, for the New Republic.

Then Moses steps forward and, for the next half hour, retells the entire story of my journey. His words help me remember parts that I had forgotten when I was trapped in the fog of the prison for so long.

Then there are more hugs, and finally Daniel and I wave to the multitudes.

"Thank you!" I say to the cheering crowd. "Thank you all!"

And two or three dozen children run up on to the stage, engulf Daniel and me, and shower us with hugs, kisses, and small gifts."

"Yes, behold!" the youngest girl of the council shouts out above the cheers of the crowd. "These are the children of runners. These are the children who escaped the Parlors!"

She turns and looks up away from the crowd. She is looking, I realize, at the people of the New Republic.

"Your children!" she shouts out with a raised fist, and there is a sharpness in her tone. "Alive and well! And I am one of them!"

I can imagine the millions in the New Republic who are watching this moment unfold. The shock on my stepmother's face! The shock on the faces of millions. And my father?

Then after I have hugged every child, after Daniel has been kissed a hundred times, it is time to leave. The people of the Free Nations reach out to touch us as we climb the steps that lead back out to the gardens.

As we reenter the plush landscape of flowers and trees and start down a stone pathway, a mango drops at my feet. I reach down with Daniel in my arms, pick up the fruit, and then look up into the trees. There, sitting on a thick limb, is Howler, grinning down at me.

"Monkey!" Daniel calls out, pointing up at Howler. "Good monkey!"

I laugh as Howler howls loudly and swings above us from limb to limb.

"We have been invited to join the Council of Twelve for lunch, Chrissie," Moses tells me as we walk.

"Where?" I ask.

Both Moses and Lucia laugh, and Lucia points straight up at the ethereal glow in the sky above. Huge structures float in the air above us that I can barely see in the warm light.

"Up there!" she answers.

Festivities continue throughout the day in our honor. Daniel and I are showered with too many gifts to count from all corners of the Free Nations. It is so good to see everyone again, but I wish that Dragon could be here too. He deserves so much of the credit for my escape, but he is still on the ship, being cared for. It will be several days, Moses tells me, before he is strong enough to join us.

And that will be in another city, Moses adds.

"What city is that?" I ask.

"The City of Gardens," Moses tells me.

There is a city with more gardens than this one?

"The City of Gardens is a very special place, Chrissie." That is all Moses will say.

That night, Lucia shares her room with Daniel and me in a quaint thatched hut owned by Moses that sits just above the beach in a thick grove of fruit trees.

"I like to listen to the sound of the ocean surf," Moses explains. "And I like the feel of sand in my toes."

I love his home. It is filled with warmth and, of course, a healing glow. Here, with Moses, I have never felt safer.

Lucia tells me about her life here. She tells me about school.

"Teachers teach us how to knit," she says excitedly, "and how to garden. We talk about everything, Chrissie. We don't have to sit and read from viewers."

It is good to settle into a big warm bed that has more than enough room for all three of us. Lucia laughs out with delight when Daniel buries his head in the sheets and plays peekaboo with her. That night, I sleep another deep, dreamless sleep.

The following morning, just after breakfast, Padre drops by with a request.

"Chrissie," he asks, "would you take a walk with me on the beach?"

Moses, who has been sitting cross-legged in a corner, deep in meditation, nods his approval with closed eyes. Lucia promises me that she will take me to her school as soon as we return. She wants to show me off to her friends.

The beach is deserted at this early hour with the sun not fully up yet. The surf rolls gently ashore, and sea gulls drift lazily through a gentle breeze blowing from the ocean. Padre looks out across the blue water and then turns to talk to me.

"Chrissie," he says, "I know that there is something we need to talk about. I can still see how sad you are."

"Yes," I answer. Padre wears his straw hat, his black suit, and his round, white collar. Daniel and I, by contrast, still wear the outfits we were given aboard the FNS *Indomitable*.

"We had to kill so many people," I say. "Is that what God wanted?"

Padre quietly stares at the sand as we walk.

"So many times I have asked myself that question," he finally answers. "And then I realize, do you ignore evil and let it destroy everything? Or do you battle against it? We must choose, Chrissie. You chose to save Daniel. You and I both chose to battle evil. I believe that we made the right choice."

We are a few hundred feet down the beach from Moses's house, walking around a big, twenty-foot-high boulder that sits in the sand and obscures our view farther up the beach. Daniel drags his hand along the rock's smooth surface as we circle around it.

"I think I understand," I say. "But it doesn't make me feel any better."

"Nor should it," Padre agrees. "And now, it is time to teach you what this is truly all about."

He reaches out to me and traces the sign of the cross on my forehead.

"It is time to teach you everything, Chrissie."

Just then, I catch a bright blue-white flash of light out of the corner of my eye. Daniel screams, and I see Padre drop to his knees, his hands clutching his chest. He has been shot.

CHAPTER FORTY-FOUR

For the last two days, I have felt like I am in the safest place on earth. That illusion is now completely shattered as I drop like a rock with Daniel into the sand and search for the shooter. I hold Daniel in one arm, slide quickly over to Padre, and pull him down next to me. He is in bad shape. He clutches his chest and gasps for breath.

I keep searching for the shooter, but no one is in sight.

"I'll get help," I whisper to Padre.

"Chrissie!" Padre says, grimacing. "It is too late. Too late!"

He is pointing at something, and I look up to see Stingray standing in the sand twenty feet away, grinning at me with a blaster in his hand, his back to the ocean. He has appeared out of nowhere, and Jason is with him, metal collar around his neck and chained to a stake in the sand. Jason is beaten black and blue and sits next to the stake, hugging his knees to his chest.

Stingray is a sight! He still wears the golden jumpsuit that I last saw him in, but it is stained with dried blood down the front of it and ripped open where Dragon ran his sword across. I can see the dark line where the flesh of his chest and stomach has been surgically fused back together.

His body looks horrendous, but his face! He is badly burned and his face has not healed. Much of the skin on his cheeks is already peeling off to reveal the raw flesh underneath. The burns extend up under his sunglasses, which reflect the light of the rising sun.

Quickly, I tell Daniel to go hide under the big rock we just passed. As he crawls away, I stand up to face Stingray.

"That was really a moving performance in the amphitheater yesterday!" he says with a grimace. "Do you have any idea how much trouble you are for me, dear girl?"

"How did you get here?" I ask as I face him.

Stingray winces in pain as he tries to grin.

"A really fast boat! And Moses isn't the only master of hiding in plain sight."

Stingray glances down at the blaster in his hand and tosses it away in the sand.

"Never liked blasters," he says.

Slowly, I inch toward him. I raise my arms and click my silver wristbands together. The arm shields deploy and cover my hands and arms up to my elbows. Stingray shakes his head.

"I had a feeling that this wouldn't be easy," he says. He raises his arms and snaps his fingers. His shields are nearly identical to mine.

"We don't have to do this, Chrissie," Stingray says as we circle each other.

"Yes we do," I mutter as I size him up. I rush in.

Stingray is inhumanly fast. He blocks my strikes and knocks me down hard into the sand. Even through my shields, his arms feel like steel rods. I roll backwards, jump to my feet, and attack again. This time, I am more effective, and I can see that he is really hurting. Several of my strikes get through to his midsection, and he steps back.

He is breathing hard and hugging his chest with his right arm.

"I won't kill you, Chrissie," he says as he tries to catch his breath. "I don't want to hurt you. I just want to take you and Daniel back. That's all."

That's all, all right! I rush in again with a rapid flurry of strikes and blocks, and Stingray is not quite as fast as he was before. I watch for it and it happens. He walks right into my trap. It is the move that Angel taught me, and as Stingray twists, I have him in the neck lock—the one that can kill him.

Then, you kill him! I hear Angel telling me. I have to get this right; it's my only chance.

Stingray answers with superhuman strength, flips me over his shoulder, and I am down again on my back in the sand. He looks down at me and laughs, but it is a quiet, almost sad laugh.

"A trick like that only works once," he says as he wraps his arm around his midsection again. I climb back to my feet and he stops grinning.

"Don't make me kill you, Chrissie!" he warns.

I have done my best against him. He is hurt bad, but I can't beat him. I know I can't; he is just too good. He is going to kill me, but maybe I can buy some time for Daniel. Maybe someone will come. Maybe.

I hunch down, ready to spring at him again. But something stops me.

Stingray is not looking at me anymore. He is looking behind me.

I slowly step to the side so that I can still watch him and see what has captured his attention.

There in the sand is Daniel, standing and holding someone's hand. Someone I recognize. It is the shining man from my vision who waved at me in that field of flowers when I sat at the table with my mother. When they all told me that I had to go back. Again, he shines so brightly, I can hardly make out his features. But I can see that he is a tall, rugged man.

Stingray continues to stare at the man and at Daniel, and he quizzically cocks his head to the side. He looks perplexed.

That is when the shining figure speaks and, immediately, I recognize him. He is the *voice*!

"Come back to us, Joshua," the shining figure says. "It is time to come back."

Stingray drops his arms to his sides, snaps his fingers, and unshields. He shakes his head. He looks sad.

"I can't come back," he tells the shining man. "I have done terrible things. I have killed too many people. It is too late for me."

"It is never too late, son," the voice of the shining figure says to him. "Never too late."

Stingray shakes his head again, looks up at me, and smiles. It is not his wicked, crooked grin. It is just a sad smile. The shining figure slowly fades away.

"Chrissie," he says quietly. "I've never told you how much you remind me of my mother."

Then suddenly, he screams out and drops to his knees. The white hot point of a laser knife is protruding from his chest. Jason stands behind him, holding the handle of the knife! He lets Stingray drop to the sand and continues to twist the knife until Stingray falls over on his side and stops breathing.

Jason jumps to his feet, runs to me, and hugs me.

"Chrissie, are you okay?" he asks as he looks into my eyes. I can't speak yet, so I shake my head yes.

Then he rears back and hits me in the face as hard as he can with his fist. Everything goes pitch black.

CHAPTER FORTY-FIVE

"Chrissie, Chrissie, give me your answer true…"

I am in horrible pain. Jason is straddling me, pinning me down in the hot sand, and singing.

"I'm half dizzy, all for the love of you…"

He is using his laser knife, carving something into my forehead. My vision is blurred, but even through blurry eyes, I can see the feral gleam in his eyes as he works.

"It won't be a stylish marriage…"

It burns! The pain from the laser is so intense, I am about to pass out again.

"I can't afford a carriage…"

He holds my head steady with a strong grip. Still, I look around with my eyes. I can make out the body of Padre lying nearby in the sand. He isn't moving. Neither is Stingray.

"But you'll look sweet…"

Daniel sits in the distance, with Jason's collar wrapped around his waist. Chained to the stake in the white hot, frying sun. I can hear him crying.

"Upon the seat…"

Jason sings and carves. I can't pass out. I have to hold on.

"Of a bicycle built for two…"

He makes one more deep cut with the laser knife. I gasp and try to hold on to consciousness.

"There!"

He sits up and admires his work.

"Perfect, my love. Your head will look perfect in its place of honor on the president's desk."

I twist violently and struggle to throw him off me. He only laughs and then slaps me hard across my face.

"Easy, sweetheart," he says with a strange voice. "That's no way to treat your betrothed."

"You traitor!" I scream.

"Traitor?' Jason asks. "Traitor? Tell me if I'm wrong, dear, but I'm not the one who decided to run."

Daniel is screaming. I have to get to him.

Jason slaps me again. Then, he grins. A wicked, crooked grin. And his eyes! He is clearly insane.

"You've been a lot of trouble, sweetheart," he says casually as he strokes my burning cheek. "But you're worth it," he adds. "Worth two hundred million credits, to be exact. That is the price on your pretty head! Oh, and guess what. You are looking at the next assistant minister of information. Aren't you proud of me?"

The pain from the laser knife is helping me wake up. I wiggle my fingers and toes. I know that I am in bad shape, but everything seems to be working.

"That is what our new president promised me," Jay continues with a hiss in his voice.

"All I have to do is bring the kid back alive and your head in a sack. That's all the president wants to see! But I wanted to add one extra, special touch, so I carved the sign of your disobedience on your forehead for him to see. "

The sign of my disobedience? I can't see it, but it burns!

"Poor little Chrissie!" Jason chides. "You are worth almost nothing alive. But dead, you are worth everything! Stingray told you the truth. He wanted to take you back alive."

Daniel has calmed down a little. His screams have settled to a whimper.

"Stingray lost his nerve, Chrissie," Jason says, ignoring Daniel. "But I haven't."

Daniel screams again, really loud this time, and Jason turns slightly to look at him.

I gather my strength and jam my knee into Jason's back. He falls forward into me and I head-butt him as hard as I can. It nearly knocks me out again, but it stuns him and he falls back into surprise. His laser knife tumbles away across the sand.

It gives me time to struggle to my feet. I feel heavy, sluggish. I try to shield up, but my wristbands are missing. I see that Jason is wearing them.

"I was hoping you would do that, Chrissie," he says as he stands up. He claps his wrists together and shields up.

"Stingray was my master," he announces proudly. "Let me show you what I've learned."

He strikes out at me hard. He has learned a lot; he moves like Stingray. It is everything I can do to keep him off me. He wades in, hunting for a death blow. I block his shields with my bare arms and try to hunt for an advantage too. But my arms can't hold up long under this abuse. Soon, his shields will break them. Jason circles and twists, beating me every time with an endless combination of punches.

I am fading. I am going to have to give everything I have in one quick attack. I scream as loud as I can and launch myself at him with a quick succession of strikes. He jumps away from me in surprise and makes the one mistake I have been hoping for.

Jason is not Stingray, and he is certainly not Angel. He walks right into my trap and, just before I black out again, I have him in the death lock. I hold tight and squeeze until I feel him pass out. Then I drop him in the sand and turn toward Daniel, who is looking up at me with wet eyes. But I am really weak now, and I faint again...

CHAPTER FORTY-SIX

"Chrissie!"

It is Moses's voice. He is cradling my head in his lap. Stingray's body is lying right next to me in the sand. Jason lies unconscious a dozen feet away. Lucia is holding Daniel in her arms and crying. Medics are sitting with Padre in the sand, applying a dressing to the burn in his chest. He is alive! He gazes across the sand at me and smiles weakly.

"We are taking you up to the hospital," Moses tells me with worry in his eyes. Slowly, I sit up and look over at Stingray's body. He is lying on his back, his mirrored sunglasses gleaming in the bright sun. Moses looks at Stingray and starts shaking, overcome with grief. I watch in confusion as Moses leans over and holds Stingray's head and shoulders in his arms. He whispers something to Stingray that I can't hear, and then lays Stingray gently back down in the sand. Through his teary eyes, he sees my confusion.

"He was your cousin, Chrissie," Moses tells me. "And he was my son. His real name was Joshua, and I loved him very, very much."

More medics arrive and slowly help me to my feet.

"Wait," I tell them. There is something that I have to see. I kneel back down next to Stingray and remove his sunglasses. What I see makes me gasp. He has no eyes! Where his eyes should be there are only half-closed, empty sockets.

"He never had eyes, Chrissie," Moses explains to me. "He was born blind."

CHAPTER FORTY-SEVEN

So this is how it ends, and this is how it begins.

I slowly open my eyes. Was that my mind or was that the voice? I don't know for sure.

I float in the air on my back in a hospital healing chamber, engulfed in that wonderful warm, golden light. Daniel huddles on my stomach, sound asleep. He was sunburned and badly dehydrated from exposure while he was chained in the merciless sun to that stake in the sand. The two of us are clothed in soft, white gowns.

The light surrounding us, making us completely weightless, reminds me of the light that erupted in a vision that I had of my mother so long ago when I slept on Moses's shoulder that first night in the underground. This light contains the same intense love and emotion. It has intelligence. I can feel that it cares for me deeply. And for Daniel.

Daniel stirs awake and raises his head to look at me. His bright blue eyes sparkle in the golden light.

"Mama!" he whispers as he hugs my neck. As I kiss him, I can see that the sunburn on his face has started to heal.

We have been in the chamber for two days and the scar on my forehead no longer burns. I still have no idea what Jason carved; I don't have the nerve to even touch it. Daniel, with a serious look, traces the rough scar with his finger, and immediately, I know what it is. A cross. Jason carved a cross, the sign of my disobedience, on my forehead.

Moses and Lucia visit us daily, but only for short periods. We need solitude in the light to heal, the doctors have said. On the third day, Moses looks hugely relieved.

"Padre is going to make it," he tells me. "That is one tough old man!"

"What about Dragon?" I ask.

"Dragon is coming along fine, child," Moses answers as he playfully tugs on Daniels hair. "Let's worry about you and Daniel for now."

My fight with Stingray and Jason on the beach took its toll on me. Nothing is broken, but everything hurts. But the golden light is soothing the pain away.

On the fourth day, I wake up and realize that someone is holding my hand. Daniel is still cuddled on my stomach, asleep. I turn my head and look right into the brown eyes of Dragon. He squeezes my hand and smiles.

Daniel is delighted that Dragon is with us. He jabbers for an hour, some of which we can understand, and fills Dragon in on the events of the past week. Dragon reaches out and traces the scar of the cross on my forehead.

"The doctors can take care of this, Chrissie," he tells me. "You won't even be able to tell that you ever had it."

"No," I tell him with deep emotion welling up inside of me, "the Cross stays. I will wear it for the rest of my life."

Dragon nods slowly and gets a faraway look in his eyes.

"And so the prophecy is fulfilled," he answers. "The prophecy foretold by a saint from my country, Japan, over a century ago. 'And the mother of the Prophet shall carry the sign, the sign of the cross. And you shall see it and know!'"

CHAPTER FORTY-EIGHT

When we are strong enough to walk, Dragon, Daniel, and I slowly stroll through the immense gardens and talk. At first, we talk about small things, what we like and dislike. Dragon tells me crazy stories about his exotic home far to the east. The Land of the Rising Sun.

"One day, I will take you there, Chrissie," he promises me. "It is a beautiful country."

He describes the mountains and crystal clear streams that are filled with colorful fish.

"This big!" He shows Daniel with his hands.

"Wow!" Daniel exclaims. *Wow* is Daniels new favorite word. He says it every time he sees sometime new. I can't blame him; Liberty City is truly a "wow" place.

"What about your family?" I ask Dragon. He looks at the ground.

"Dead, Chrissie," he answers quietly. "All dead. I come from a family of guides."

I don't press.

Evenings are spent with Moses and Lucia in Moses's beach house. I find out that Moses is also an extraordinary cook. Not an evening goes by that his home is not overrun with friends: mamas and papas from San Hidalgo, friends from the city above us, and other guides who know where to find the best food around. Only Padre is missing, still recovering in the golden light.

As the days pass, Dragon and I start holding hands as we walk, and our talks turn more serious. We talk about the future. I want to be a guide and, like Angel, he disagrees strongly.

"Sooner or later, almost every guide dies, Chrissie," he tells me. "And you are the mother of Daniel. Your place is with him."

"Of course," I argue. "But when he is older, I can start."

"But you wear the sign," he points out. "And it will always put you in danger."

"I will wear a headband like Angel's," I say. "It is pointless trying to talk me out of it, Dragon."

He smiles and shakes his head.

"A gift runs strong in your family, Chrissie," he finally says. "Who am I to tell you what you can and cannot do?"

Daniel has wandered ahead and is calling for Howler to come out and play. Quickly, I pull Dragon close and kiss him.

"I like it when you try," I whisper.

Finally, Dragon teaches me what Padre was going to teach me. He teaches me the meaning of the cross and whom it symbolizes. He teaches me everything. Finally, I understand.

Padre has recovered and sits with us at dinner.

"Next week, we will travel on, Chrissie," he tells me. "To the City of Gardens."

I think of all the massive gardens Dragon and I have strolled through in the past weeks here in Liberty City.

"So, there is a place where there are more gardens than here?" I ask.

Moses laughs from across the room where he is busy cooking fish.

"Liberty City is just a small seaside village, Chrissie," he says, "with tiny gardens. There is so much out there for you to see."

After dinner, Moses's tone grows serious.

"Tomorrow morning, we have something to do, Chrissie," he tells me. "The Council of Twelve met today and decided to send

Jason home to the New Republic. Captain Perez will take possession of him and fly him back."

I shake my head.

"That isn't wise," I disagree. "Jason is insane. He tried to kill me."

And he is incredibly dangerous, I think to myself as I remember how well he fought.

"The Council of Twelve decided to send him back as a message to the new president," Moses explains. "Jason's sanity is slowly returning. For the past month, he has been treated in a healing chamber like yours. He will be returned as a witness to what he has seen here."

"But still…," I protest.

"The council has ruled" is all that Moses will say.

The next morning, just after breakfast, Moses walks with me down to the beach. I carry Daniel in my arms as we make our way down the steep path that leads directly to the sand.

This is not right, I argue in my mind. *Jason is one of them. We can't let him go back.*

Out on the beach, close to the rolling surf, Captain Perez waits patiently in front of one of his away boats. The disc-shaped boat glows brighter than the sun. Four of his men surround him. He smiles and waves to us when he sees us.

After we hug each other, we wait together until finally I see an armed guard of men leading Jason up the beach toward us. As soon as I see Jason, the roar of the ocean waves, the piercing cries of the seagulls, the brisk wind in my hair, all cease to exist for me.

Too many memories are rushing back. Too many horrors.

I stop breathing. Then I feel Daniel hug my neck.

"Mama," he whispers.

His gentle whisper calms me, and I finally take a breath.

Even though he still carries scars of his own from our fight, Jason is as handsome as ever. They have replaced his torn clothes with new ones. His bindings prevent him from moving freely, and he walks with an awkward pace.

"Attention!" Captain Perez commands, and his men form up to receive Jason from the guard.

Moses eases over close enough to touch me as Jason passes by. Jason refuses to look me in the eye, and even if he tried, I would look away. I can't stand the sight of him.

"Mama!" Daniel whispers into my ear again. He starts squirming and struggles to be put down. I look questioningly at Moses, and he nods yes.

I lower Daniel to the sand. As soon as I do, he turns and walks awkwardly on his new prosthetic leg to Jason.

"No!" I exclaim as I realize what he is doing. Moses reaches out and grips my hand.

"Don't worry, Chrissie," he whispers. "It's okay."

I know that he is right. Jason is securely bound and hand-cuffed. He is incapable of harming Daniel. And we surround him on every side…still, I am on edge.

Then it happens…and all at once, everything in my life changes forever.

Daniel walks straight up to Jason and reaches out to him with his handless arm. I gasp as I watch Jason drop to his knees.

Gently, Daniel touches Jason's forehead and carefully traces the sign of the cross on it; all the while looking deeply into Jason's eyes. Jason starts to weep.

Jason looks up at Daniel through anguished eyes and shakes his head over and over again. Daniel smiles at him with a smile far too wise for a two-year-old.

Then ever so slowly, Daniel closes his eyes and bows his head. He is praying. A two-year-old, praying! There is not a doubt in my mind because I feel the power of his prayer. I can hear his silent words. He is praying for Jason, for forgiveness, for mercy, for a safe journey.

Jason sobs uncontrollably now, and I look up to see that Moses, Captain Perez, and the others have also bowed their heads. Tears stream down their cheeks.

Daniel wraps his arms around Jason's neck and hugs him. Then he looks up at me and smiles.

For the first time in my life, I whisper a prayer to God. A prayer of thanks. A prayer of hope.

"Amen," Captain Perez says quietly as he takes Jason by the arm and leads him through the hatch of the away boat. Jason is still sobbing as he enters the glowing craft.

"Amen," Moses echoes, smiling down at Daniel as my son walks back to us across the sand.

Through wet eyes, I watch the away boat as it rises, skims across the ocean waves, and then shoots straight up into the deep blue sky.

CHAPTER FORTY-NINE

The City of Gardens lives up to its name. It is also known as the Jewel of Africa. It is sits directly in the heart of the great continent, and it is truly a jewel. The gardens are easily ten times more vast than the gardens at Port Liberty. And like Port Liberty, every building in the city floats hundreds of feet above the ground.

As I have done for the past month, I stroll through the quiet gardens with Dragon. He continues to heal from his wounds, and he is strong enough now to carry Daniel and hold my hand at the same time. We talk about a lot of things. Every single day, I am amazed to learn something new about this world and about all the worlds.

I learn that Dragon was there with me and Daniel the entire time we were in prison. Moses had foreseen it all; he had planned ahead.

"I'm so sorry, Chrissie." Dragon shakes his head. "I wanted to do something sooner. Stingray and Hydra were just too strong. We had to get you out in the open first."

"What about Daniel?" I ask. "Did they do anything to him?"

"I don't think so," Dragon tries to assure me. "Once they realized who and what Daniel is and what he is actually capable of doing, they left him alone. They were afraid of him, Chrissie. I took charge of Daniel's supervision. I hired my own nurses to watch him. I did my best to keep Stingray and Hydra away from him, and to my knowledge, they had very little contact with him."

"But they did have contact with him," I emphasize, wanting to get this all straight.

"Unfortunately, yes," Dragon lowers his head. "Some contact. I could not control everything."

I don't blame Dragon for that. I am glad he was there all along. I am glad he was there to watch over us. I squeeze his hand. Then I look deep into his eyes, and there is no doubt in my mind that I love him.

Later, we are gathered in a vast graveyard that is hidden deep in the gardens. Everyone who is left is present—Moses; Padre, who sits in a wheelchair; Dragon, complete with his swords; the two old papas; the three old mamas; Daniel; Lucia; and me.

Moses is the last to join us. We have waited for him for over an hour, and when he arrives, I wince at the cuts and bruises on his face, and I see that his left eye is nearly swollen shut.

"It was a rough night," he tells me. "I'll tell you later."

We have come to pay our respects to Rachel, my aunt. We have also laid Stingray to rest here. His gravestone is fashioned in the shape of a cross like all of the gravestones here. It lies next to my aunt's, on the left side; but "Joshua," his real name, is inscribed on it. To the right of my aunt's grave is a gravestone with "Angel" inscribed on it. Moses quietly explains.

"When your aunt ran, she carried twins," he tells us.

"I was her guide. It was a hard run, Chrissie, and we nearly died. We had two of the toughest closers after us that I had ever run across. Medusa and Hydra. And there was someone else who was even more ruthless than them."

"And he died long, long ago," Padre breaks in.

Moses looks down at Padre, who is sitting slightly hunched in his wheelchair, and a strange nod of acknowledgement passes between the two men.

"Yes," Moses agrees, "he is dead now."

Moses continues.

"Rachel gave birth to her twins in the town of San Hidalgo. She named the boy Joshua, after a great warrior who saved his people from extinction. He was born without eyes, and yet as he grew, it was clear that he could see. The baby girl, she decided, was as pretty as an angel. San Hidalgo's priest had taught her all about angels, so that became her daughter's name. The little girl was mute, and yet we could hear her words clearly in our minds. Both children were incredibly gifted, Chrissie, just like your aunt, like your mother, like you. And, of course, like Daniel.

"Eventually, we made our way to the Free Nations. Like you, your aunt wanted to become a guide. As I taught her the ways of guiding, we fell in love and married. I adopted the twins as my own. Eight years later, your aunt went into the New Republic to guide a runner out. She saved the mother and child, but she had to face Medusa alone, and before we could get help to her, she died from that encounter."

I nod in understanding. Medusa almost killed me with just a slight glance. I had the help of Padre and the villagers. What if I had been alone?

"I raised Joshua and Angel after that," Moses continues. "And in due time, they chose to become guides themselves even though they knew better than anybody that most guides die terrible deaths. See all the graves around you, Chrissie? For the past one hundred years, this has been the honored resting place for guides."

I look at the endless rows of crosses that surround us. The gravestones extend out into the distance, in perfect symmetry, as far as my eye can see. So this is what makes the City of Gardens so special.

"By the time he was eighteen," Moses continues, "Joshua was the most gifted guide the Free Nations had ever produced. He could sense the thoughts of a runner almost before she decided to run. He rescued runner after runner from Parlors across the New Republic. He saved so many mothers and children. Always, as soon as he brought them out, he turned around and headed back in. Angel was nearly as good a guide as he was. I could never have been prouder of the two children. Between the two of them, they saved so many lives."

I think back and picture Angel's lovely face. I remember the day she stroked my cheek and told me how much I reminded her of her mother. It all makes sense to me now. Stingray, however, is another story.

"What happened to him?" I ask Moses. I see the tears wetting his cheeks now as he continues to tell his story.

"Joshua was too effective, too good as a guide, so the president of the New Republic pulled out all of the stops to capture him. He succeeded. Joshua was finally captured and taken to the same prison that held you and Daniel for the past year, Chrissie. But Joshua stayed much longer. Medusa and Hydra worked on him with their evil powers and drugs for three years. They turned him, twisted him, and he became the monster known as Stingray. He became the greatest closer the New Republic had ever seen."

"Why didn't you go in after him?" I ask gently. Moses sadly shakes his head.

"They cut off his thoughts with their terrible drugs," he answers. "And I thought he was dead. When I finally did see him again, we were enemies."

"I understand," I say. I know what it was like in that prison. Without Dragon, they would have turned me too.

"I would like to think that maybe there was some part of my son left in Stingray, some tiny spark," Moses says. "But I just don't know."

"I think there had to be," I assure him. "He could have killed Daniel and me at any time, and yet he chose not to. And he could have killed you too, Moses."

I remember how he went berserk when Angel died. I remember how he dropped his arms to his sides and unshielded when he saw who was holding Daniel's hand. The shining man! And I remember how he told me how much I reminded him of his mother. Of course I did; his mother was Rachel. Is that why he could not kill me at the end?

"Maybe so," Moses says quietly. "But I just don't know."

Later, after Padre has given a special prayer for my family, we walk together as a new family out of the graveyard.

"I had to kill a closer last night," Moses finally tells us, explaining his injuries. "It was too close for comfort. Even here, in the City of Gardens, you and Daniel are not safe, Chrissie. And in the New Republic, things are changing rapidly."

"The new president is insane," Dragon quietly informs me. "He has ordered twice as many Parlors, new tests for any child up to ten years old, with orders to terminate those children, born or unborn, who he deems undesirable."

I gasp at what I am hearing.

"He has to be stopped!" I exclaim.

"Yes," Moses agrees, "he must be stopped. He will kill the innocents because he is afraid, Chrissie. He is afraid that Daniel, or another child who is like Daniel, will appear to challenge him."

"Can't you sweep in and defeat him?"

"He is too strong," Moses shakes his head. "And spies for the New Republic have accessed the secrets to our technology. They are catching up, Chrissie, and sooner than later."

"What do we do?" I ask Moses.

"We have already done it," he smiles. "Daniel is alive, and you have started a movement. Remember the day when we stood on the platform with Africa's Council of Twelve? Every single person in the New Republic saw you that day. You made the right choice, Chrissie. Today, the number of runners is tenfold what it was before. And every day, the number increases. Mothers are defying the Parlors. They are choosing to run to save their babies. They want to be like you."

"Which makes things especially dangerous for you and Daniel," Padre adds. "Much too dangerous to remain here with us. More closers like the one Moses fought last night will come.

They will stop at nothing to find you and kill you. We cannot allow that to happen."

"I have already made the arrangements," Moses says. "Tomorrow, you and Daniel will depart on the last leg of your journey to Haven."

"Haven?"

I thought that this was Haven. Dragon steps forward with his hands resting on the hilts of his swords. Now I know why he is wearing them.

"I am still your guide, Chrissie," he tells me. "I am coming with you."

I nod my head in agreement. Daniel reaches out for Dragon, and Dragon scoops him up in his arms. Daniel reaches up and playfully yanks at Dragon's jet-black hair.

"Dwagon!" he says.

"Dragon will guide you to Haven," Moses agrees. "But I shall remain here. There are so many runners now, Chrissie. We need every guide we can get."

I nod my head, and then I turn to Dragon with a question.

"You are my guide," I say to him. "But is that the only reason you want to come with us?"

Dragon reaches out and gently takes my hand in his. His eyes gleam at me, and he smiles shyly.

"No, Chrissie," he says, "it is not the only reason."

"What about me?" Lucia asks.

PART FOUR:

HAVEN

CHAPTER FIFTY

I am back on the beach, holding Daniel in my arms. Daniel is a baby again. The waves behind me are crashing into the sand with a deafening roar.

An older man faces me with his back to the ocean. This is the place. This is where it happened, where everybody died. The man has slicked-back gray hair, and he is wearing mirrored sunglasses. He is grinning at me with a wicked, crooked grin.

He is wearing an expensive gray suit with a golden crest embroidered on his breast pocket. Only one man in the world is entitled to wear that crest.

His grin turns into a scowl, and he takes off his sunglasses. I freeze, expecting to see eyeless sockets where his eyes should be. But this man has eyes. He has my father's eyes.

"You little witch!" he growls at me. "You can run, but you can never hide from me!"

I fall to my knees, and I scream and scream and scream.

"Chrissie!" someone is saying, shaking me awake. "Chrissie, wake up!"

I wake up and sit upright in bed. Dragon, my husband, studies me with worried eyes.

"It's the dream again, isn't it?" he asks. I nod my head yes.

Restless now, I climb out of bed and walk past Lucia's bedroom to the children's room. Outside of their bedroom window, the lights of our beautiful glass-domed city, Haven, twinkle beneath the limitless stars of the Martian night sky. Phobos, the faster Martian moon, is racing high across the sky, washing the beautiful Martian landscape in a stark relief of light and shadow. Slower Diemos cannot be far behind.

Beautiful Haven of Mars. The city that Moses built!

Daniel, five years old now, sits up in his bed and smiles at me with his sparkling blue eyes. His baby sister, Ruthie, is sound asleep in her crib.

Daniel frowns for a brief moment, climbs out of bed, and walks over to me. When I kneel to hug him, he takes my face and holds it with both of his hands.

"Don't worry, I'm not going to let that bad man hurt you!" he tells me and kisses my cheek. I try not to cry, but the tears come anyway. Daniel wipes the tears from my face and traces the sign of the cross on my forehead as I carry him back to bed. Before he lies back down, he turns to me and gives me a look that is far too serious for a five-year-old.

"When I grow up, I will go to him, Mama," he says to me. "And when I meet him, I will make him read the writing on the wall!"

I climb back into bed next to Dragon, snuggle up to him, and try to sleep again. But sleep does not come easily.

❧ The End ❧